FOREVER INNOCENT

DEANNA ROY

casey shay press

Forever Innocent

Copyright © 2013 by Deanna Roy. All rights reserved.

No part of this book may be used or reproduced by any means, graphic, electronic, or mechanical, including photocopying, taping, and recording without written permission except in the case of brief quotations embodied in critical articles and reviews.

This is a work of fiction. All the characters, organizations, and events portrayed in this novel are either products of the author's imagination or used fictitiously.

Casey Shay Press
PO Box 160116
Austin, TX 78716
www.caseyshaypress.com

Hardcover: ISBN: 9781938150203
Paperback: ISBN: 9781938150180
Ebook ISBN: 9781938150197

Library of Congress Control Number: 2013914926

Other books by Deanna Roy

Stella & Dane
A new adult contemporary romance

Baby Dust: A Novel about Miscarriage
Women's fiction on baby loss

Jinnie Wishmaker
Marcus Mender
an adventure series for 9-12 year olds under the name DD Roy

Dust Bunnies: Secret Agents
an iPad story book app for children ages 3-9

Learn more about the author at

www.deannaroy.com

For my angels
Casey (1998)
Daniel (2001)
Emma (2001)

And two very special angels
Cordelia (2007)
William (2010)

And three angels whose mothers
nominated their names to be
the main characters in this book.
Corabelle
Gavin
Finn

You are not forgotten.

1

CORABELLE

I had finally arrived at the first day of the rest of my life, and I was late.

Clumps of students broke apart as I ran along the sidewalk. I had memorized the campus map since I was too old to be wandering around like a lost freshman, but I hadn't considered how long it might take to find a parking spot on the first day.

The counselor who reviewed my transfer records warned me that some classes dropped no-shows to make room for other students, so I could not miss roll call. I'd waited so long. I couldn't screw up *now*.

I turned by the glass library built in honor of Dr. Seuss and barreled toward Warren Mall. Faces and colors blurred past me. I noticed with some satisfaction that I wasn't the only one in a hurry. A young couple also ran across the grass, hands grasped between them.

My heart made a tiny pang, but I was used to that. Relationships weren't anything I let myself have time for, not even in the last year, when I had little else to do but serve coffee and wait until I qualified for in-state benefits at UC San Diego. One day, I told myself. But not now. My refusal to date had earned me the nickname Frozen Latte at work, but I wouldn't crack, even if the hottest man in San Diego sauntered up to the counter at Cool Beans and asked for chai with a side of Corabelle.

Not worth it. I knew that better than anyone.

I pushed past several leisurely walkers and burst into the engineering hall. The door to the stairwell required a hard yank, but once inside, I took the steps two and three at a time. I needed this class to make up some credits I lost when I left New Mexico. An expensive loss, now that all my scholarships had been forfeited, but I'd been saving. I'd squeak by like everyone else, working crap jobs and racking up student loans. I was lucky admissions took one look at my status as a National Merit Scholar and asked no questions about my sudden departure from my last school.

Or my arrest record.

I paused in the hallway to catch my breath and get my bearings. The room was dead ahead. I jerked open the door. The professor looked up in a smallish lecture hall with about one hundred seats. He shuffled the papers on his podium and resumed calling out names. "Study Group Two will work with Amy Powers." He pointed at a blond woman in jeans and a UCSD T-shirt. "She'll be your TA for the duration of the course. Last names G through P will check in with her when we break."

I flattened myself against the wall, looking for Jenny, a girl I worked with at Cool Beans who had convinced me to take astronomy. "The star parties rock!" she said. The class was apparently fun and easy. I could use a little of that, especially since my lit courses were serious and doused with lengthy writing assignments.

I spotted her hot-pink ponytail in the center of the back row. She waved me over, lifting a backpack from the seat beside her. As

I moved that way, the professor pointed out another TA, a scrawny boy who looked like a '90s throwback in lumberjack plaid and ripped jeans.

"I was getting worried!" Jenny hissed.

"Did they take roll?" I yanked my iPad out of my backpack and breathed deeply, trying to get my heart to slow down.

"No, the TAs are going to do it." She pointed at the lumberjack. "He's cute, and he's yours."

I appraised '90s boy a second time but still didn't feel it. Jenny had been leading the charge to get me to lose my nickname and date somebody, anybody. She read online profiles to me like an auctioneer might extoll the virtues of a 1920s cigarette case.

"I don't think so," I whispered.

Jenny rolled her eyes. "You're forgetting the second most important reason to go to college — da boyz."

"I'm just going to graduate in a year and move on. No point starting something now."

"Yeah, you said the same thing when I met you six months ago." Jenny chewed on the end of her pen. "I think I've gone through four relationships since then."

I raised my eyebrows. "Relationships?"

Jenny jabbed the pen at her notebook. "Okay, bang-fests. It's all semantics."

The professor laser-pointed at a book title on the projector screen as I surveyed the room. Lots of freshmen, judging by their expressions, which varied from panic to bravado. I'd probably be the oldest one here at twenty-two.

"Students, let's break so you can meet your TA, and they can talk about the study groups and external labs. We will have six meetings outside of class hours for measuring celestial occurrences."

Celestial occurrences. My favorite poem came to mind —

When I Heard the Learn'd Astronomer, a comparison between the scientific and romantic views of the heavens. I often felt the two extremes at war within me — the stargazer and the pragmatist. This class should satisfy both, and maybe one day when I stood in a lecture hall to talk about what inspired literature, I would have a brilliant example.

The room got noisy as students gathered their things to move.

"I got the straitlaced blond chick," Jenny said. "Just my luck."

I stuck my iPad in my pack. "You between boyfriends again?"

"Nah. I'm just always on the lookout for my next ex." Jenny shoved her bag on her shoulder. "If you're not interested in lumberjack boy, send him my way!"

I shook my head as I headed toward the scrawny guy. The room segmented and clustered around the three TAs. I felt another pang as I thought about how, if life had gone normally last year, that would be me right now, a new grad student rather than twenty credit hours away from my bachelor's degree. I hung back at the rear of the group.

"I'm Robert," the TA said. "Our group will be stargazing every other Thursday. If you miss one, you can make it up with another study group." He passed out a stack of papers. "On this list, you'll get your spectrum lab assignments. Five of you will work together and be graded together for those."

A girl passed a page back. I scanned for my name but caught something else. I gripped the strap of my bag, not believing it. Impossible. Gavin couldn't be here. He hadn't even graduated high school. Just took off without telling anybody where he was going.

I searched the cluster of students until I saw him, holding the paper to his face, also not believing. He looked up, no doubt to find me.

His face was partially obscured by a ball cap, but he pulled it off as he scanned the cluster of students. Then he saw me and our gazes clashed.

The rest of the room dissolved. I had forgotten everything — his hard jaw lined with stubble, his fierce expression. Shock splintered through us both. I could see it in those unsettled blue eyes, the drawing together of his brows. He swallowed and I could only stare at his neck and chest and arms, the places where I once felt completely safe.

"Corabelle," he said, and then, as if he'd been expecting me all along, "you came to the school by the sea."

My head whipped around to the door as if I could x-ray all the way through the walls, across campus, and down the short path to the Pacific. Our school by the ocean. The pictures we had drawn when we played teacher as children. Of course.

How had I not realized the real reason why I had come here? And how had I not known he would too?

2

CORABELLE

I couldn't do this.

Screw this elective, screw getting dropped. Hell, maybe screw this school. I turned and dashed for the door.

"Wait! Who are you?" the TA called out. "I need to check roll."

"She's Corabelle Rotheford," Gavin said. "And I'm Gavin Mays. Don't drop us." His voice had an edge to it, like he was not to be messed with. The Gavin I knew never talked that way, but I had no time to think about it.

I wrenched open the door and hurtled into the hall. He'd follow me, and I had to lose him, had to think. I darted down the corridor and flung myself through the exit to the stairwell.

I slipped on the third step and began sliding, but managed to clutch the rail before I hit the ground. I pulled my backpack around to avoid crunching anything I couldn't afford to replace. This was crazy. I had to pull myself together.

My sneakers found a solid step, and I wriggled back to standing. The door blew open above me, no doubt Gavin. I sat down. If he wanted to talk, we would talk. It wouldn't kill me. Hell, he was the one who deserted me on the worst day of my life.

I heard his footfalls on the stairs and sensed him sitting beside me even though I looked away, down the hole of the stairwell.

"I can't believe you're here," he said. "Did you come for me?"

I whipped around at that. "Is that what you think?"

He frowned. "I just assumed you found out."

"If I had known you were here, I never would have come."

His jaw tightened. "Right. Makes sense. Stupid kid thing, us wanting to teach by the sea."

I could see he'd changed, was jaded inside. I couldn't blame him. I fought the urge every day to hate everyone and everything, to hate life.

The air grew stuffier, hotter, as if we brought too much emotion inside the concrete walls. My chest hurt from holding it all in, the anger threatening to dissolve into grief.

Stay mad, I warned myself, but all the things I wanted to forget came back, moments I'd shoved into the back of my brain. Impulsively, I touched my stomach, still bearing stretch marks, tiny white rivers like lightning bolts from my hips to my navel. And without wanting to, I saw that little face, his sweet cheeks and nubby nose, the tiniest perfect fingers.

I sobbed out loud, a horrid sound that echoed against the walls.

"Corabelle. Come here." Gavin tried to put his arm around me.

I jerked away and stood, accidentally smacking his face with my backpack as I went up. Damn it, who cares, I had to GO.

I raced down the stairs again, trying to be more sure-footed this time. I couldn't take a class with Gavin. I couldn't be around him at all. Even if I could find a way to suck it up, to stuff our past down and away, he'd be a distraction. We never were able to keep our hands off each other, back when we were together. Of course our birth control failed. We pushed every limit.

Then pregnancy had failed. Then parenthood itself.

This was too much. I couldn't be in his group. Stargazing. Spectrum lab. Graded together. No way. No no no no way.

I couldn't help but look up as I descended the stairs. Gavin was above me, blue eyes piercing in the yellow light. He had so much rage coming off him, like he had earned it. Well, I had too.

"Why did this happen?" My voice was powerful in the chamber, stronger and bolder than I felt.

"Which part?" he asked.

I knew what he meant. The baby or his death? Gavin's desertion or finding each other again?

Disgust with him burned in my belly. Gavin had been my best friend since I was a child, the one person I thought would be there for me all my life. But he walked out of our baby's funeral, shucking his jacket and tie as he stormed out, missing graduation, disappearing completely. Gone from my life, just like little Finn.

He came down the stairs, slowly, like he wasn't sure he should. "Do you believe in second chances?" he asked. His voice had gone soft, losing its edge.

No way. Our baby had not been given a second chance. And Gavin had left me, discarded like his clothing in the aisle of the church. A person capable of that was not the sort of man I could depend on for anything.

But he was holding out his hand, those fingers I had once known so well. My gaze moved up his arm, darker and hairier than it had been, to the sleeve of his T-shirt, and his shoulder, broader now, like a man's instead of a boy's. Then back up to that chiseled face. And those eyes, piercing blue. I was sure the baby would have them. But I never got to see. He never opened his eyes.

Life rushed at me too hard then and I felt light, like I was floating. My old habit of holding my breath too long when I was in distress kicked in without my thinking about it. I was going to faint, escape into black oblivion, my one safe place.

My knees buckled and I bent over the rail. Gavin rushed down the last steps and held on to me, pulling me into that familiar embrace. He smelled of outdoors, boyish soap, and the life I once loved.

As my vision turned to spots, I realized that maybe I'd arrived at the college by the sea just to come home.

3

GAVIN

Corabelle had to have known I'd be here. She HAD to.

I held her against the rail, making sure she didn't fall. Her black hair was all tied up, and her face was so pale. She'd never been super sturdy, and the whole time she was pregnant I feared she would just slip away.

I had no answers for her. Why I left. Why I stayed away. Or why I came to UCSD, which was a risk. It had always been our plan, and we were both accepted our senior year. But then we found out about the baby. New Mexico State had been closer to people who could help us out as we navigated work, college, and family.

Her breathing was shallow and fast. I held on to her, waiting for her to come back around.

I figured I knew what she was seeing behind those closed eyes, her lashes curled against her cheek. Finn. Despite what Corabelle might think, that I wanted to erase the memory of him and those seven days we had him, I still had his picture. One was always with me.

When she began to move around again, I used my free hand to

tug my wallet out and flipped it to the center. "I never forgot."

Corabelle's eyes fluttered open, but when she saw the picture I held out, she pushed away from me, despite her unsteadiness. "Why do you have that? You don't deserve it!"

I jumped in front of her and took her arm. "I was Finn's father. I do too deserve it."

"You didn't do ANYTHING! You took off!" Her eyes were going red, like she'd cry. Damn it, I hated it when she cried. But I had nothing to say to that.

She jerked her arm away from me, and I actually felt relief that she was angry rather than in tears. Anger I could deal with.

"I'm dropping this class," she said. "But I can't leave here. I have to finish my degree."

"Wait. You didn't finish in New Mexico?"

"How did you know where I went?" Corabelle stood straight as a crowbar.

"I assumed. I planned to find you."

"But you didn't." Her brown eyes flashed with little sparks of light, like they always did when she got mad. She was the most beautiful girl I'd ever known, something I'd taken for granted when I was a numbskull teen.

"It was too late by then," I said. Too late on all counts, even the ones she didn't know about.

Her hand shook a little as she gripped the metal slats of the railing. "Probably so."

I wanted to ask what happened at NMSU, but she had changed from upset to fear, as if she had something to hide. She never did have much of a poker face.

I didn't want to be the cause of any more distress for her. "I'll drop the class. Hell, I'm on the ten-year plan already. It won't matter."

"Why aren't YOU finished yet?" she asked.

"Work. I have to pay every dollar for school myself."

"I didn't think you'd be here," she said. "I thought you'd be done with college."

"Yeah, well, when you ditch the school that was giving you a free ride, it's hard to convince another one to cough up any dough."

She nodded, and I figured something similar had happened to her. At least she was calm again.

"Can I walk you somewhere?" I didn't really want to leave her alone after all this.

"No, I need to figure things out." Corabelle squeezed the bridge of her nose, a little gesture I had forgotten, something she did when she was stressed.

"I'm serious. I'll drop the course," I said.

"Don't you need it? What's your major?"

"Geology."

"Rocks? Seriously? What happened to teaching?"

I didn't answer, and she looked away. She knew why. Kids were not my thing, not now, not anymore.

She twisted at her ponytail. "I switched to literature. I plan to teach college instead of elementary."

That made sense to me. "Professor suits you."

"Maybe. I'd hoped to be a TA by now. This is just an elective. I can pick another."

"So can I."

She sighed. "I'll go talk to my counselor, see what I can get into."

I squeezed her shoulder, relieved when she didn't flinch. "You were always doing that."

"Doing what?"

"Inconveniencing yourself for others. You always took care of everyone else first."

She brushed her hair out of her eye. "Old habits die hard."

"Let me do it this time."

Corabelle gave me a hard look. "I have to make sure it happens. So I'm going to do it."

She didn't trust me. But then, I hadn't given her much reason to. "All right."

"I have to stay here. I can't transfer again, lose more credits, another year. But it's a big campus, right?"

I nodded. "Plenty big enough for two undergrads to get lost in."

She went around me and descended the last few stairs. I thought she might look back again, like she had earlier, but this time she pushed through the exit door and was gone.

I sat back down. Hell, I was more wound up than I'd been in a long time. Corabelle was mine. She'd always been mine. Going without her had been easy when she was out of sight, but thinking about crossing campus and spotting her, or worse, running into her on a date with some other jerk undergrad —

I smashed my fist into the metal rail. She hated me enough to avoid me at all costs. I had to get out of here. Had to make sure we didn't cross paths. I'd just drop out this quarter. Or more. Let her finish the year, and then I could come back.

I reconciled myself to losing the fees I had paid, and the damn textbooks. I'd have to just sell these back and take the loss.

I jumped to my feet. It took me months to save up for each class, and now it'd be lost. More hours at the garage. My life was eternally screwed.

I pushed the exit door too hard and it flew open, startling a couple girls just inside the hall. I yanked my hat from the side pocket of my backpack and pulled it low over my eyes, ignoring their interested expressions. Young and stupid, thinking I was someone they should tangle with. They had no idea what life could deal you. What I could deal them. What I'd been dealt.

The quad seemed full of color, green diamonds of grass cut by white stripes of sidewalk. I knew if I could see past the buildings, the big blue of the Pacific would spread wide like the giant crayoned pictures Corabelle and I used to tack to the wall when we set up our pretend school. Growing up with unrelenting New Mexico dry spells, most kids got into fantasies about the sea.

In high school, we discovered San Diego had a college that overlooked the ocean and decided to apply there. Marriage was a long way off, with miles of growing up to do in between. But we wanted to stay together as long as it made sense.

Then came the baby, and disaster after disaster.

But now she was here and wanted nothing to do with me. Just as well. If she knew what all I'd done since leaving that funeral, she'd hate me even more.

4

GAVIN

My boss never missed a thing.

"Roll all the tires out to recycling," Bud said. "They're filling up the back."

I stuck my punch card in the sleeve dangling beneath the clock. "You hatin' on me today?"

"You look like you need a chore that won't cost me money if you screw it up." Bud coughed into his elbow. "Class that tough?"

I tossed my backpack beneath a scuffed-up desk by the door. "You have no idea."

"Don't need no degree to hold a socket wrench." Bud wiped his hands on his overalls, leaving a long black smear.

I forced a laugh. "And that's a good thing, since I'll be sixty-five before I graduate."

"You got your schedule? I'll figure up your hours."

"Nah. I'm dropping out."

Bud pulled off his hat and wiped his head with a red rag. "That's bull."

"Nope. Not feeling it this year."

Bud's meaty hand gripped my shoulder in a vise. "I know I just said you don't need a degree. But you're not cut out for this work long-term. I like you, and you've got a job here as long as you need one, but I'm not going to stand by and let you quit school."

I turned away, shrugging off his hand. "Then fire me."

He spun me back around. "Get out there and roll tires until you change your mind."

"Not enough tires out there for that."

"You ain't been back there in a while."

Fine. I stormed through the bays where Randy and Carl were changing oil on a couple SUVs. Mario had the guts of a 1997 Camaro spread on a tarp, shaking his head over a gunked-up intake manifold.

I stopped short, seeing the car. Why would this car be in the shop at this very moment?

Mario lifted a gasket and peered through the hole. "People don't treat their babies right."

I ran my hand along the roof, shiny and clean. "They kept it waxed and purty on the outside."

Mario grunted. "The engine is beyond gone. These people should be lined up and executed."

I thumbed the door handle, unable to resist a look inside. I had saved up and bought a very similar Camaro when I turned eighteen. Corabelle and I had broken it in pretty fast, and just looking at the slope of the passenger seat brought up visions of her, sweaty hair sticking to her forehead, looking down on me as she straddled my lap.

I slammed the door closed.

"Easy, friend. Everything's loose and hanging." Mario reached for a rag. "You don't like the car?"

"I used to have one."

"Ah, a woman. Always a woman."

"How did you get from the car to a girl?"

"A man slams a door, it's always about a woman." He grinned.

I had to be wearing my damn past on my shoulders. First Bud, now Mario. "I got to go roll tires."

Mario laughed. "You piss off the boss man again?"

"Apparently I've pissed off the world."

Mario chortled as I walked on through to the back, where the old and new tires were stored. Some we repaired and resold as used. The ones too far gone were rolled behind the shop and heaved into a short dumpster that would be picked up by a recycler when it got full. It was a backbreaking chore, tumbling the flat and sometimes shredded tires and tossing them over the side wall.

I tugged the first tire off the stack and braced it on my shoulder. It was too thrashed to wheel out, and I knew from experience to take these first, as once you got worn down, you wanted to be rolling, not lugging.

A girl with long black hair stepped out of a car on the side lot as I pushed through the back door. I stared so hard that I stumbled off the curb, sure it was Corabelle, and my heart nearly thumped right out of my skin.

But when she looked my way, I realized she was just some other girl. She peered up at the sign to Bud's Garage and headed toward the front door. I wondered if Corabelle had already gone to see her counselor and dropped out of astronomy. I picked the class because of the star parties, like most undergrads. I didn't really need more science electives, as my geology courses were plenty, but it seemed a good balance, the earth and the heavens, staying grounded but looking up to the infinite.

I tossed the tire into the bin. Damn, I hadn't waxed all poetic like this in years. Life had been practical for a long time. Work. Class. Beer. Studies. Occasional women, when I could afford one. I didn't have much of a clue what I'd actually do with a degree in geology. But rocks were solid. They didn't change, not easily. If they got worn down, it took time.

Then there were geodes. My grandpa, way back when I was a kid, had bought me one once. He cracked it sharply on the step in front of our house, and the dull smooth exterior revealed something fantastic inside, a sparkling burst of colored crystal — the opposite of what it had once appeared to be. I immediately ran to Corabelle's to give her half, leaving my grandpa behind to laugh at my surprise.

Life had turned out exactly the opposite of that rock. What once had been so bright and full of promise had gotten buried in the dull grays of the daily grind. I still had that geode, though, and it had inspired me to get my high school diploma squared away and take up geology at UCSD. Pick a new dream, as far from my old life as possible.

I wiped the sweat off my neck, glad for a hat as the sun was more like summer than fall. Honest work, my mother would have said. I should call her. I hadn't spoken to her, hell, since Christmas. I yanked open the back door, feeling guilt but pushing it back. I knew why I didn't call. Dad would jerk the phone from her hand, start yelling about when I was going to pay him back for that semester he covered when I took off. Four years and he wouldn't let it go. He never let anything go.

I decided to roll the next tire, and chose one so bald it showed the tread ghosts. Still, I wasn't seeing the rubber or the stack, but Corabelle's face, not the features of a girl any longer, but sharper and more defined. I'd looked into that face more than anyone's, even my mother's, from the time we could walk. We lived back to back across an alley, and the path from my house to hers was one I could do in the pitch black, the driving rain of a monsoon, sick, angry, lost, or desperate.

I smashed through the door, already tired of rolling. Corabelle had been my whole life for eighteen years. The last four without her had been nothing. I hadn't seen it until I looked up from that piece of paper listing her name, and there she was.

Right now, it was her choice to reject me and that had to feel good to her. She was getting me back for leaving and for all the things she didn't even know.

Maybe I shouldn't quit. Maybe I should keep letting her throw punches at me. If she gave a good hard shove that truly and finally hurt, maybe I'd finally stop wanting her back.

5

CORABELLE

The strap to my backpack was going to break clean off if I jerked on it any more. I sat across from my counselor, who looked frazzled from dealing with first-day mishaps. Folders and loose pages covered her enormous desk. The office was small and hot, and a rivulet of sweat trickled from her hairline down her temple as she typed.

"Corabelle, you have three choices. Pick a different time slot for a class. Drop below a full load for the quarter." She glanced up at me. "Or stay in astronomy."

My fingers tightened on the strap again. "I have to ask my manager if I can change my hours. He has to work around all our schedules."

"Well, I can't help you if I don't know any other times. There's nothing else useful to you on Mondays at 9 a.m. unless you want another PE-type credit. I can get you into interpretive dance or weight lifting."

I groaned.

"Enrollment is way up this year and classes have started. Pickings are slim." She tapped more keys. "I've got seven students hoping you'll drop astronomy. It's a popular class."

"How long is the waiting list for the speech class, or what was the other?"

"Ancient Rome. Too long. Those are small classes and I don't think enough could possibly drop." She swiveled in her chair. "Corabelle, if you want to graduate on time, you should just take this class. I don't understand why you're suddenly so opposed."

I couldn't tell her it was about a boy. "It's got too much extra work for an elective."

"The star parties are what make the class. You knew that going in."

I swallowed. "I have to get out."

She pushed a folder aside. "Let me pull up your actual records rather than this printed overview. We can take a good hard look at your transfer history and see if maybe we can wiggle some class over to cover this one."

I slammed my hand on the desk. "No!"

She looked up, startled.

I forced myself to relax. "I mean, no, it's fine."

She turned from the keyboard to study me. "I'm just trying to see where you might switch something around. Maybe there's an online course."

My face burned. I'd gone this far without anyone finding out what happened in New Mexico. I couldn't risk the consequences if that professor had saved any note in the system. "I'll stay in astronomy."

The woman nodded. "That's a good choice. You'll find the star parties fantastic." She closed my folder full of official printouts I painstakingly kept, all bearing seals and formal letters, anything I could do to avoid people digging too deeply into my electronic past. So far, I had been able to count on people being busy or lazy.

"Thank you. Sorry for wasting your time."

She waved me away. "It's all right. See you at the end of the quarter so we can establish your final coursework."

I slung the backpack over my shoulder and opened the door, stepping over the line of students sitting along the wall, waiting to get in.

My head buzzed as I stormed through the building. Maybe I could switch TAs. Yes, if I told them I had a permanent conflict with Thursdays, it would make more sense to switch study groups now than to constantly do makeups. Gavin would be in the classroom, but I could avoid him. As long as we were at different star parties, it would be okay.

The day was still bright and colorful outside, making it difficult to stay upset with a world full of birdsong and eucalyptus. I was back on track, in school again, and the last thing I needed was to let Gavin Mays derail my life a second time.

Jenny caught up with me at the quad, her pink ponytail as vivid as a blossom. "You ran out of class. And that hunkalicious man-meat followed you. What was that all about?"

"Someone I used to know."

"Ahhhh! Someone you used to bang!" She grabbed my arm and stopped me from walking. "Is this the boy who chilled off Frozen Latte? Tell! Tell! Tell!"

"He's from my hometown."

"And…"

"We dated."

"And…"

"I just can't be in his study group."

Jenny plunked down in the grass, setting her messenger bag beside her. "I can get that. I don't have a single ex I want to see again unless it's in a body bag."

I sat next to her. "I tried to drop just now, but the counselor couldn't get me anything but interpretive dance."

"Really?" Jenny jumped back up and held out her arms in a ballet pose, spinning neatly in a circle. Just as I wondered what the heck she was doing, she dramatically dropped her head and shoulders, like a puppet whose strings had just broken.

"What are you doing?"

She peered up at me. "What, you don't like my interpretation of a flower in the rain?"

"Seriously? You took dance?"

She plopped back into the grass, lying down with her head on her bag and her black leggings crossed at the knee. "The teacher was so freaking hot."

I had an idea. "Hey, you wanted lumberjack boy, right? The other TA?"

"Yeah, sure." She tugged on her orange miniskirt and straightened the crop top, like she was arranging herself for display. Jenny always looked like she had stepped out of the shop window of a trendy store.

"Why don't we switch? Then you could do the star parties with lumberjack boy, and I wouldn't have to be in the same group as Gavin."

She lifted her sunglasses to peer at me. "Gavin. Is that hunk boy?"

Surely she wouldn't go for him. The thought of her fawning on Gavin made me feel sick.

"Don't look all distressed." She took my hand and crossed an "x" on my palm. "Girlfriends don't date girlfriends' exes. Period."

I swallowed, pushing against the pain of picturing Gavin with any other girl. He'd been my first and only, and I had been his. But no telling how many he'd been with since then.

"Hey! Cora! I'm serious!" Jenny sat up and waved her hand in front of my face. "I can see how upset you are. Girl, you've got to learn to keep that face in check."

I looked at her, all color and tight clothes, vivid lipstick, big shades, and colored hair. She was cute and fun. Gavin just might eat her up.

"I'm saving myself for Lumberjack," Jenny said. "Don't worry about it. And sure. Their e-mails are on our paper whatsits. We can get them to switch. Say we have to work."

My shoulders relaxed a bit. "Thank you, Jenny. You're saving me here."

She waved at some guy who was checking her out as he walked by. "Oh, no, you're saving me. I'll be rolling logs with Lumberjack in no time."

6

GAVIN

The last damn tire was in the bin.

Mario had already taken off, telling me to call him later if I wanted to shoot some pool. Bud was still inside, closing up.

My back was screaming, and I stretched my arms high in the air, trying to head off a cramp. I wouldn't need to work out tonight, and I'd be hurting tomorrow. But it felt good.

Bud waited inside the back door. "Brace yourself for a lecture," he said as he flipped the lock.

Great. I passed on by him to head to the tiny break room, just a little closet where we had a fridge and a sink. I yanked a bottle of water from inside and chugged the whole thing in one long gulp. Bud had mostly been hands off as a boss. He brought me on two years ago when I was flat busted and going to have to drop out of school.

I'd been hauling groceries but my car had crapped out and I couldn't afford the parts. I sold the Camaro early on to pay for my first year of school, replacing it with junkers, but I'd run slowly in the hole with college expenses. Mario and I knew each other from the pool hall, being about matched for skill, and won money off each other at an even clip. He brought me to Bud, who hired me to rotate tires and change oil for twice the pay I earned as a sacker.

Bud filled the doorway, stinking of grease and sweat and a long day.

"So you gonna tell me to stay in school?" I asked.

He wiped his hands on a rag, slowly, with deliberation. "I know you got a shit dad."

I exhaled in a rush. "Who the hell thinks that?"

"Nobody had to say it. I can see it. Chip on your shoulder as big as my dick."

I snorted. He had a way with words, that Bud. "So you're stepping in?"

"Don't get smart with me." He pointed a finger at my nose with an intensity I'd never seen in him. "I got a boy at home."

"I didn't know you had a son."

"Don't talk about him much." He fumbled in his overalls and pulled out a wallet. Like me, he had a single picture in the center. The boy in the shot was a man, full grown, but with a kid quality to him. His eyebrows were high in the air, like he was surprised, and his goofy grin was infectious.

"He's all grown, but he lives with me still. Thirty now, but his mind…" He pointed at his forehead. "His mind is like he's about five."

I looked down at the picture again. I could see it.

"Marci and me, bless her soul, we only had the one." He turned the photo around. "Never could seem to get her pregnant again." He tucked the wallet in his pocket. "Don't get me wrong, Andy is enough. And now that she's gone, I'm glad he's with me. Gives me something to come home to."

I leaned on the fridge, staring at a big scratch across the freezer door. I wasn't sure about his point, but I had a feeling it was coming.

"What I'm saying is that if you've got the opportunity, you take it." He cleared his throat. "When I hired you, you wanted your degree. You needed a job that got you the extra to get you through. I know you ain't got nobody to fall back on. So don't throw away what opportunity God gave you, 'cause the Big Guy don't go around giving it to everybody."

He turned away and stormed across the empty bays.

I closed my eyes and leaned my forehead against the cool fridge. I couldn't tell how much of what Bud said was blowing smoke and how much he meant business. Maybe I could find some other way. I mean, if Corabelle was dropping astronomy, then that would be fine. I just had to make sure I didn't run into her anywhere else. Lie low. Eyes to the ground.

We were adults. We could do this. It was just the shock of it, seeing each other again after all those years.

I pushed away and headed to the time clock to punch out. Bud was sitting at his desk by the front window, locking up the register.

He turned to me as I passed through. "You all right?"

I nodded. "Yeah."

"You going to give me your schedule so I can work you in?"

I unlocked the door and pushed it open. "I'll bring it tomorrow."

"Good." He stood up to lock the door behind me.

The gravel crunched beneath my boots as I headed toward my Harley, the only transportation I could manage these days, gas being what it was. Mario had found the body as a junker, and I built it piece by piece. I wondered if Corabelle had ever ridden a motorcycle, if she had had a chance in the intervening years.

The motor vibrated between my legs as the Harley roared to life. Something unfurled in me, coming down like I'd been coiled up. Staying in school was the right thing to do. Bud was right. I'd make it work.

I wasn't particularly looking forward to Wednesday and astronomy class. My Harley cornered hard as I circled into my usual spot. Students needed to wise up to bikes. Way easier to park and no buses or schedules to worry with.

A girl smiled at me, holding a couple books to her chest, long blond hair flowing down her back. I yanked off my helmet and dropped it in the saddlebag. Chicks and bikes. Secondary benefit, although not one I availed myself of, at least not with girls like her. I had no use for them. No matter how much precaution you took, things could go south. I had very precise taste in women these days, and sweet sorority girls didn't qualify.

As I secured the bag, Corabelle flashed back into my memory, her hair across a pillow. We lived together for two months, two sweet damn months, once we figured out we were staying in New Mexico to raise the baby. We had a little apartment, and hell, the whole town was helping us out. Low rent, used furniture. And I had her all to myself, all the time.

We had this back window in the bedroom, big as the wall and no curtains, since it faced a crazy tall fence and nobody nowhere could see in. In the mornings, light would stream in. I'd wake Corabelle up for school, give her a glass of water, and a cracker if she was feeling queasy, but by then she was better, not as sick.

Some mornings, she would look at me a certain way, and I'd know she was feeling all right, and I'd kiss her, and that connection would just charge through us like the sun blasting across the bed. It all got tied up together, loving on her and the beams of light on her hair, the swell of her belly and having all her skin to touch and look at. Mine. She'd been mine. We'd been crazy with it.

Enough.

I slung my pack over my shoulder and shoved sunglasses on my face. Keep it down. Even if she had dropped my class, she probably was walking to some other morning course. Seeing her would not improve my mood.

The jaunt to the engineering hall was mercifully short. I skipped the stairwell where we talked two days ago and hustled all the way to the other end of the building. Then I realized I was being stupid and went back down the hall, opened the damn door, and went up the damn stairs. I was acting like a sentimental ten-year-old girl, and I knew what they were like. My little sister had been ten when I took off.

My jaw tightened as I passed the spot where I caught Corabelle on the rail. She felt so different, lean and strong. The last months we'd been together she'd been pregnant. I'd forgotten her body.

Like hell I had.

The door yielded to my shove and swung open with another slam. At least there weren't any moon-eyed girls this time. The classroom door was propped open, so I headed in and plunked down at the end of a center row.

"I don't think that one's yours," a girl said, raising her eyebrows at my sunglasses.

"What do you mean?"

"We got assigned seats by the TAs."

Shit. I stood up and looked around. Students dotted random chairs. Up at the podium, one of the TAs pointed a guy to a row. She must have the chart.

I strode up to her and yanked off my sunglasses. "Mays," I barked.

She jumped a little. "What?"

"Mays. Where do I sit?"

Her face bloomed red as she consulted the page. "Fifth row, tenth seat."

I turned away to head back, but then stopped. Corabelle was in the doorway, watching me with anger and disgust. My fist clenched, then relaxed, then clenched again. She'd seen me acting like an asshole. Whatever. I'm sure it made ditching me easier.

She took tentative steps along the back aisle, and I could see in her face how much she didn't want to be here. I guessed she wasn't able to drop the class. Didn't surprise me really. Of all the years I'd been enrolled at UCSD, this one had been the worst in terms of getting the classes I requested.

I sank into my seat, unable to take my eyes off her. So much for lying low. She seemed a little lost, but some girl with pink hair pointed her toward the podium. Corabelle took the long way around to the other side of the room rather than pass me again. She asked the blond TA about her seat.

The pink chick watched me with distrust the whole time. I figured she had to be a friend of hers. She held that stare so long that I finally waved.

Corabelle looked at my row, and I realized we were going to be close to each other. My last name and Corabelle's were only six letters apart, and in our hometown, we often were seated close together in school. With barely a hundred people in the class, I wasn't surprised when she ended up just a few seats down.

She didn't look at me, and I knew I had to stop staring. I shoved my sunglasses back on my face, not caring if it made me look emo or that the room was really too dark to see.

The professor came in and powered on the projectors. Students began piling through the door, wandering around, some forgetting exactly where they sat and having to shift around. The girl with the chart straightened everyone out. It looked to be the way she was taking roll, also typical. My enthusiasm for the class was all but gone.

Robert, the TA for my group, went up to the girl TA and they compared lists to the chart. Robert crossed a name off his list and the girl wrote it on hers. That gave me an idea. If I told Robert I had to work on Thursdays, maybe he'd put me in another group. That way, Corabelle and I would only have to suffer being near each other during lectures. And who knows, maybe I could skip half of them and still pull a decent grade. It would be a lot easier going to the star parties knowing I wouldn't have to be up there with her.

I'd catch up with the TA after class and make that happen.

7

CORABELLE

I tied my Cool Beans apron around my waist and yanked my hair into a serviceable ponytail. With a year's worth of seniority, which at a coffee shop was plenty, I'd been able to take off the first two days of class, but now work beckoned.

Jenny dumped the tip jar onto one of the tables, sorting through the change to trade for paper. "I forgot how cheap the students were."

I nodded, snagging the empty tip jar on my way to the counter. "We're bottom-feeders."

The shop was mostly empty, just a couple students with noise-canceling headphones working on laptops in the corners. One of them was a big-time regular, a clearly impoverished student who always bought one tea bag then asked for so many mugs of hot water that he had to be drinking nothing but wet sugar in the end. A couple of my coworkers teased me about him, saying he only came for me, but I didn't see it. He always ordered, then asked for more water, and that was it. Not like it mattered. Dating was out, and with Gavin around, I'd be way too riled up to pay attention to anyone else.

Jenny came up behind me to the register, dumping in a pile of pennies. "First star party is tonight! You ready?"

"I'll have to bust my butt to get there." Now that my labs were on Wednesday, I had to take morning classes, put in my afternoon shift, and race back to campus. "Thank goodness it's only every other week."

"Tomorrow is my date with destiny and the lumberjack." Jenny braced her elbows on the counter.

"You mean Robert?"

"I like him better as the lumberjack." She stared up at the ceiling. "I like to think beneath those plaid sleeves lies raw muscle."

Hardly. I had more bulk than that boy. But it was Jenny's dream. "Did you break it off with hipster dude?"

Jenny popped up and untied her apron. "No way. Never jump ship until you have a lifeboat."

I dropped some change into the empty tip jar to get it started. "Jenny's life axioms. They are my favorite thing about you, you know."

She stuffed her apron in the cabinet below the register. "Good. 'Cuz I've got a million of 'em. Are you excited? Tonight you will be at one of the most romantic spots in San Diego, on top of a building overlooking the ocean, gazing at the stars."

"If we can even see them in the city."

Jenny shoved me playfully. "Can't you be romantic for at least a minute?"

"You wouldn't want me romantic. I'd steal all your men."

"As if!" Jenny laughed, then sobered. "Actually, maybe I do like you because you are a safe wingman. You never look at them." She snatched her purse from the cabinet and slammed it shut. "You HAVE to call me and tell me what it's like up there. I'll want to know exactly how to dress."

"Lumberjack will be busy, you know. Instructing." I sorted

through the customer numbers on little wire stands, organizing them into neat lines.

"I'll make sure he notices me." She headed for the door. "You better text me!"

The shop seemed quieter after she left, less colorful and bright. I didn't think I ever lit up a room quite like Jenny could. I sank onto a stool, knowing I should get to the tasks I had to perform before a rush hit, but really, for the first time, I let it sink in that I was still in class with Gavin.

He looked so different with his sunglasses and black clothes. He'd changed since high school, no doubt. I didn't know him anymore.

Tea-bag boy got up from his table and brought his empty cup to the counter. "Can I get some more hot water?"

I nodded, turning with the mug. As the steam curled up toward my face, I wondered if maybe I had been wrong to stay completely away from dating. If I had some other person in my life, Gavin probably wouldn't have such an impact. This guy seemed normal.

Smile. Turn around and be nice. Give yourself something else to think about. I picked up the mug and carried it back to the counter. The boy wore a white shirt and cargo shorts. His hair was shaggy and dirty blond, his eyes hazel. When I didn't let go of the mug, he raised his eyebrows. "You okay?"

"Sorry. Here you go." God, I'd messed up already.

"Thanks." He took the mug and headed back to his seat.

Some start. I watched him walk away, a little on the lean side, but intriguing and deep, like he could be an indie musician or maybe someone who wrote dark stories. There was an intensity in him, just below the surface of his laid-back ease.

He sat down and looked back at me, catching my stare.

I whirled around. Hell. I was mucking this up something awful. I sat on the stool and began a mindless task, picking up a bottle of syrup for Italian sodas and wiping it down with a damp cloth.

Fact was, I'd never dated, ever. Gavin was my best friend from before I could remember. We grew up together, and our relationship transitioned from talking about cartoons and games to who was starting to pair off and how far they were going.

My first kiss had been when I was twelve. We watched *Hello, Dolly!* and I was full of romantic expectation. I asked Gavin what it must have been like for those couples to kiss, and he hadn't said a word, but took my hand and led me to my room, then my closet, shutting the door behind us.

A little light came in through the slats, crossing his face with fine lines. "What are we doing?" I whispered, even though I had known, my belly fluttering.

He placed a palm against each of my cheeks and leaned in, brushing his lips against mine.

The closet burst into color like the Fourth of July, sparks flying behind my eyes. I closed them without knowing I should.

Gavin leaned back. "Do you think we did that right?"

I put my hands on top of his and nodded. Something started that day. This happiness I always felt around him changed from something simple to a yearning, and I didn't know what for.

But we kept kissing, a lot, more and more. In fact, with that head start, we jumped ahead of the curve for most of the things boys and girls did together.

"Miss?"

My head snapped up. Tea-bag boy was back.

I hopped off the stool and set the syrup bottle down. I had never gotten past the first one.

"Yes! Can I help you?"

He didn't answer right away, and I could see he only came up to talk to me. "I just thought," he began and looked back at his table, as if it might give him a clue to what he was after, then turned back to me. "You seemed…something."

Panic rose in my chest. Jenny and the others had been right about him, and now I'd given him a reason to think I was interested. I had a hard time breathing, and I wondered why I had considered seeing anyone. It had just been too long since I felt this way, this crazy horrifying fear that I might be attracted to someone, that I might rely on them, and that they might just disappear.

The boy tipped his head. "Are you okay?"

"I —" Crap. I what? "I have to go turn something off."

I raced along the counter and burst through the door to the back room. God, god, god. What was wrong with me? Would I be ruined forever? I leaned against a wall, one hand to my chest. My coworker Jason was supposed to be here, to help. Where was he? I wasn't up for being out there. I should be doing my setup work in the back.

My chest had gone all tight. I knew what I should do, breathe slowly and relax, but instead I did the same thing as always and held my breath, making it worse, watching the spots flash in front of my eyes. Everything started going dark and my knees buckled. Without anything blocking my airflow, I knew I'd just sink to the floor, conk my head, and then come back around. I'd done it a thousand times in the last few years. It helped. For a few minutes, I always felt like I knew what it had been like for baby Finn, after the ventilator went off, and his little chest stopped moving up and down —

My head hit the floor.

The cold of the concrete against my cheek started bringing me back. The room returned in degrees, first dark, then lighter, then slowly gaining color. I sat on the floor, my back against a wire rack of mugs. Stupid. I shouldn't have done this here. I could have brought down a whole pile of dishes and lost an entire paycheck.

Or someone could have found me and seen just how crazy I could be.

I heaved myself up and headed to the sink. The water splashing on my face and neck helped me relax and regain control. I didn't know any other way to cope.

I didn't have to accept or reject that boy out there. I was going to be fine.

When I walked back out, another customer, a girl, was in line behind the boy. I couldn't believe he was still standing there.

"You all right?" he asked.

"Did you need something?"

He looked confused and anxious. "I just — you seemed —" He stopped talking and stepped to the side so the girl could come up.

"I need another mocha latte," she said, casting a quick glance at the boy.

"No problem," I said and whirled away. The moment was gone. The boy would move on. I would never look at another one again, not until I knew I could handle it, whenever that might be.

When I turned around, the girl was pulling out one of those digital cigarettes. "We don't allow those inside," I said and pushed her latte across the counter.

"It's not a real cigarette."

"I know, but still, we ask you to take those things on the patio."

The girl frowned. "I know my rights. There is no ban on these right now."

This was making my day even better. I took in a deep breath, still feeling the constriction in my chest from my episode. "I don't make the rules. I just get fired if I don't enforce them."

She dropped a five on the counter and picked up her latte. "So kick me out." Her heavy footfalls on the hardwood floor echoed through the room as she stomped back to her table to make a big show of lifting the e-cig to her lips.

I couldn't bear to look at the boy, who was still standing by the counter. This was humiliating, plus a problem. Martin wouldn't really fire me, but he'd be upset. We kept asking him to put up a sign about the e-cigs, but so far he hadn't done it.

"Hey." The boy's expression was full of sympathy. "If you could use a break from all this later, this is me." He pushed a napkin toward me. "It'll go straight to my phone."

The napkin stuck to my damp hand. Austin Thompson. OneQuirkyDude44 was his e-mail handle, which struck me as funny.

"Made you smile." He tapped the counter twice and turned back to his table.

Jason burst through the back door, his dreadlocks flying behind him. "So freaking sorry. Traffic was a bugger."

I folded up the napkin and stuck it in my apron pocket. "It's fine. Only two people here."

He caught me tucking the note away, but had the sense not to say anything about it. Instead, he pushed an errant hunk of hair out of his face. "Old Man Martin is going to sock it to me if I'm late anymore."

"He won't hear it from me," I said.

"You cool with me saying I was here on time?" He reached around me for an apron below the counter, but I saw him glance at my pocket, as if he was dying to ask about the folded napkin.

I stepped out of his way. "Sure. No point getting fired."

"That's why everyone likes you." His fingers flew as he tied the strings. "Even if you are a Frozen Latte."

I winced at the nickname and glanced over at Austin, hoping he hadn't heard.

But Jason caught me looking. "Awwww! Is the ice queen thawing out?" He looked at the pocket yet again.

I backed away toward the door to the storage room. "I have to do the setups."

"We'll be calling you Hot Pumpkin Spice before it's over!" he called after me.

Austin was bound to have heard that. I bolted to my sanctuary and set to grinding the beans that would get us through the evening rush, wishing I could remain invisible forever.

8

GAVIN

A pair of giggling girls moved aside as I took the steps several at a time from the top floor of the building to the roof exit. My boots on the concrete made a sharp echo, like striking metal.

A rock propped the door open a few inches. I yanked it wide and the gravelly tarred rooftop seemed to absorb all light. I waited a moment to adjust, my eyes automatically moving to the edges where the city twinkled beyond a gleaming white ledge, and the blackness of the ocean was like the end of everything, like night itself.

Amy, the girl TA I talked to that morning when I switched labs, was lit like a statue by a heavy-duty floor light identical to the ones we used in the shop. "Gavin, right?" she asked. Her face blushed a little as she handed me a popsicle stick. "This will be your cross-staff for the lab."

I held the little piece of wood between my thumb and finger, flipping it over. Not what I expected. "Rudimentary, my dear Amy."

She laughed and her face burned even more red. Wisps of blond hair stuck to her cheeks as she reached down into her bag and pulled out a sheet of paper. Her skin was ghostly in the searing light, her legs blown out. She was cute, in a nerdy sort of way, the complete opposite of my type.

"Here are the instructions. You'll have to calibrate your stick and map out the Big Dipper using it as a measuring device." She passed me the page. "The calibration chart is around the corner past the door. The degrees on your stick will depend on the length of your arm, so you won't have the same length as other students."

"Thanks." I started to walk away.

"Hey, Gavin?"

I turned back around.

"If you need something, I'm glad to help." She stared at the paper in my hands. Shy girls. I couldn't work with them. They seemed so easy to break. I felt heavy with the weight of their expectations, and I knew one misstep could crush their hopes. That was something I was damn good at.

She looked up, cheeks on fire, and I realized why she was so willing to switch me even though it meant more work for her. Good old-fashioned boy crush. "I appreciate you letting me in your group," I said.

Amy nodded. "Sure."

A few other lamps had been set up along the roof, the cords snaking every direction. I angled my page toward a light. Draw lines on the stick, yada yada. Calibrate with the wall chart. I glanced at the poster tacked on the wall, where several freshman-looking types were aiming their sticks. Got it.

I dug around in my bag for a marker to divide up the stick. Making a straight line while free-holding something that small would be impossible, so I walked over to the lip of the roof to sit and hold it steady.

The building was one of the dorms on the extreme west side of campus. The city spread out in a twinkle of lights, the roadways like ribbons threading through. All of it was bordered by the black of the Pacific, as though it were a monster bumping up against the edge of civilization.

My stick was barely visible, so I dug a tiny key-chain flashlight from my bag. I held it between my teeth as I drew a line lengthwise on the stick. Passable, but I felt I could do better with a straightedge, so I flipped the stick over to use the cardboard cover of a notebook to try it a second time.

That's when I heard her voice.

Corabelle stood in the cone of light that shot up next to Amy. She looked like an angel, lit up from below, and her dark hair was bright to the tips.

Holy hell. Why was she here tonight? I had switched to avoid her, to help her out.

Then I realized with a sickening sensation — so had she.

I knew she couldn't see too far past all that light. I could watch her a moment, so sad looking, so serious. Even doing something as ordinary as accepting a piece of paper, she looked tragic, like a fragile, beautiful doll.

Despite all my work to drive that need of her out of me, it roared back with an ache so powerful that for a second, I really thought it might be easier to swing my legs over the ledge and jump. I couldn't have Corabelle, not anymore, and if I thought for a minute I ought to try, I had to remember all the things she'd eventually find out. I was simply setting myself up to lose her again.

She stepped out of the light and I was torn between focusing on my task or letting her see that I was watching.

But then it was too late, and she looked straight at me. Her mouth fell open in an astonished "o."

I left my stuff on the ledge and hurried over to her. "I switched groups."

She couldn't seem to tear her gaze away from me, so I kept

talking. "When I saw you were still in the class, I thought it would help."

She closed her mouth finally and gripped her assignment so hard that it crumpled. I took it from her and straightened it against the leg of my jeans.

When I handed it back, she said, "I did the same thing."

"I'll talk to Amy," I said. "I'll switch back."

Corabelle's jaw clenched, and I had to resist the urge to run my finger under her chin, like I always had when she was upset.

"It's going to be fine. I'll be fine." She spun away from me and headed toward the calibration chart.

Bloody hell. Life seemed to be throwing us at each other. Hadn't it done enough already?

9

CORABELLE

My hands were shaking so hard that there was no way I could draw a line on a stupid popsicle stick.

Gavin was somewhere behind me. I didn't believe anymore that I'd be able to shake him. Whatever whim of fate or karma that blasted us apart four years ago apparently felt we should not be separated now. I didn't know how to fight it.

The feeling I might hyperventilate came over me again, but instead of feeding it, I fought it. Not here, not now. I had to stay in control.

But just looking at Gavin took me back to the days before we were so damaged, when we had no clue that anything could go wrong. We were a family in progress, and our future spread out before us like the stars. I thought we'd be that happy and innocent forever, and that nothing would ever come between us.

I passed the calibration chart and sank down on the roof next to one of the lights, where a couple other girls were reading over the lab instructions.

If I sat just so, Gavin was visible from the corner of my eye. He looked so lean, so strong, and his thighs filled out those jeans like they never had before. I wondered about the rest of him, how he might have changed, and the image of his face over mine, his body propped on his arms, made all the chilly parts of me grow hot. Everything I held tightly inside, my desire to be held close, to lose myself, began to unfurl.

For just a moment, I let myself remember how happy I'd once been. I hadn't basked in those memories for a long time, not since New Mexico and the disaster there, when I discovered a shocking side of myself, how in a split second despair could turn to violence.

I set my backpack down on the roof and pretended to read the assignment, although Gavin was still in my field of vision. I didn't want to think of the bad things, just the good ones.

When Finn was just born, literally the first few minutes, I felt completely and utterly blessed. Labor hadn't been anything like the horror stories everyone had been teasing me with. Sure, the baby was pretty early at 32 weeks, and small. But he was plenty old enough. Babies that age survived all the time.

His little lungs managed just fine at first, and even though they had placed him in an isolette with his eyes covered and monitors on his tiny body, no one seemed overly alarmed.

Gavin sat on the edge of the bed, holding my hand. "He's beautiful. He's perfect."

They wheeled him down to NICU and I remembered sinking back on the pillow, exhausted, but there was no reason to worry. The last happy memory, possibly my very last happy memory, was Gavin leaning down and pressing his lips into my hair and whispering, "You are so amazing."

Up on the roof, I couldn't help it, but I turned so I could see him clearly. He was hunched over his popsicle stick, a shadow against the bright lights of the city. Emotion welled up, and for a moment I thought, he can just look up, and I can smile at him, and it can be like it always was.

But then he frowned, struggling to line up the cover of a notebook on his popsicle stick, his eyebrows drawing together. His expression reminded me of how he acted during the funeral, agitated and bitter, getting up before the minister said, "Amen." He stormed down the aisle, shrugging the too-large jacket off his shoulders and dropping it to the floor.

Nothing good could stay pure, not even a memory.

I forced myself to look back at my instructions. This was why I didn't want to have class with him. It would take so much mental energy to manage with him so near.

The girls by the light leaned their heads together.

"Amy is totally losing it over that guy," one said to the other.

"Out of her league," the other said.

"Sort of sad how she keeps staring at him."

"I'd stare at him."

I didn't want to pay any attention to their gossip, but still, it was a distraction from my thoughts. I looked over at the TA. She was trying not to be obvious, but every six seconds she glanced over her shoulder at the ledge. I followed her gaze. Good Lord. She was obsessing over Gavin.

I turned back to my page. Draw a line. Do your assignment. Get your degree. Get the hell out.

I unzipped my bag and fished around for a ruler.

The two girls headed for the wall chart, and damn it, I sneaked another peek at Gavin. He was strung out. I could tell by the way his chin jutted forward. He kept setting and resetting the cardboard on the tiny stick, trying to keep it straight. His frustration was growing, and he was going to explode any minute.

Too bad. I aligned the ruler with my stick and drew a thin solid line. Next, I measured out the five sections and ticked off the centimeters. I would not look. I would finish this. Go home. Forget.

I stood up and headed to the wall chart to calibrate the cross-staff. I held out the stick and determined the degrees that corresponded to the lines I'd drawn. Now to map out the Big Dipper and I could go.

I turned around, and God, I couldn't help it, but my gaze went back to him. Gavin was still sitting there, elbow on his knee, chin in his hand. He looked at his popsicle stick again and suddenly it was winging its way out into the night sky.

Amy apparently saw it as well, as she walked over to him and handed him another stick. "Need help?" she asked.

He shook his head, but the TA persisted, standing close. Too close.

I yanked the ruler from my bag. I was going to do something stupid. I closed the gap and held out the ruler. "You never did have the right school supplies."

Gavin swallowed, his Adam's apple starting high, then bobbing down. "You always were there with your organized binders and perfectly sharpened pencils." His eyes didn't seem so blue in the dark, and his lips were quirked in that little lopsided smile I teased him about when we were small, but not so much later, when kissing it became my primary obsession.

Amy set the new stick on the ledge and backed away. I should leave this alone, let her have him. Anyone had to be better for him than me.

He accepted the ruler and laid it on the stick. I picked up his little flashlight and held it for him. The new line halved the piece of wood neatly, and he quickly marked off the five segments. When he was done, he returned the ruler. "Thanks."

I held the plastic, still warm from his hands. I didn't know what to do or say, so as he moved toward the wall chart, I followed, like a groupie dying for any acknowledgment from the rock star she obsessed over.

He held out the stick and closed one eye. His arm really wasn't too high, but still, I reached out and lowered it to the optimum level for calibration, my hand burning where it connected with his skin. He sucked in a breath and I knew he felt it too. How could he not, with all our history?

"Did you make your map yet?" he asked.

"No."

Without the least hesitation, he took my hand and led me to my backpack, scooping it up, then around the rooftop to the far corner. No lights were hooked up there, so it was quiet and dark. "Lie here with me," he said and set his backpack on the ground. He squeezed my fingers as he let go, and I wished we had walked some great distance, just to feel his hand on mine a little longer.

I laid my pack next to his and we stretched out on the bumpy surface, staring up at the stars.

"So how long have we both lived in the same city and not known it?" he asked.

"I got here a year ago."

"A year."

I couldn't believe he was here the whole time. "It's a big city, I guess."

"Doesn't seem big now. Do you work?"

"Yeah. At a coffee shop on Broadway. You?"

He shifted next to me. "At a garage. Changing oil. Easy stuff."

"Not what we planned, is it?"

"Hardly."

A breeze kicked up and our papers fluttered. I pressed down to keep them from flying away. "I guess we should do the lab."

He pointed to the sky. "There's the Big Dipper."

"We should measure it," I said, but neither of us made any move to fill out our worksheet.

This was so easy, lying next to him, just *being*.

"Did we ever do any stargazing when we were kids?" he asked.

"I don't think so."

"Should've."

"Yeah."

"Not like we were in some metropolis."

"Nope. I remember the stars." I shifted on the rough roof, the bits of asphalt biting into my shoulders. Still, I swear it was the happiest I'd been in a long time. Stupid. Ridiculous. But true. I tried to think of Austin passing the note across to me at the coffee shop, but he was nothing, just no contest compared to all the emotions that surfaced with Gavin.

I felt doomed. I couldn't be with him. Too much had happened, and everything since. God. If he knew why I hit my professor, why I quit school. If he put it all together, he'd hate me. Right now, he still thought I was perfect and good.

Even though he left.

If he had all the facts, he'd leave again.

Go away, I told those thoughts. Live in the moment. Feel something for once.

I closed my eyes, reveling in the warmth of Gavin next to me and the comfort of sharing space with someone who knew me.

"Corabelle?"

My name sounded familiar when he said it, as though no one had used it since him. "Yeah?"

"Seems like the world wants us to at least be friends again."

I didn't know which words to get stuck on. *Friends.* Or *at least.* "Seems like it."

"You think we're the only ones who still think about Finn?"

Just hearing his name out here, in the open, with the heavens wide above, made my throat close up. "I don't know."

He turned his face to me but I kept my eyes up on the stars. The Big Dipper rested neatly in the sky, surrounded by lesser bits of light, and I understood how it all fit together. Some moments of our lives were vivid and strong, hanging among all the other memories, not to be forgotten. Our baby was that constellation for us, and no matter where we looked, no matter what other stars dotted our sky, he would always be there, the biggest and the brightest of them all.

10

GAVIN

Damn, this worked.

I made sure I kept my head straight, no worries about tomorrow. Just the night sky, the Big Dipper, and Corabelle next to me.

Something had shifted in her. I could see it, feel it. And as soon as I realized she wasn't going to go away, that she'd reconciled with us being around each other again, I'd adjusted too.

She lifted her arm to point at the constellation. "I'm still reeling from the lecture on those stars."

"Really? Why?" I'd been so distracted during class that I just transcribed the words, barely letting them penetrate. Corabelle had been so close, and I'd been so anxious to get to the TA and switch labs.

"He said two of them were Horse and Rider, orbiting together." She dropped her arm. "They look like one star but really are two, endlessly circling each other."

I figured Corabelle was using metaphors, like she always had. We'd been as close as one person until I'd walked. Or possibly she was just talking about stars.

"If you'd been listening today," she went on, "you'd know that after all these centuries, a couple other astronomers decided that there were actually three. They discovered one more small star in their gravitational pull." Corabelle still looked at the sky as she said all this, but the emotion was thick in her voice.

"That was 2009," she said, barely holding it together, and my urge to pull her close was crazy strong. "They discovered this exactly four years ago."

I felt the punch in my gut. That was when we last saw each other. When Finn was born. When he lived and died in his little plastic bed. I could hear the beeps of the monitor again, a steady stream of his heartbeat and random alarms. The only thing worse than those sounds was when they stopped.

"That's a powerful coincidence, finding that third star right then," I finally said.

Corabelle turned on her side, watching me. "When he said it in class, I could barely breathe. And you sat there, all defiant in your chair, just as stiff and angry as you got at the end."

I'd been angry. I knew that. The doctors had no more told us Finn would die than everyone was looking to me to make the decisions. To be strong for the whole lot of them, as if this wasn't as hard for me. Just thinking about that day made the rage boil over and before I could think about what I was saying, I blurted out, "You made me sign the papers to turn off the machines."

Corabelle sat up. "What are you talking about?"

I should shut this down, but I'd started it. I had to finish it. "The damn forms. The ones allowing them to shut down his ventilator." Bitterness coursed through me. I hadn't thought about this in years, but she was making me. She was dredging it all up.

Corabelle tried to touch me, but I jerked away.

"Is that why you left?" she asked. "Because you had to sign?"

I couldn't breathe, much less answer. Everything was rushing at me, like it had in those final days.

Corabelle dropped her hands in her lap. "We did what the doctors told us to do."

I couldn't take this anymore. I sat up and snatched at my bag. "I signed the paper. I decided when it ended. I was the one who told them when to let him die." I kicked at the fluttering page of the lab assignment and stepped on the stick as I strode away. This wasn't going to work. Too much history. Too much misery. Too much everything.

I shoved through the door and hauled ass down the stairs. Only when I was on my motorcycle, the roar of the motor drowning out all sound, did I start to feel any better. Distance. I needed miles to separate me and Corabelle again. Nobody could go through all this and come out okay. No one could be tough enough. I sure as hell wasn't.

The lights of the city began to fade as I tore through Torrey Pines State Park and to the ocean. Just the quiet there, and the lack of strip malls and concrete, calmed my fury. I hated blowing up at Corabelle for something that wasn't her fault. If she'd signed the papers, nothing would have been any different. The nurse would still have come in, and Corabelle would still have sat in that chair to hold the baby her first and last time. They would still have removed the ventilator. And the whir of the machines and the beeps of the monitors would still have gone silent.

Finn would still have died.

I turned off where the highway made contact with the beach and killed the bike. The water crashed against the shore, its endless wake a lulling sound, like the white-noise monitor some friend had given us for the baby. When Corabelle was still pregnant and couldn't sleep, I played it for her at night. We laughed that since we couldn't go to the college by the sea, we'd bring the sea to us.

Everything was flooding back, a trove of memories deeper than the ocean in front of me. I couldn't handle it any more than I had back then. I'd run again and ditched Corabelle a second time.

I yanked my helmet off and ripped the gloves from my hands. What was I doing? Where was I going? I wanted to hurl something at the moon, all serene in the stars. My classmates were on the building still, doing their lab work, and now I was going to start with an incomplete on the first assignment. Hell, maybe college was a waste. I had experience at Bud's. If he wouldn't promote me out of the oil changes and tire repair, I could find a place that would. My family boasted a long line of blue-collar workers. I didn't have to be any better.

I couldn't run from the stars, the whole ceiling winking at me like a mockery of my time on the roof with Corabelle. There didn't seem to be any place where I could escape.

11

CORABELLE

The sugar jars clanged together as I shoved them all in a bin to be filled. Whoever closed the night before was officially on my bad side. Prepping the coffee stand for the next day was the job of the evening crew.

I opened on Thursday mornings, a crazy early shift that started at 5 a.m. The shop would open in half an hour and Jason and I were manic, grinding beans and starting all the coffees, filling the bagel bin and bringing in the pastries from the dawn delivery.

But the work was brainless, so I could think through all the events of the night before. After Gavin stormed out, I caught the page of his lab work, filled out mine, adjusted for his, and turned them both in. I didn't really want to help him, and even as I did it, I burned with anger that he let something as small as a signature ruin everything. If he hadn't left me then, I would have been okay. No blackouts, no arrest, no leaving my old college.

Sugar slid over my hands as I overfilled a jar. "Shit!" I said, pulling back on the jug.

Jason paused as he walked by with a tray of biscotti. "Frozen Latte knows curse words?" He shook his dreadlocks. "The world is upside down."

I flicked sugar at him. This seemed so unbelievably simple. I'd spent half the night trying to remember that day, the parts I could bear. I really had no recollection of the conversation about the paperwork. We sat in some little conference room, and they'd gone over the results of Finn's heart test, and his brain scans, and how there was no longer any hope and the surgeon would not operate.

I closed my eyes for a moment. The room was so clear, the gray walls, black chairs, fake wood table. The doctor's beeper had gone off incessantly, but he ignored it, at least.

Finn was already lost. They hadn't saved him. His heart defect would not be repaired, and the lack of oxygen had already taken its toll. He would die, now or later, and we should prevent him from suffering.

I couldn't remember where I had been when the papers were signed, only that it was prom night, and people who had no idea what was happening were sending me texts asking if we would get away for the night, if I had a dress to wear. Facebook was blowing up with pictures of corsages and hairdos and limousines.

The shadows of a couple customers darkened the windowed door. I had to move, stop thinking, and work. I wiped down the sugar jars and set them out on the coffee bar. Jason came toward me, lugging the first two coffee tureens of the day. "You can let them in," he said. "We're set up."

I crossed the shop and twisted the lock on the door. Several early regulars in suits and work clothes hustled in. Jason waited behind the counter, and I rounded the pastry display to man the machines. I already knew what several orders would be.

In New Mexico, I had a cushy job working in the dean's office, filing and answering phones. Sometimes here in San Diego, early in the morning, during the rush, when customers were late to work and we couldn't make their coffee fast enough, I wished I had taken the risk to use my experience to get something better. I still could. If I went for an office job outside of the university, probably no one would look very close. And even if they did find out about my altercation on campus, the worst that could happen would be to get fired, and I could try the next place.

But I'd been too rattled when I first arrived. It seemed easier taking a job like this where no one cared about your past or even your present outside of the hours you were in the shop. Show up, do your job, and don't steal anything. That was about as much as anyone asked. Baristas could be surly and still be considered just to have character. Friendliness didn't necessarily get better tips, as regulars were set in their ways on ordering and dropping in change or adding to it. It was easy to be unmotivated.

The first three customers grew into a line to the door, and two hours passed before we got a break. The shop was still pretty empty, as the students who filled the tables weren't up yet. Everyone had taken their coffee to go.

Jason leaned on the counter. "At least it goes by fast."

I opened the back of the pastry case to see what needed replenishing. "I'm going to grab some more strudel," I told Jason. "Be right back."

Alone in the storeroom, my thoughts went right back to the star lab. I had to take great gulps of air. Gavin had brought all this emotion back to the surface. I'd have to do something about it soon, maybe really push. I kept all the plastic bags out of sight, but now, I didn't think I could resist. I looked forward to the black. I wanted it, the one thing that always connected me to Finn.

I snagged a tray of strudel and headed back up front. Jason still leaned on the counter, his cell phone in his hands. "I've got news for Frozen Latte!" he said.

I tugged a plastic glove on my hand and began loading the strudel into the case. "What are you talking about?"

"Found something in my apron pocket and decided it was a sign to take some action!" He laughed.

Whatever. I started a new row of strudel, but something nagged at me. Apron pocket. Oh, God. That e-mail address for Austin, the boy yesterday. I must have left it in one of the aprons in my hurry to get back to campus.

I whipped around so fast that the last few strudels on the tray flew off, one of them bouncing off Jason.

"Pastry attack!" he shouted, still laughing. "Don't panic, Latte, I didn't act like the e-mail was from you."

I snatched at his phone. "What did you say to him?"

I fumbled with the unfamiliar settings. I couldn't afford a smart phone, so I had no idea what all the icons meant. The envelope seemed logical, but those turned out to be text messages.

Jason scooped up the errant strudels and dropped them in the trash. "All I said was that he should come by the shop today. That you were here."

"Why did you do that?"

"He likes you. You need to get out more."

"I want to be the one who decides that."

"He's a good guy," Jason said. "We all approved."

"What?" I looked around the empty shop. "Who's we?"

"Pretty much the whole staff who was around last night."

The phone dinged and I held it away when Jason reached for it. "I should be able to read it first if it's him."

Jason shrugged. "Okay, but if you get an eyeful of my sexting, don't say I didn't warn you."

God. I walked away from him and sat at one of the tables. After a bit of button pushing, I found the e-mail. It said to come by, as "the girl you gave your e-mail to" was working today. He hadn't given him my name.

As I suspected, the reply was from Austin. He had class until noon, but then he'd come by.

It would be close. I got off at one to head to class at two. If he came right away, he'd make it. Maybe I could spend my last hour in the back, doing setup. Jenny would be here by then, not Jason, and she'd cover for me.

I stood up and slid the phone across the counter to Jason. "I'm going to stack mugs."

Jason laughed again. "We're going to get you laid whether you like it or not."

Right. That's exactly what I'd been avoiding all this time. I wasn't going to break now. In the year after Finn died, I studied the failure rate of every form of birth control. All of them had chinks in their armor, including the shot, which I'd been on.

The only way to avoid it was to side with the Catholics. Full-on abstinence.

Jason pushed a broom around, catching the crumbs from the pastry incident. His eyes were full of mischief as he pretended to dance with the handle and sweep it into a dramatic kiss. I wasn't mad, not really. These people wanted something good for me. They just didn't know any better.

And I wasn't going to enlighten them.

My heart started hammering the moment the clock struck twelve. Jenny came in through the front, looking harried. "Stupid traffic jam on 52. No accident or anything. Just slow people."

Jason tucked his apron under the register. "Too many people. Always too many people." He tied his dreadlocks into a ponytail. "I'd stick around to see the happy reunion, but I have class."

Jenny leaned on the counter. "What's he talking about?"

"Nothing," I said. Austin probably wouldn't show. No use feeding futile gossip.

Jason halted, his hand on the door. "It's not nothing! Latte here has a hot hookup with one of the regulars." He saluted us and headed outside.

"Are you holding out on me?" A customer came in, so Jenny moved around to the back, shoving her messenger bag in a cabinet.

I ignored her and smiled at the middle-aged man asking for a cappuccino. I'd serve him, then head to the back to do setups. Austin could arrive at any time. On a good day, you could get here from campus in about fifteen minutes. In traffic, it might be longer.

Jenny waited for me to hand the man his change before launching into questioning. "Who was Jason talking about? Why don't I know about this?"

I shrugged. "Some guy gave me his e-mail address yesterday. I left the note in one of the aprons. Jason found it and e-mailed the guy."

"WHAT? That is a blatant disregard of the hookup code!" She tied an apron around her waist. "Contacting potential boy toys is at the sole discretion of the best friend!"

I moved past her. "I'm going to do the dishes."

Jenny grabbed my arm. "What does he look like? How will I know he's here?"

"It doesn't matter. I don't think I'm up for that."

She let go. "It's because of hunk boy, isn't it? He's got you all wired up."

"Maybe."

Jenny shook her head. "I guess I'll be seeing him tonight. Maybe I'll give him a piece of my mind."

I walked to the end of the counter and lifted the overflowing tray from the busing station. "Actually, you won't. Gavin switched too, thinking he'd get away from me. We were both there last night."

A girl walked up to order something, but Jenny held up her hand. "Just a minute." She turned back to me. "So you're saying you had to be on the roof with him after all?"

I shrugged. "There was nothing romantic about it. Just a lab mapping out the Big Dipper."

Jenny frowned. "But weren't there stars? Night breezes off the ocean? Anything?"

I pictured Gavin on his back, head on his pack, lying next to me, my fingers still warm from where he held them. My stomach turned, and I could feel my breath threatening to kick up. "No," I managed to say. "Just lab work."

Jenny blew a puff of air at her frothy pink bangs in disgust. "Then that class is a total waste." She finally turned back to the girl. "What can I get for you?"

I pushed my elbow into the door, trying to avoid spilling any of the mugs or cups on the tray. Plenty of dishes to deal with until the end of my shift, unless Jenny got swamped and needed someone to make the drinks while she took orders. Hopefully that wouldn't happen. We didn't serve anything substantial here, so lunch tended to be quiet.

Rinsing dishes to load into the industrial washer was good, mindless work. My Tuesday/Thursday schedule was tough, two upper-division lit classes with a murderous reading list, but the first novel quiz wasn't until next week, and I had all weekend to catch up. I didn't have a bead on the profs here yet, but I figured most classes were the same. Read the books, figure out the instructor's preferred interpretation of the text, and spit it back at them on the midterm.

I swore if I ever got a class of my own, free thinking would be required, not regurgitation. But maybe one of these professors would surprise me.

The door to the back opened and Jenny peeked through. "Someone's here for you."

I glanced at the clock. 12:32. Not close enough to the end of my shift to sneak out.

"Can you get him to leave?" I asked.

"I don't think this one is going to be easy to put off." She pushed the door open wider, and Gavin's frame filled the doorway.

I backed up a few steps. "What are you doing here?"

"You told me you worked at a coffee shop on Broadway. I've been to six today, trying to find you."

"We have class tomorrow."

"I didn't want to see you in class."

"Oh, boy!" Jenny said and ducked under his arm.

He let the door close behind her.

I held a damp rag out in front of me like a pathetic shield. "I don't know you anymore. The Gavin I used to know wouldn't just take off like you did last night. Like you did at the funeral."

"You're not the same either."

I lowered my arms. "What are you talking about?"

"You're so sad all the time."

Rage bolted through me. "How dare you come in here and judge how I feel, now or ten years from now!" Jesus, he'd walked right out. How could he stand here and ask me why I was sad?

"I lost everything too!"

"NO!" I could tell my voice was hitting a shriek, one that would penetrate into the shop. I forced it down. "You made your choice. I was the one who had to live with it."

His jaw was so tight that a muscle in his cheek started twitching. The only time I ever saw him like that was after his dad had done something awful, thrown things or threatened him. How many times had he run to my house after a shouting match?

God. I would not cry. Would. Not. I was strong. I was a survivor. I had gone four years without him, and I could go plenty more. This time I would walk away. I no longer cared about my shift, or the hours. Martin wasn't going to fire me over leaving a little early one day.

I whirled around to sign out. Forget that, Jenny could forge my name. I'd text her later. I just wanted away from here.

But Gavin still blocked the door.

I walked up to him. "Let me get my things. I need to go to class."

He didn't budge. He wore all black again, a Dead Kennedys T-shirt from a 2011 concert. I didn't know that band. He'd been to a show, and I had no idea where or when or what music he listened to. I knew nothing about him anymore.

"Gavin, please, let me go."

Suddenly his arms were around me and he jerked my head into his chest. His heart hammered against my ear, and I could feel how overwrought he was, even though he was trying to hide it.

We stood there, glasses clinking in the room next door, the damp rag in my hand now between us, getting us both wet. I could feel time ticking along with the beat of his heart, slowing, revving down. I knew this was where I belonged, but there was no way to stay there.

"I have to believe we found each other for a reason," Gavin said.

I shook my head against his chest. "No. It's too late now. We can't do this." I tried to pull away, but his arms were a vise.

"Look up at me, Corabelle."

I didn't want to. Those blue eyes, that face. They were too familiar, too perfect.

But he made me. His hand came under my chin, and he lifted my head. I closed my eyes, refusing to look, but then his lips were on mine and the shock was so complete that I cried out against his mouth.

He pressed me against him. His kiss was fevered, hot, and everything I remembered from when we were young, plus so much more. He held my head against him and dove in deeply, his tongue parting my lips. When we fitted against each other every muscle in my body reacted and blood pounded through my veins in places I'd long since left for dead.

And I did feel utterly alive, kissing him back, my arms coming around him, letting the rag fall to the floor. He felt my response and his mouth became frenzied, his hands reaching down behind my thighs and lifting me up so that I straddled him. My arms curled around his neck, and I let go of everything, my fear, my anger, my grief, and just reveled in the heat blasting through me, the connection of our hips and his mouth trailing across my jaw and along my neck.

One of his hands cupped my bottom and squeezed, the other wrapped around my waist. He shifted me down, connecting us in that intimate way I'd only known with him, the roughness of his jeans bulging against my skirt, trapped between us. Despite everything we'd been through, I wanted nothing between us, and to find that place that had always bound us. Passion. Emotion. All the things I held away from myself since Finn, and the hospital, and that misery.

He groaned against my throat, pushing harder against me. Even with all the denim and fabric, I could feel it building, intense and hot and full of need. I clutched him, the strap of my sundress falling off my shoulder. Gavin nudged it with his nose, bending as much as he was able with me riding his hips, flicking his tongue along the lace edge of the bra. He stepped forward, resting me on the high dish counter, freeing his hand to cup my breast, still maintaining the rhythm between us.

I ached, desperate for more contact, for all of him. Every rational thought about where we were, who he was, what had happened was way beyond the glow of how I felt right now, explosive and hot.

The temperature shifted as the door opened, and Jenny's "Oh, shit!" forced us to break apart.

She pushed her pink bangs out of her eyes. "Just needed to tell Corabelle something." She appraised Gavin. "Not that it matters now." She switched her gaze to me. "Loverboy is here."

Oh, God. By the time I turned to Gavin, his eyes blazed. "You have a boyfriend?"

"What's it to you?" The words snapped out of me before I could think about how he'd take it.

His fist smashed into the metal counter by my hip, rattling all the dishes. Jenny suppressed a shriek.

"Get out of here, Gavin," I said.

"I had no idea you were so easy with everyone," he spat out.

He backed away, and I struggled to catch myself as I slid off the high counter.

The door banged against the wall as he smashed through it to the shop. I hoped Austin wasn't too obvious out there, because there was no telling what Gavin would do if he figured out which one he was.

"Holy shit, Corabelle!" Jenny said. "When you get back to business, you are BACK."

I smoothed down my skirt, my hands shaking. I never had scenes like this in my life. "We have a history."

"I'll say! Wow! Nobody's ever pinned me on a dish counter before!" She headed back to the door. "Should I put this guy off? Say you left already?"

I nodded. "I think that's for the best."

Jenny disappeared through the door, and I hurried for the

loading-dock door that led out into the alley to make sure Gavin had left. Just as I turned the back corner, I saw him roar down the street on his motorcycle.

I pressed my fingers into my lips, tender and swollen. Everything had happened so fast. I didn't know what to think, except Gavin had reawakened something in me, a dark hunger that was far more dangerous than the passion we explored as teens. I was in trouble, big trouble, and I couldn't see any way out.

I pressed against the wall. Focus. Remember school. Your goals. Get done. Get out.

Class. I had to get to class.

But my legs ignored me, and I slid down until I was on the ground, knees to my chest, a stupid vulnerable pose in that skirt, no doubt flashing anyone who cared to glance back toward the alley.

Austin appeared in the gap between the buildings, and I prayed he wouldn't look this way. I scrambled to my feet, ready to flee, but of course the bits of rock and brick crunched beneath my shoes and got his attention.

"Corabelle?" He peered into the shadows.

I ran for the door but damn it, I forgot it locked on the outside. I could hit the delivery buzzer, but if Jenny was busy, she wouldn't come right away.

He appeared around the corner. "Corabelle, are you all right?"

I pulled myself together and forced a smile. "Jenny told you my name?"

He nodded. "Did something just happen?"

"No. I'm fine. Really."

Austin looked at the door. "You're locked out?"

"Yeah. I accidentally let it shut."

He leaned against the brick wall. "You have a minute?"

"Not really."

He ran his hand through his hair, looking anxious. "Okay.

Sorry. I just got that e-mail."

I forced a clipped laugh. "Oh, that was Jason. He meddles."

"You gave him my e-mail address?"

"He got hold of your note to me."

Austin fiddled with the strap of his backpack. "He seemed to think you wouldn't mind me coming by."

"He shouldn't have done that."

He looked down at his shoes, and my sympathy surged, but I didn't know what else to do. I practically dry-humped my ex in the dish room not five minutes ago.

And he'd called me easy. Right. Four years of abstinence was easy.

Austin held out his hand. "Well, here's to being friends. I order cheap tea, and you give me warm-ups until the leaves give out."

I reached for him, noticing right off how gentle his fingers were compared to the frenzied grip of Gavin. "The sugar's free, you know." I instantly blushed, realizing the double meaning.

"I'd already have starved half to death if it wasn't. Student poverty."

"I know how that is."

"Can I walk you back around?" His hazel eyes were earnest. Once again I realized that if I could just feel something for someone else, maybe Gavin wouldn't hurt so much.

"Okay."

Austin settled his backpack on his shoulder and we wandered out of the shadow of the building and into the sun. If Gavin thought I was easy, maybe I should just be easy. If he hated me, then maybe we could stay apart.

As we turned to the front windows, Jenny looked up from inside, her eyebrows shooting up in surprise.

Probably nobody had ever lost their nickname faster than I had just lost mine.

12

GAVIN

Bud looked up from the receipt book as I walked into the front office of the garage. "You're late."

"Had a school thing," I said and walked on through to clock in. I spent all morning looking for Corabelle instead of working, just to find out she had some boyfriend.

I punched my card and actually wished for tires to throw and work off some of this tension. I could still feel Corabelle beneath my hands, her skin feverish, her body writhing against me. Was she doing it with that pipsqueak? Just thinking about it made my head want to explode. She was mine. She had to be. I had to get her to see that we belonged together.

But damn it, I upset her. Called her easy. Damn it.

Mario approached and shouted, "Heads up!" as he tossed me a set of keys.

"What's this?"

"Another Camaro came through. Told the boss you could take one apart in your sleep. He says for you to change out the motor mount."

That was a decent job, jacking the motor and pulling the

mount, then realigning the engine. "He got the parts?"

"Yeah, came in while you were out. You're moving up. Take Bay 3."

I jingled the keys as I went out front to find the car. Bud was hard to figure out. First he threatens to fire me if I drop out of school. Then he moves me out of routine and into mechanics.

This Camaro was only a couple years old, and sitting in the driver's seat didn't fire up memories the way the other car had. I picked up the work order from the passenger side and saw it had come in for a tune-up when the motor-mount problem was discovered. With the other issues on the sheet, it looked like whoever owned this car rode it hard over rough terrain. The shocks were shot, tires out of alignment, and two of the axles were cracked. Those had all been fixed while I was scouting coffee shops, but the motor mounts were circled and Bud had scrawled, "Leave for Gavin."

The motor clunked on starting up, a telltale sign of a misaligned engine. I glanced back at the work order to make sure they'd checked to make sure nothing else had been damaged. Fans could get chipped, hoses torked, a whole host of problems. I'd go over it all again after everything was back in place.

I pulled into the bay, starting to feel grateful for the task, work that would require more concentration than changing a filter, maybe get Corabelle out of my head for a while. Mario came up with the box containing the mount bracket and waited for me to step out. "Lemme know if you need a hand on the realign."

"Will do."

The hood popped up smoothly, and I peered into the Camaro's guts. The inside of the motor mount was cracked clean through, but the bracket was easy to access. I just had to jack the block for support. The job would take less than an hour, if it all went well.

The clang of other mechanics working this end of the garage was a soothing sound. I rolled a jack under the car and steadied the engine. Everyone did their jobs with competence and skill. I could see the appeal of this sort of work. Finite, black and white, cut and dried. Unlike studying in school, where it seemed half the time you were spinning your wheels, memorizing something you'd never need to know again, or writing the same essay on Milton that a million other undergrads had done before.

I should just quit, lie to Bud about it, and pretend to go to class. I could keep up the ruse until December and if Bud kept feeding me real work, I'd be qualified for a better job. Mom might not like it, but hell, I wasn't around them anymore. And my asshole father never approved of anything I did anyway. Screw that. After that scene with Corabelle, maybe I was turning out to be just like him.

The socket wrench fit neatly on the bolt. I remembered watching other boys with their dads, fixing bikes or playing ball with easy camaraderie. Mine had always been intense, angry, disapproving.

Once when we worked on my mother's overheating Oldsmobile, I thought I was being so smart by using a towel to open the hot radiator. But when it spewed boiling water and antifreeze, Dad backhanded me so hard that I fell over my sister's bike, breaking the wheel.

My life seemed like a series of missteps that pissed off my father. Now that I'd been around the block a few times, I knew some kids had it worse. They got in the line of fire just for existing.

When I was little, I felt like I deserved it, punishment for doing something stupid or wrong. Only later did I start to push back. If I went home now, we'd probably kill each other within five minutes.

The bracket came off easily, and I set it aside. Now to remove the long bolt to the mount.

Even when we got old enough to walk around the neighborhood without our parents, I never let Corabelle come over to my house, preferring the quiet simplicity of her family — mother, father, one little girl. But in that middle space when I was small enough to push around, but big enough to take a harder lick, the asshole sometimes really unleashed, like the day I got knocked across the driveway.

Corabelle had seen those bruises and looked up at me with wide sympathetic eyes. She started showing up and hanging out when my dad insisted I help him, reading or poking at the straggly flowers my mother tried to plant by the front steps. Her presence kept my dad in check, just one of the many ways that she saved me.

The mount was out, and I had to do the tricky part, get the new one to align.

Dad caught on pretty quick to when Corabelle and I shifted from little-kid friends to a boy and girl who were messing around. Early on, when I was thirteen, he grabbed me by the collar and flung me into the wall, telling me I better not go around knocking up any girls, or he'd throw my ass out.

By the time I was in high school, and Corabelle and I were crazy tight, I hardly stayed home at all. Her parents saw the handwriting on the wall and got her on that birth-control shot. Once that barrier was crossed we were insane, at each other every minute, and I couldn't get enough of her. Now, sweating over the engine, I could picture every inch of her body.

Finding out about the baby was a huge blow. Because of the shot, we didn't know what was going on for several weeks. She thought she had the flu, then that she was tired from staying up too late. I bought the test and stood over her while she peed on the stick. The sight of her astonished face as the two lines appeared is one of those moments seared into my memory.

We never bothered telling my parents about the baby, letting the town gossip handle it. I moved in with her and vowed never to let my father cast an eye on my son.

The new bracket wouldn't align, so I shifted the jack up a notch, trying to find the sweet spot. I could call Mario over, get him to eyeball it while I worked the lever, but only if it took too long. I'd done it by myself before.

Clearly the work wasn't occupying my mind well enough. I tried to shake off the past, how I worried about what sort of dad I could possibly be, having the worst possible example. When the baby was sick, and then when they told us he wouldn't make it, I figured the score. The universe knew I wouldn't do any better. The bad-father gene would end with me. After the funeral, I went to Mexico to make sure of it, even though I knew it meant I had to give up Corabelle.

Bud came out of the office. "How's it coming?"

I walked around the side to check the screw mounts. They were aligned. "Just putting the last bolts in."

"Good, 'cause the owner's here to pick it up already, and I don't think I can endure that woman one more minute."

I chuckled. "Bud menaced by a woman. Never thought I'd see it."

He looked under the hood as I locked in the bolts. "I don't see anything damaged. She got lucky."

The sockets were solid, so I backed away from the engine. "She should be good to go."

"Start her up. Let's take a listen."

I hopped in the seat again and fired up the motor. The clunk was gone. Bud dropped the hood and came around. "She's good. Pull it around."

By the time I came back into the office, Bud was leading an old lady to the door. "And here's the man who got her ready for you, Mrs. Peters."

I handed her the keys. "Ma'am, you must live near some rough roads."

"Oh, posh," she said. "I live in La Jolla. I just hate speed bumps."

Bud coughed to hide his laugh and I kept a poker face. "Well, I guess we'll be seeing you again in about twenty thousand miles," I said.

"Works for me!" She winked, the blue eye shadow over her eyes as bright as a peacock's feather. "Maybe I'll mess up something else just to come back and get another gander at you!"

Bud passed her a clipboard. "Sign here, Mrs. Peters."

I turned to head back to the bays, but the woman grabbed me by the arm. "It wouldn't be very gentlemanly of you if you didn't see me to my car and make sure it is in good working order, now would it?"

Bud waved me on. "Start it up for her, Gavin."

Mrs. Peters continued to hang on my elbow as I opened the door and led her out to the Camaro, all red and sparkling in the late afternoon sun. "What a grand day!" she said. "I don't guess I can sneak you away for a drive!"

I pictured her wrecked and broken motor mount and imagined jumping creek beds with Mrs. Peters behind the wheel, her white hair flying. "I'm afraid I am much needed here."

"Well, poo." She waited by the car as I opened the door, then she slid inside. "Let's see what she's got."

I handed her the keys and winced as she cranked the motor, stomping the gas so the engine revved loud enough to make people across the street turn to look. I leaned in the open door. "You might want to take it easy."

"This car is going be around longer than I am!" she shouted over the roar. "Life is short. Go after what you love and ride it as hard as you can!"

I barely managed to close the door and jump out of the way before she shot backward across the parking lot, then slammed it into drive and careened past me again, heading for the exit.

That woman was going to kill someone. Still, I had to laugh as I headed back inside. Bud was stuffing her papers in a file folder. "She'll be back. Drivers like her mean good money for us." He turned around. "Let me guess, she gave you some sort of advice about life being short, and she was about to die?"

"Yeah." Of course, that got me thinking about Corabelle. Hell, everything did.

"She's been saying that for a decade. She's going to outlive us all." He glanced at the clock. "You can go ahead and head out. I'm sure whatever kept you all morning is still nagging at you now."

I suppressed a smart-ass reply. "All right, Bud. See you tomorrow." I wondered where Corabelle might be, at work still, or on campus. Maybe I could get that pink-haired girl to tell me where she lived.

I should leave her alone. I knew it. But something in me just couldn't let it go.

13

CORABELLE

I crossed the quad, anxiety rising as the engineering building grew close. Gavin would be in there, just a few seats down. The two feelings for him warred inside me. Anger that he'd called me easy, when I hadn't been with anyone but him. And an urgency to get him alone, to feel, if only for a little while, the way we had when we were young and innocent of all the ways life could fail us.

The stairwell echoed with my footsteps, and I couldn't help but run my hand over the part of the rail where Gavin caught me trying to black out. I had to get control of that now. Gavin showing up again was the sign that my little fits of crazy had to end. I needed some other way to cope.

I thought I'd be able to sneak in close to the start of class and slip into my chair without having to talk to him. But Gavin was waiting outside the door, his lab assignment in his hand. He looked more amazing than ever. Every detail about him was seared into me, the blue T-shirt fitting across his chest and arms, the dark stubble on his jaw, the sideburn near his ear.

He held out the paper. "You turned this in for me?"

I nodded, grasping hard on the strap of my backpack.

"Why?"

"I felt bad that I upset you." I drew in a deep breath. "By talking about Finn."

It was so hard to say his name. And not easier on Gavin to hear it. I could see it in how his eyebrows drew together.

A couple other students cut between us to enter the door. "Thank you." He hesitated. "Can I see you later?"

Panic rose from my belly. "No. I can't. Please, Gavin. It's too hard."

He pressed his lips together. "This isn't over."

"It is. It has to be."

He whipped around and went back in the room.

I leaned against the wall, eyes on the ceiling, trying to pull myself together. I didn't know what to do. I couldn't be with him. There was too much past, and I was barely holding it together before he showed up.

Unless maybe Austin really could help. He seemed so much easier to manage than Gavin, and my secrets had no power with him.

I pushed away from the wall and hurried to my seat, trying not to look Gavin's way. While the professor talked about supernovas, I tapped out an e-mail to Austin on my iPad. "Are you on campus today? I get out of Jacobs Hall at 10. Corabelle."

I could feel Gavin's eyes on me as I took notes and tried to focus, already regretting involving an innocent boy to make life easier for me. I stole a guilty glance down the row. Gavin was still watching, intense and brooding. His eyes dropped to the strap of my tank top, and I knew he was remembering the moment at the coffee shop.

Fire licked through me again, and I focused back on the screen. Gavin always had that effect on me.

After that first kissing session in my closet, we were crazy with it. Every chance we got, we pressed against each other feverishly. When a movie or television show showed a couple clutching each other, we'd stop everything to pay attention, only to act the scene out later in my room.

The first time Gavin touched me was completely by accident. I'd just started wearing training bras. He teased me about it and threatened to pop the elastic. When he reached for the back, I whirled around and his fingers grazed across my chest.

The touch had been so electric, I almost screamed. Gavin immediately backed away, sure he'd done something wrong. All I really wanted was for him to do it again.

A lot like now. The scene in the dish room had played over and over in my mind all night. Surely Gavin wasn't the only way to feel so intense. I had always been too afraid of giving any other boy a chance.

My screen popped up with an e-mail notification. Austin. I kept my head down as I opened it. He didn't have class, but he'd come down anyway. He lived close to campus.

So it was done. I'd engaged him, and I couldn't just back away. This was for the best.

I suffered through the lecture, taking frenetic notes to avoid looking at Gavin. At last class ended and Jenny bounded over to me. "You haven't asked me how I am!"

"Oh, that's right! Star party! How did it go with Lumberjack?" From the corner of my eye I could see Gavin loading up his backpack. I wanted him long gone before I went outside and met up with Austin.

"He was a dream!" Jenny glanced over her shoulder. Robert stood talking to Amy and the third TA. Jenny pulled me toward the door. "I have to tell you about him!"

This would work. As long as Jenny and I were absorbed in a conversation, Gavin would pass on by and I could wait to go outside to meet Austin.

When we were out of earshot of the TAs, Jenny said, "I got him! We're going out Saturday night!"

"That's great. Is he okay with you being a student?"

"Rules are made to be broken. We're discreet."

Jenny was about as discreet as a fire truck. "You sure about that?"

She hugged her messenger bag to her chest. "Completely. After all the other students left the lab, we stayed up on the roof until midnight!"

"Wow."

"He kisses just like Westley in *The Princess Bride*."

"You kissed him already?"

"Of course!" Jenny slung her strap over her shoulder. "I'm not into taking things slow." She threaded her arm around mine. "And based on the dish room, neither are you!"

The hall was clear, so I let her lead me down the steps.

"So what about the guy from the coffee shop? You seemed all serious coming from the alley with him despite serving up suds with hunk boy." Jenny sighed. "I should have been taking notes from you."

"Austin is meeting me here."

Jenny halted by the door to the stairwell. "Seriously? Man-meat looked ready to kill him yesterday, and you're putting them in the same zip code?"

"Gavin's probably already halfway across town on his Harley by now."

Jenny tugged on the handle to the stairs. "Your funeral. Or his."

I winced at the word, refusing to let the image of a powder-blue casket stick in my mind. "It'll be fine."

Still, we took our time on the stairs, killing a few more minutes.

"Let me scout ahead," Jenny said. We walked down the hall and approached the main doors. "I'll come back when the coast is clear."

"Corabelle?"

I turned to the voice. Austin was coming down the hall.

"Hey," I said, not sure at all I was doing the right thing. But I'd committed.

"Hey." He reached out like he would take my hand, then pulled back, closing his fingers around the strap of his pack.

"So you said you live close?" I asked.

He nodded. "You want to go there?"

My face burned. "No! I — it was just conversation."

Austin laughed a little. "I'm glad you wrote me. I'm glad I could come."

A few other students passed by us, and we moved to a corner. I relaxed a little. Finally I'd do something like normal girls. Meet a regular guy, have a normal conversation, and just be another college student. This was going to be all right.

14

GAVIN

I didn't really want to leave campus. I hung around the door, waiting on Corabelle, but she kept talking to that girl she worked with. Finally I gave up, heading to my Harley. But instead of driving off campus, I decided to go past the engineering building. Maybe I could convince her to take a ride with me.

Corabelle's pinked-up friend was standing at the entrance, looking around.

I braked in front of her, and she stuck her hip out, all full of attitude.

"You need to roll right on by," she said.

"Nice to see you again, too." I pulled off my helmet. "Where's Corabelle?"

"Not anywhere you can get to her."

"She and I have a history."

"Yeah, that was pretty obvious in the dish room."

I assessed her. She met my gaze pretty steady, not intimidated in the least. "How long have you known her?"

"Since I started working at Cool Beans."

"You her friend?"

"I'd take her over you." She jutted her hip out. She was a live wire, completely the opposite of Corabelle.

"Fair enough. I need to be able to contact her."

The girl laughed. "You're crazy if you think I'm going to give up her number."

"It's important."

"So is her privacy. You look like a stalker to me." She tossed her hair behind her shoulders.

"I could say I got it from the TA. She's in my study group. But it's serious. Corabelle, she —" How did I persuade this girl? "She's getting upset with me around."

"That's not exactly convincing."

"I'm the only one who can help her."

She looked back to the door, and I knew Corabelle was still inside.

"All I know is that she's been hurt by somebody." She moved in close and poked my shirt. "And I'm figuring after that scene yesterday that the somebody is you."

"We grew up together."

"And she wanted to get away from you. That's why she changed groups. So I don't think she wants to hear from you."

"But this guy?"

"Not your business."

"They been together long?"

"Again, not your business."

I couldn't crack this girl. Corabelle would get mad at me for this, but I had to give it a shot. "We had a kid together," I said.

The girl's jaw dropped. "What?"

"He died when he was a week old."

Her bag slid down her shoulder and rested on the ground. "I didn't know."

"We were eighteen. I sort of left her. I shouldn't have." I stuck my helmet on the handlebars. "I want to make this right. Help me do that. You saw her yesterday. I think we have a shot at this."

The girl pushed at her bangs, upset, and I could see she was struggling with what to do.

"What's she been like?"

She shrugged. "Sad. Alone. She doesn't go anywhere, do anything."

Her words were a blow to the gut. "You two? Do you do things?"

"Sometimes. Mainly I see her at work. And we signed up for this class." She twisted her bright hair in her fingers. "She doesn't go out."

So that guy had to be something new. "Corabelle used to light up a room. Her laughter was the happiest sound in the world."

"I've never heard her laugh."

Another blow. "We were supposed to get married, but the baby came early. Then I left." I had to get to this girl. I needed to talk to Corabelle, before she got all tied up in that other guy. What was going on with me was pushing her toward him, I was sure of it. "If I could just talk to her, outside of class, I think I could make things right."

The girl pulled out her phone. "I tell you what. You give me your number, and I'll give it to her. If she wants to talk to you, she'll call."

That was probably about as good as I could get for now. I told her my number and waited as she tapped it in. "You will tell her?"

She shrugged. "If I think it's a good idea."

The doors behind her opened and her eyes went wide as Corabelle and another guy came down the steps.

"Shit," she muttered.

Corabelle saw us and froze. The dude seemed oblivious and tried to lead her away, but she wouldn't move.

Everything inside me wanted to claw its way out — rage, disgust, and somewhere way down there, despair. I was going to be too late.

She grabbed the boy's hand, and he looked surprised. They took off along the front of the building and down a path away from us.

I started to swing my leg off the bike even though I was in the middle of the sidewalk, but the girl punched my arm. "Don't you dare," she said. "I'm not going to let you mess with her unless it's what she wants."

"I'm what she wants."

She shook her head. "That's not what it looks like to me. You need to back off. I don't care how well you can put a girl up against a dish counter, that boy is bound to be better for her than you."

I snatched up my helmet and shoved it on. This was pointless. I needed away from all this, and the fire in my belly wasn't an easy one to quench.

The Harley roared, startling a bunch of birds in the tree next to us. The pink girl backed away. She'd probably delete my number. I'd gotten nowhere. I probably wasn't going to get anywhere.

I left campus behind to head to the garage. I had a short shift this afternoon, then the night was free. I could see if Mario wanted to shoot pool, but really I knew what I had to do. Scrounge up a bit of cash and head to Zona Norte in Tijuana. There, the girls were easy and paid to like you, and I didn't have to think about real life at all.

The border guard glanced at my ID and waved me on with a halfhearted "Be careful."

The half-hour drive from San Diego to Mexico helped put the scene with Corabelle behind me. I felt like I was at my second home as I left the searing lights of the border complex and rolled down Segunda Benito Juarez toward the red-light district.

I knew my way around Tijuana and the women there. No attachments. No risks. Just a simple ease of a simple need by a seasoned pro.

I turned off the highway and onto the main strip. The streets were pulsing with neon signs for hotels and *taquerias*. Cars rolled slowly, trolling for girls. They stood in their territorial spots, and if one was picked up, another took her place.

They waved as I zipped past, flashing a lot of skin. High heels, leopard prints, red vinyl, and fishnet. Not my scene whatsoever.

The best girls weren't there, just the ones aiming for *turistas*. Overpaid and under-interested. And mostly managed. I hated the girls with pimps. They had too many bruises, and I struggled to kill my urge to drag their asses out of there.

Just a couple streets over would be the ordinary girls, the professionals-on-the-side kind, many of them wives or students or making their way on the streets on their own. They kept quiet, avoiding attention, not wanting to catch the eye of anyone who might try to claim them or make their lives more difficult than they already were.

Tonight I wanted Rosa, and the thought of her already had my mood downshifting into something more manageable. Rosa lived with her brother, or so she claimed, and worked in a little *farmacia* during the day.

In fact, that's how I met her, just a couple weeks after I left New Mexico.

I'd driven my Camaro through the border states, aimless, exhausted, stopping nowhere. The picture of Finn they passed out at the funeral sat on my passenger seat and I glanced at it often.

The only real thing I'd done as a parent was sign away my kid's life. And after my stupid exit during the funeral, I was pretty sure the world had decided I was no more fit to be a dad than my own father had been.

Somewhere in Utah I decided that a vasectomy was the way to go. Corabelle had been on birth control, and it hadn't mattered.

Once I got the idea in my head to do it, I couldn't think about anything but finding a doctor and getting it done. I had no other goals, no other place to go.

I went to three clinics stateside, trying to find a doctor willing to do a vasectomy on a teenager. No dice. I remembered my grandpa used to get his denture work done in Ciudad Juarez because it was cheaper and there wasn't any hassle with insurance or paperwork.

I was already west by then, so I sold my laptop for cash and drove along the border until I got to Mexicali. A doctor there sent me on to Tijuana, where I finally found someone who didn't want to see ID, and cash on the table was good enough to get snipped.

The procedure itself wasn't too bad. They gave me some pill that made me loopy and sluggish. I felt a needle and some pinching. Afterward, though, walking was impossible. I couldn't really understand the nurse's instructions and had no idea what I was supposed to do for pain.

I ended up at the *farmacia* in hopes of scoring something stronger than Tylenol. The girl behind the counter was beautiful, long black hair curling down her back, not unlike Corabelle's. She spoke enough English that I could explain what had happened, and she consulted with a man in the back. She gave me a cold pack and a jockstrap and a bottle of pills with the stern instructions to take only two per day.

I was saved. I stayed at a hotel across the street, unable to go any farther, and I remember looking out the window and seeing her close up the shop. The nightlife was colorful and the pain, while duller, kept me up for hours.

In that hot little room, though, the magnitude of what I'd done started to hit. I couldn't go back to Corabelle, not ever. She'd take it personally. She'd assume I didn't want a baby with her after all. I would have to stay away. I'd finished us.

I don't think about those first few hours after the surgery any more than I replay that span of time after the ventilators went silent. But when I pulled myself together enough, I tried to find a diversion inside those four filthy walls.

All the TV channels were in Spanish, so I pulled a chair up to the window, surprised when I saw the girl back again, lounging on the corner, wearing a low-cut stretchy blouse and a short skirt.

She seemed uncertain about what she was doing, and that innocence caught my attention. A man approached her and they argued a moment, but she sent him on his way. Probably wanting something for free. When an hour passed and she had no luck, I made my way painfully down the stairs and out onto the street.

She saw me coming and pressed her hand over her cleavage. "Feeling better, *señor*?"

"How much?"

"*Perdón*?"

Suddenly I worried that I was dead wrong. She was just hanging out here, waiting for someone, someone who was really late. I waved my hand at her. "Sorry. Never mind."

I turned away, but she caught my shoulder. "You are not well for this." She glanced down at my pants, bulging from the cold packs.

"I know." My ache for Corabelle was suddenly fierce, and the comfort of this woman seemed like it might help.

"Okay. I come. You are up there?" She pointed at the hotel.

I nodded.

We walked back across the street and up to my room. I had to take it super slow, and she held my arm, keeping me steady.

"This doctor. Was he good?" she asked.

I shrugged. "I have no idea."

She helped me get settled on the bed. "Why you do this? You are so young."

"I have my reasons." I reached out for her hair, tweaking the strands between my fingers. When she faced away, taking off her shoes, I could almost believe she was Corabelle.

We still hadn't agreed on a price, and I had no assurance that she wouldn't rob me blind if the drugs knocked me out. But most of my stuff was in a locker on the other side of the border. I could probably afford to lose everything I had on me. I twined my fingers through her hair, relieved I could touch her without worrying about her reaction, and closed my eyes.

Her body fitted next to mine and now I could really imagine that Corabelle was next to me. We were on a holiday, our honeymoon maybe, and this was all we could afford. Her parents were watching Finn for a couple nights, and we'd gotten away. The girl laid her hand on my chest and I held it.

"Rosa," she said.

"I'm Gavin."

"You rest, Gavin."

And so I spent my first night with her in a seedy hotel room and slept through the haze of pain medication and sore balls. I stayed in Tijuana for a week, until I figured out that I wasn't going back home and I needed to find a job. Settling in San Diego made sense, and since I was already accepted to UCSD, I could easily get admitted, take a GED for my diploma, and start my coursework.

At first I went back to see Rosa just to get a sense that I had taken a few steps into my past. I always paid her, but it was probably my fourth or fifth visit before we finally got to business, when my loneliness hit a peak. After her I found other girls, closer, in San Diego, and realized that prostitutes were a perfect solution. No strings. No mess. No mistakes.

Over the years, I got to know Rosa better. She always seemed happy to see me, and now that I was restless about Corabelle, I wanted only her.

The apartments where she lived were stacked in rundown buildings with adobe facades. Normally I wouldn't enter one alone, being so obviously an outsider, but every time I thought about what Corabelle might be doing with that baby-faced punk, I couldn't give a shit about any of it. Bring on the switchblades, the fistfight, even the gunpoint. Anything was easier than trying to be the good guy again just so Corabelle could finish me off.

I knew better than to leave my bike on that street, so I rolled it right into the corridor between the two halves of the building. I kept my back to the wall as I pulled out my phone to text her.

It took a few minutes, but she finally responded with "I'm coming down." I didn't know if that meant she was rushing someone out, but I didn't much care either. Rosa was my top choice, and tonight it would take more than any ordinary girl to settle me.

The locks began twisting and creaking as someone fumbled with the other side. When Rosa opened the door, I didn't respond like I expected. She looked the same, long black hair now laced with blond, her curvy body strapped into things that pushed up and squeezed in. She motioned me inside, looking both ways down the corridor into the night. I grasped the handlebars of my bike and rolled it in as I always did, and we shoved it into a little room under the stairs where people stuffed their trash until collection.

"*Mi amante*," she said. "I am glad to see you." She wrapped her arms around me and pulled me in to her lips. I couldn't shake the feeling that something was off, but I managed a passable kiss. She led me up the stairs to her door.

Some people would probably have considered the place squalor, but to me it was typical for the district. The walls were peeling and the rail rusted out. A weak light sputtered at the landing.

Inside the apartments, the tenants took care of their spaces. Rosa covered her walls with large woven tapestries in red and gold and green. Candles burned in every corner, and a CD turned low just covered the street sounds with rhapsodic love songs in Spanish.

"Sit," Rosa said, pushing me to the sofa, also covered in bright blankets. She moved to her kitchen and returned with a Corona. "Bad day?"

I nodded and knocked back half the bottle. Rosa could handle this. I'd come here in bad shape before.

"Ah, *pobrecito*. Let me fix." She knelt and began to untie my boots.

I laid my head back on the sofa and tried to relax. Her ceiling was covered in stains. We were all born into such different circumstances. I hadn't been that much better off than Rosa, a tumbledown house on a bad street in a small town. My biggest luck had been to back up to middle-class row houses across the alley, and Corabelle.

Damn it, I'd come back to her again. I took a long pull of the beer and watched Rosa set the heavy boots aside. She wore some tight contraption of a shirt with lace strings up the front. It pushed her breasts up so that they started spilling over. She caught me looking and tugged on one of the strings, letting it loose.

Normally I'd already have my hands on her, pulling that off, burying my face against her skin, but today I felt so detached, like she was on a screen rather than in the room. She seemed to understand this and stood up, turning in a slow circle as she plucked at the rest of the laces. They came out, one by one, until the shirt fell open and she shrugged the whole thing off her shoulders.

Her dark naked breasts were kissed by candlelight. I should have been feeling it, and alarms started going off that I wasn't. This couldn't be about Corabelle. I wouldn't let it. Rosa had been my escape for years, easy and friendly and open to whatever I wanted.

Damn it, it was already happening. I couldn't help but compare them, Corabelle's innocent beauty next to Rosa, who seemed to be trying so hard with the eyelashes and rouged cheeks. Where Rosa was ample, Corabelle was slight. I should have had my hands and mouth on the feast in front of me, but I just sat there like a chair, nothing stirring in my pants.

I'd make this happen. I would force it. With a growl, I grasped Rosa's hand and pulled her toward me. She tumbled into my lap with a light laugh.

I pulled her into a kiss, plumbing her mouth with my tongue. She met me with practiced ease, and as soon as I sensed her working to please me rather than responding on her own, I jerked away again. Bloody hell. She'd been fine before.

"Very bad day," she said, smoothing down my hair. "Let me fix." She reached between my legs and squeezed.

It wasn't going to work. Not today. I lifted her off my lap and set her on the sofa. The window beckoned and I stood beside it, looking out on the streets. People walked down below, making deals, passing cash for women or drugs or wagers. I didn't used to know any of this. If none of the crap had happened four years ago, I still wouldn't know. I'd be out of school, teaching kids like we'd planned. Finn would be wandering around, a year away from kindergarten, and WHY THE HELL WAS THIS ON MY MIND AGAIN?

"Something's different, Gavinito."

I shrugged. "Old life came back."

"Like the day we met?"

"Something like that."

"The reason why you get cut so young?"

I whirled around, tugging out several bills — money I couldn't really afford to be wasting — and left them on the table. "I have to go."

Rosa nodded, picking up her shirt as I shoved on my boots. "I see you again soon, when day not so bad?"

"Yeah, definitely."

She worked the series of locks on her door and pressed against the doorframe. She seemed to know I wouldn't be back. "*Adios*, Gavinito."

"Good-bye, Rosa."

I rushed down the stairs, anxious to be out of there. I shouldn't be messing with Corabelle for the same damn reasons. It's not like her learning about the vasectomy four years later would make it any easier. She'd want kids eventually, and I'd screwed her over.

But then, what if she didn't? What if she felt like I did? Maybe this would be the right thing.

I had to talk to her. I had to know what she wanted, where she was going. And if there was any place for me. I'd make one. I'd make her see.

My anxiety rose as I headed for the trash room. Of all the times I'd been in Tijuana and hadn't cared what happened to me or what could go wrong, this night I just knew the bike would be stolen or I'd get thrown in an alley. Murphy's Law, my dad used to say when something went south. "Shit that can go wrong, will go wrong. Right when you need it not to."

I was relieved as hell to see the Harley sitting where I left it. I rolled it out and opened the outer door more cautiously than usual, watching to make sure I wasn't interrupting a deal. I normally rode through with swagger that made people leave me alone, but right now I felt like a nervous tourist trying to get the hell back home.

The corridor was empty so I walked the bike down to the street. I'd go to the coffee shop, live there if I had to, until I saw Corabelle again. I didn't think for a minute that that pink-haired chick would give Corabelle my number, not after she ran off with the other guy.

When I popped out on the street, a pair of men just a few feet away looked up. Damn it, I'd been distracted. You couldn't do that in Zona Norte.

"Who the fuck is that?" one of them said, some college kid from stateside, and he took off running.

Shit.

The other man, short and thick and blasting machismo in a leather jacket, strode up to me, smoothing his long sideburns with his fingers. "Who the fuck are you?"

"Just moving on." I threw my leg over the Harley, but I misjudged his intention. Sideburns rushed me, arms around my chest, and dragged me off the bike.

"You lost me a fine customer." He delivered a sharp kick to my gut, and sparks flew behind my eyes. He ran his hand along the chrome. "Nice ride."

When he started to lift it from the ground, I swung my boot around to knock him off his feet. By the time he recovered, I was up again and ready to finish this out. No way was someone going to screw me over this late in the game.

Sideburns seemed to relish the thought of a fight, and I caught the glint of a set of brass knuckles. That was good, I thought. He felt he needed an edge, which meant he wasn't a street fighter.

He lunged first, and my fist connected with his jaw in a crunch of bone. I had no time to think about the pain, because he was back, delivering several sharp blows to my ribs.

He could hit me there all day. I whipped around, grabbing him by the shoulders and shoving him into the street. He stumbled off the curb, shook himself, and charged again.

I'd had enough of this bullshit, so I let him get close enough to take a poorly aimed shot at my chest, then I aimed low and hard, a forward punch into his gut followed by two in a row to his face. He blew backward, falling into the wall.

He raised his hands in the air and stumbled toward the curb like he was leaving. He seemed calm, too calm, and that's when I knew he was packing.

This was no good. A sorry-ass punk like him would take a potshot at me when I rode away. I had to shut him down.

"Hey!" I shouted.

When he turned back around, I ran at him with a growl, knocking him into a car. Four rapid punches to his face kept him still long enough that I could reach around and feel for the gun stuck in the back of his waistband, under the coat. I jerked it out, knowing I'd have to ditch it somewhere before I got to the border.

I aimed it at his head. "Back off. I have no issue with you."

I kept the gun trained on him as I moved to the bike. I couldn't lift the Harley without lowering my arm. If he had a second one, this was over. Adrenaline soared through my body and I wondered for a moment if Corabelle would notice if I disappeared, rolled into some ditch in Mexico.

Sideburns watched me as I lifted the bike. Normally I would have pocketed the shells and tossed the weapon, but my prints were on it, and the last thing I needed was for him to kill somebody later and drag me into it.

The Harley roared, and I kept the gun in my left hand as I took off down the street, watching him for as long as possible. I had to give the universe credit, she was going to direct me the way she wanted me to go, closing off other avenues until I followed her path. I couldn't come back to Zona Norte anytime soon. Sideburns would be watching this street, assuming I'd be back, and next time wouldn't go so easy for me.

I took the most direct route back to the main highway and as soon as I hit the stretch that was unpopulated, mostly trees and brush, I pulled over.

I yanked an oil rag from my saddlebag, and in the light from the headlamp, I emptied the gun, a Glock, letting the ammunition fall onto the rag. I was careful not to touch any of the bullets as I used the rag to toss them into the thick brush.

Then I wiped down the gun as best I could, letting the oily rag take off any prints. I pushed aside a thorny bush and kicked at the dirt to create a shallow hole. Once the Glock was buried and the brush back over it, I breathed out a relieved sigh. That had been too close. Way too close. I'd been in fights before, back when I'd shoot pool in Tijuana and sometimes some punk didn't want to give up his losses. But this was more. This was another sign that my life was going some other direction.

I got back on the bike and headed toward the border crossing. It wasn't until the guard checked my ID and waved me back through that I realized how lucky I'd been.

Now it was time to take that luck and make it work on Corabelle. Time to man up and face everything.

15

CORABELLE

The day had actually gone pretty well.

Austin and I had walked through campus, gotten cheap noodles from a cart vendor, and hung out near the Sun God statue, staring up into its colorful protective face. I suspected he might have skipped a class for me, but I didn't ask him about it. Fridays were my clear days, catch-up days, but this early in the quarter I could goof off still.

When evening came, he asked if I wanted to walk over to his place. "Don't worry that I'm trying to get you alone," he said. "I have six roommates and nobody ever gets anybody alone."

"Six!" I appreciated, as I had throughout the day, how easy Austin had made everything, as if anticipating my every point of concern.

"If you're after me for my money, I might as well just give it all to you now." He pulled a quarter from his pocket and pressed it into my palm.

I swallowed at the contact. Austin had been super hands off, even though I had grabbed him when we hurried out of the building as Jenny stalled Gavin. There was nothing about this guy I hadn't liked. The world seemed to understand that at this very moment, I needed something like him. I'd doubted fate for so long that it was a relief to actually believe in it again, if just for a day.

He let go and I closed my fingers around the quarter. "So poverty means you live in barracks?"

"It's a townhouse with three bedrooms. So it's not too bad."

We walked along a path through a forest of trees, past the towering library and away from the roof where I spent time with Gavin. I chided myself for thinking about him when the day had been so easy.

"So tell me something," Austin said, and his change of tone made my heart hammer. Don't ruin it, I begged. Let it be.

He stuck his hands in his pockets, as if trying to stall for time. My anxiety rose.

"We've had a good day, right?" He looked out over the diagonal panels of the sidewalk instead of at me. A few other students were heading out toward the parking lots. We were almost back to the engineering hall, where we'd started.

"Yeah, sure. It's been good."

"So why do you seem so sad?"

Back to that. I remembered when he gave me the note. He knocked on the counter, as if knowing he'd done something special by making me smile for a second. Everyone was right, he had been watching me all along.

"Is that too personal?" He stopped walking, still not looking at me.

I came up beside him. "Might be a story for another day."

"Okay." He turned finally, gazing at my face. "I guess making you laugh will just have to become my new goal in life."

I forced a smile, for his sake, even if it wasn't too convincing.

"See, I'm halfway there." He reached out and took my hand. "Is this okay?"

I had to smile that he asked permission. "In some countries, I think it means we're betrothed."

"A joke!" He slapped a palm against his forehead. "I'm better than I thought!"

I punched him on the arm and he grasped my other hand, facing me like we were about to say wedding vows. His tone got all serious and I swallowed. What would he do now? Try to kiss me in the middle of the quad? I glanced around nervously. Gavin could be on campus somewhere.

Austin let go of my hands. I'd messed up the moment. I'd probably do that a lot.

"Let's go see what trouble everyone's into," he said. "Someone's bound to have ordered cheap pizza, and then I can feed you."

"Do you work?"

"No time for a job," he said. "Engineering kills me. I'm just trying to get done before my loans overrun my earning potential."

We resumed walking along the mall, past the engineering building. I could picture Gavin on his motorcycle, talking to Jenny. I hadn't had a single free moment to call or text her and find out what they had discussed. Maybe she'd reneged on her deal and gone off with him. My belly burned.

"Still with us?" Austin asked.

Dang it. He deserved more than my scattered attention. "I am," I said. "I may be more ditzy headed than you figured."

He bumped his shoulder against mine. We were almost the same height. "I'd go for deep over ditzy."

We left campus behind and wandered a few streets into the adjoining neighborhood, a mass of apartment complexes. "You live near campus?" he asked.

"Oh, no. I'm way out."

"Did you bus in?"

"I have a car."

"Hoity-toity, are we?" He turned us down a side street.

"I have a job. It helps." And, of course, three years of school paid by scholarship. My debt would be minimal as long as I was careful.

We walked along a sidewalk to a row of townhouse condos that looked to be mostly rentals, judging by the scraggly lawns and ill-kept hedges, all signs of students who couldn't care less about curb appeal.

The buildings looked identical to me, but Austin turned us in at one near the middle of the street. "See, not too tiny. We can probably find some little corner to ourselves."

The wood steps were peeling and scarred. A tower of pizza boxes filled one side of the porch, awkwardly stacked in a way that couldn't possibly stand on its own.

"The leaning tower of pizza," Austin explained. "Impaled on a center stake. Our little student engineering joke." He opened the door and stepped aside to let me through.

The smell of beer and stale bread accosted me as my eyes adjusted. We were approaching full dark now, and only a few small corner lamps lit the living room.

A girl sprawled on a ratty recliner, her face glowing from the light of her laptop. She didn't look up. "That's Daryl's girl," Austin said in my ear. "I'd introduce you but I can't remember her name."

To the left was another large room, wall to wall with sofas. In it, several guys sat around a television, playing a video game. "You want to meet them?" Austin asked. "Or save it for later?"

I suddenly wasn't up for being friendly to a roomful of strangers. "Show me around first."

We went straight back to the kitchen, cluttered with paper cups and more pizza boxes. "This is a good day," he said. "Usually you can't find the sink." Off to one side was a dining room with a huge rough-hewn picnic table in it. "Seating for ten," he said. "For all our grand occasions."

"I'll keep it in mind for my next formal banquet."

He reached for my hand and squeezed. "You want to see my room? Ben might be there, so we'd have a chaperone."

I swallowed. What if he wasn't? Being alone with Austin didn't feel right, not yet. But I was being silly. I was twenty-two and not exactly a virgin.

Austin sensed my hesitation. "Or we can sit here." He pointed at the table.

"No, it's fine. Show me your space."

We crossed back into the kitchen and through a narrow hallway that led to a set of tightly turning stairs. "I'm on the second floor. All the bedrooms are upstairs."

I followed him up. On the walls were posters of scientists, cheaply framed. Einstein with his shock of crazy hair. Madame Curie looking serious and smart.

"Door closed, no sock, looks like Ben's there but not in any compromising positions."

"Seriously? You use the sock method?"

He twisted the knob. "We do. Yes, we're juvenile." The door stuck a minute, then popped open. The smoke and smell hit me instantly.

"Hey, guys!" Austin said. "I brought a girl!"

"Bullshit!" someone said. "Did you lay a trap or something?"

Austin tried to pull me inside but my feet were rooted to the floor. Weed. They were all smoking marijuana. I began to back away, yanking my hand from his.

"Corabelle, you okay?" He looked inside. "Shit, guys, can you put those out?"

I couldn't believe it. I thought all this time that fate was putting me here. That Austin would help. That Gavin was just a coincidence. That I'd be better.

I turned for the stairs. But no, it was worse. I could see it now. Things weren't getting better. I was getting caught. Everything was catching up to me. The world wanted its punishment. I was going to pay again, all over again, and probably again and again and again throughout my whole life.

I started running, crashing down the stairs, knocking Einstein sideways, and hurtled back through the house. Austin was close behind, but when I crashed through the door and out onto the lawn, he called out. "Corabelle, stop! Please! I'm sorry! I didn't know it would upset you! I should have checked first!"

My feet pounded the sidewalk in a full-on sprint. Hell was on my heels. I knew if I looked behind me, I would see it, a black cloud creeping up, like the way the ocean had bumped up against the lights of the city from the roof. My past was coming for me and this time there would be no way to escape it.

16

CORABELLE

I didn't start to breathe again until my car pulled up to the apartment complex. There had been too many signs today. I always felt my life was like an intricate story, crafted so carefully that every moment had symbolism and every action carried the weight of a great and important truth. Today was foreshadowing. Disaster ahead. A tragic ending.

I already had that. What more could happen?

I unlocked my door, the blackness of the familiar room a comfort. Maybe I just needed a bath, a dark room, warm water, to float in silence until the world dissolved into nothingness.

I felt my way across the tiny living room, leaving my backpack on the sofa and discarding clothes along the way. The tiles bit into my knees as I knelt in front of the bathtub, reaching blindly for the knobs.

A car drove by outside and the muted headlights penetrated the block of bottled glass in the wall of the shower. The water spilled over my hands, cold and shocking. I pushed my hair back, a tangled mass after the crazy run.

When the temperature turned warm, I flipped the drain

stopper and waited for the tub to fill. The fiberglass felt good against my throbbing temple. Austin would write me, ask me what happened. I didn't know what I'd tell him. He probably thought I was some sort of anti-drug nut, a weed prude. He had no idea. No one had any idea.

I stood up and stepped into the water. My hair grew heavy as it soaked and I slid beneath the surface, getting good and drenched.

Not true. One person knew. Katie, a friend back home who gave me my first joint in high school. I was strung out about my SAT score. I'd gotten to be a National Merit Scholar based on my PSAT, but my regular score hadn't come back as high. Early in my senior year, I had one chance to retake it, do better, and the long nights were killing me.

Gavin hadn't cared about his score as long as he could get in. He knew he'd have to work through school, but I hoped to get scholarships and focus on studying.

Katie and I had been prepping together, both going for as close to a perfect score as we could get. With my emphasis on literature, though, my math wasn't topping out.

I'd never done any sort of drug. My parents were straitlaced. Most of my friends were all serious students, not the sort to party on weekends with anything more than beer, if that. Gavin didn't do it, although he knew guys who did. Our drug of choice had been sex.

But a couple weeks before the retake, Katie had shown me her stash, spreading the little papers to roll and the baggie of weed out on her kitchen table. She got it from her brother, she said, who got it from someone at college.

"I think you're just too uptight about your score," she said. "Take a practice set lit up and see if you do any better." She handed me the fat roll and a lighter.

"I don't smoke cigarettes," I told her. "I'll have a coughing fit."

"It's different. Smoother. Try it."

I looked at my last practice score. I wasn't getting any better. I just couldn't answer things fast enough. I felt the weight of the clock, the pressure to get every question right.

I stared at the joint. "I don't know what to do with it."

"Here, I'll start it." She lit the end of the roll at the twist and it blazed with light for a moment, then the burnt end went black. She sucked in, held it, then blew out a long clean line of smoke that dissipated elegantly into nothingness.

The smell hit, the sickly sweet smoke. She passed the joint to me. "Just take a couple puffs, then stop until you see what it does."

"Do I breathe it in?"

She laughed. "Of course."

Katie made it seem easy. I tentatively put it to my lips.

"Just suck it in," she said.

I inhaled, and immediately felt the urge to cough, but it wasn't too bad, and I could suppress it.

"You're doing all right," she said. She took the joint from me and puffed. "Don't forget to exhale!"

I let it go and the smoke went everywhere in an ugly cloud. Katie laughed. "You'll get it." She passed it back. "One more and then we'll wait. It takes a few minutes. You may not feel much the first time."

I briefly flashed to middle school and the anti-drug lectures. No one had paid the least bit of attention then. I hadn't been around drugs, ever. Katie acted like it was no big deal.

"How you doing?" she asked.

My mouth tasted strange. I had a sense of being a little hot and my heart might have been beating faster, but then, I was nervous. "Nothing," I said.

"One more." She passed it over again.

I took another puff and gave it back. "I'm going to do one

more timed section and call it a day," I said.

She examined the joint. "I have no idea if this is any good or not. Nothing to compare it to."

I shrugged. Figures it wouldn't do anything to me. I probably did something wrong.

But somewhere about question six, I felt a lightness come over me. My stomach turned, just a tiny tweak, and I felt buoyant, chilled out, like everything was good.

I glanced up at Katie. She'd kicked her feet up on the table. I wondered if her parents knew about her habit. She was doing it right here in the kitchen. Either they approved or they weren't coming back anytime soon.

I moved through the questions. The extra work was paying off. I could almost predict the answers they would use for options and easily eliminated the wrong ones. I forgot about the clock entirely, feeling a rhythm with the equations, not completely caring if I got them right or not, moving from one to the next with ease. I ticked off the last one and noticed I still had time left. Crazy.

I flipped through to the answer key, realizing the room was getting hazy. Katie was really going at it. The first few questions checked off fine. I ran my fingers down the line. Correct. Correct. Correct.

Holy crap, I hadn't missed a single question. It was just a set, twenty problems, but still.

"That's what I'm talking about," Katie said. "You killed it, didn't you?"

"Might be a coincidence." I packed up my books, feeling happy and loose. I'd walked over, thankfully. I wasn't sure I was up for driving. Now that I was done concentrating, I could feel something off, like I noticed each step a second after my foot hit the ground.

Katie followed me to the door. "Let's try it again tomorrow.

Do a longer bit. It's an experiment."

I walked out into the night. "Maybe."

Katie laughed. "You'll be back!"

In the bath, I rose from the water with a gasp. I'd been holding my breath again, waiting for the black.

Not in the tub. Shower sometimes, but a bath was dangerous. I never knew exactly how long it took me to come back around. Possibly long enough to drown. Another car drove by, illuminating the room for just a moment.

The boys in Austin's bedroom were a flash of memory, sitting around a table, a big glass bong in the center. Austin probably smoked. If I were around it again, if things progressed, the whole thing could start all over. Relationship. Sex. Pregnancy. Death. Secrets. Guilt.

I wiped my eyes. No more Austin. No more Gavin. I had to get back to where I'd been on Monday, before I saw him again, before everything caved in.

My phone buzzed in my jeans, lying somewhere in the bathroom. I could make out a lump on the white rug and I reached for it, wiping my hands on the denim before I tugged the phone out.

Sixteen texts from Jenny. Good grief. I scrolled through. Most were about Gavin, how he was persistent, desperate to see me. She listed his phone number and said she refused to give him mine.

The next message almost made me drop the phone.

He told me about your baby.

I read it twice then flung the phone away, not caring if it cracked. What was he doing? Why had he done that?

Water flew across the tub as my hand smacked the water over and over again. I came here to get away. I needed to escape.

My face was wet, and I wasn't sure if I was crying finally or just splashed. I rushed with hate for my high school friend Katie, for her idea, because it had worked too well. I smoked and smoked and smoked and learned exactly how much weed I needed to maximize my test taking. We went through her stash so quickly that we had to drive up to her brother's college to get more.

I sank below the water, looking up into the blackness. It was almost as good as holding my breath, but not quite. The water was cooling off, and my mind still whirred. I wanted to shut it off, stop thinking.

If only I hadn't smoked so much. If only I had trusted myself to take the test without it.

I held my breath, bubbles flowing from my lips and rising to the surface.

Spots filled my vision. My body wanted to come up for air, but I didn't let it.

I stayed away from everyone for a reason. Too many triggers. Too much history. Small things, like college boys with a bong, became huge, looming over me like the ocean swallowing the stars.

Gavin couldn't know. He could never know. If Austin talked. If Gavin heard. If he connected the dots.

My lungs were bursting but then suddenly they weren't. I exhaled everything in my body and sank farther against the hard curve of the tub. Would my body save itself in this black water?

I opened my eyes and saw Finn, curled up like he'd been in the sonograms, and how I'd imagined him to look while he was still tucked safely in my belly. He floated, the curling line of his umbilical cord snaking between us. I reached for him, hoping maybe he'd open his eyes this time, and breathe without a machine. But we were underwater, and he couldn't breathe. His lungs wouldn't work here any more than they had when he was in his little plastic bed, the ventilator taped to his mouth, forcing air in and out in a loud mechanical whine.

He shifted, rotating, almost as though he were coming closer, then opened his mouth and blew out a long exhale of gray smoke.

I gulped water and everything went quiet, so black, and I couldn't see anything at all.

17

GAVIN

I flung my helmet on the sofa, glad to be home from Tijuana. The phone buzzed and my heart raced, thinking maybe Corabelle's friend had given her my number, but it was just Mario, asking if I wanted to shoot pool.

Saying yes would be wise, get out of my head, stop thinking about Corabelle. But instead of heeding my own advice, I put Mario off and pulled out my ancient laptop, wondering if a web search might help me locate her.

Corabelle Rotheford had plenty of hits, mostly hometown articles. National Merit Scholar lists. A piece on where students were going to college. I saw my name with hers, saying we were going to UCSD, before we realized we couldn't. The article had been right in the end, because now we both were.

I scrolled through, looking for anything more recent. Corabelle had worked in the admissions office at New Mexico, it seemed. She was quoted in some article about student employees by the school paper. Seems strange she would leave a university where she had such a great job and contacts. I remembered the fear that crossed her face on the first day we talked in the stairwell. If someone there had tried to hurt her, I would hunt them down. Anger flared through me. I had to get to her. Had to find out about the years we lost. We could fix this, I knew it. We were meant to be together.

Only one more link was about her, before the searches were for different people.

I didn't want to click on that last one, but I did.

Finn Grayson Mays, infant son of Gavin Mays and Corabelle Rotheford, died on May 9, 2009.

My eyes burned. They hadn't run a picture. Corabelle didn't want one, since they all had tubes and wires on him, except for the last few, after they turned off the machines.

Finn was born May 2, 2009, in Deming, New Mexico. He is survived by his parents and his grandparents Arthur and Maybelle Rotheford and Robert and Alaina Mays of Deming.

When I saw my father's name, I closed the link. He'd been at the funeral all right, jovial, relieved, and when he told some member of Corabelle's church that at least the kids didn't have to get married now, I asked him to leave.

He refused, and I should have left it alone. My mother was grieving, and the two of us going at each other was making it worse for both her and Corabelle. But I hadn't left it alone. Then I ended up walking out.

Then not going back.

I shut the laptop. I didn't want to think about these things. I wanted Corabelle. No one else was going to work, but she was being so darn stubborn, walking off with that other guy right where I could see it.

Rage surged and I fought to bring it down before realizing,

hell, no one else is here. What did it matter if I walked around in a pisser? The room was scattered with secondhand barbells and hand weights. I stripped off my shirt and began working through my circuit. Getting physically exhausted would burn off this edge.

After a couple rounds, I wanted music, something loud and pounding. I stuck my phone into a pair of cheap speakers and set the playlist to punk. I switched to squats and ditched the boots and jeans. When the burn got good and solid, the anger started shifting to determination. I wasn't going to let Corabelle go so easily. If that pipsqueak boy interested her, fine, but I could be unrelenting. And I knew every button to push.

Corabelle and I had been pretty heavy on the sex, and I snuck in her window most every night. Because of that, we could never agree on when Finn had been conceived. To make matters worse, her being on the shot and not finding out for a while meant everything was a big question. When she was about three months along, the doctors pegged the date as mid October. I remembered that period, right in the middle of this crazy time when she was trying to retake the SAT to qualify for one of the big national scholarships.

She was studying with Katie, another super-brain who was going for a perfect score. Corabelle was completely different for a while, alternatively manic and utterly chill. When I slipped into her bed, she'd be so willing. Not like she wasn't always. Once all that started, we could scarcely keep our hands off each other. But during that time, she would try anything, do anything. We cracked open the *Kama Sutra* and just went after it, laughing at some of the more impossible positions. I felt like we'd never been closer.

I always insisted that Finn was conceived the night in the park. When I arrived at her house around midnight, she was bouncing off the walls. She'd taken an entire practice test and only missed three questions, and this was the closest she'd gotten to perfection.

Instead of crawling into her bed, we left, running down the street in the cool autumn moonlight like two kids finally escaping their parents. The little neighborhood park was silent and mostly dark. I pushed her on the swings and chased her through the monkey bars. Everything seemed possible, our future so close we could almost reach it, and Corabelle believed she could achieve this goal of the perfect score and a scholarship that would pay her way completely.

Eventually we tumbled in the cool carpet of grass. The night had chilled down, and she snuggled into me, her black hair a curtain across my chest. We had looked at the stars, I remembered suddenly, lying like we had on the roof. I'd have to remind her of that. I didn't know any constellations other than the Big Dipper, and we didn't really talk about that then. I just know she turned into me and slid her hand under my shirt and across my belly, and we were lost.

Too much. I set down a barbell and wiped my face with a towel. I hadn't known how good I had it with Corabelle then, so willing, always matching me. That night had been beyond amazing, stripping down in the grass, the moonlight on her body, highlighting the curves of her breasts and waist and hips, brightening her hair as she crawled up to sit on top of me, straddling my waist.

Her face and the stars were all one picture as I touched every part of her. My thumb went between us and found that sweet spot. Her eyes closed and she leaned back. I could see all of her skin, smooth and beautiful. She gripped my free hand, squeezing, and by paying attention to her sounds and movements, I knew when I had her close to peaking.

I slid her body down, then up, until we were almost joined. Her eyes opened wide, and she smiled, adjusting so I slipped inside. I worked her faster and now she was frantic, leaning forward, her breasts near my mouth, bracing herself on the ground as she moved in a rhythm so hard, so perfect, that I could scarcely hang on myself.

I knew when it all burst in her. She forgot where she was, crying out loud enough to set a few dogs to barking beyond the trees, grinding herself down on me with such force that I had no choice but to let go, filling her up, hanging on, breaking free of the need to hold back right as she dropped flat against me.

We shuddered against each other, the quiet settling into the low hum of crickets and a faraway highway. I held her close and this time something came over her and she started sobbing. I thought maybe I'd hurt her, but she whispered "I love you" in my ear and the emotion was so intense that it flowed into me.

I swear I felt that night as though some light began to glow, like something changed inside us both. Later, when we learned about Finn, and after the shock had worn off and we were settled into the revised version of our future, I brought that night up. Corabelle insisted it was impossible, that it happened later, but always, I felt that I knew, and for a long time I hoped it meant that I had a connection with the baby that meant I'd be a decent dad.

18

CORABELLE

I was on fire. Everything inside my chest was burning like it might ignite.

I broke the surface of the bathwater, coughing, gagging, and sucking in air. My arm and leg went over the side and I tumbled out onto the floor, shivering, naked, and in unbearable pain.

Water dribbled from my mouth and nose and I sobbed uncontrollably, tightening into a ball on the floor, head to the rug. Calm down calm down calm down. You're okay. You're alive. You're fine.

The corner of a towel brushed against my hair and I yanked it down, rolling up inside it. The screaming heat was dying down, but still I hurt, my head pounding, my chest throbbing.

Is this what I wanted? To die?

Maybe.

I considered this, trying to pull away from the pain, to concentrate on my thoughts instead. Did I want to die? Was it really that bad?

Gavin. Jenny. Austin. I felt my past closing in.

A square lit up in the dark, inches from my face. My phone. Another text from Jenny.

Coffee shop boy must be a live one.

I closed my eyes. I couldn't handle her right now. Besides, she knew. Gavin had told her.

Gavin.

The need for him began to pulse like the pressure in my head. He became my breath. Gavin, Gavin, Gavin.

I couldn't move forward. I couldn't go back. I wanted him here.

I wanted him now.

I reached for the phone, bypassing all of Jenny's chipper messages and stopping on the one with his phone number.

I shouldn't call him. It was too much. His voice. What to say. Had he wanted to die at any point?

Of course not. He wasn't the guilty one.

But he had walked away.

So maybe he knew. Maybe he could help.

He might be the only one who could help.

I clicked on his number and then tapped out one word.

Come.

As soon as I sent it, a calmness flowed over me. I stopped shivering and lay still on the floor.

Within seconds, I had a reply.

Corabelle, is this you? Where? I'm coming.

I typed the address. Once it was sent, I realized what a mess I was, wet, naked, clothes throughout the apartment. I scrambled up and wrapped my hair, hurtling through to my bedroom.

As I yanked on a shirt and shorts, I regretted bringing him in. Nothing good could come from this. He had seen me with Austin. He couldn't be happy about that.

I picked up the clothes and stuffed them in the hamper. My hair was a disaster and couldn't be combed, thick and tangled and wet. I twisted it into a messy bun and shoved a half-dozen bobby pins through it.

I had a feeling I was going to spill my secrets. Maybe it was time to lay it all out. The weeks of the SAT. What happened in New Mexico. I'd already lost him once and survived. At least this time there would not be any lies or guilt.

The doorbell buzzed. Too late to back out.

I opened the door. Gavin stood on the porch, shirtless, sweaty, wearing only a pair of workout shorts and tennis shoes. My heart caught. His chest was as smooth as ever, but now he was so muscled, the hard pecs leading into his shoulders and broad sinewed arms. His lean waist disappeared into the band of his shorts, and I had to step back, blood rushing in my ears. All day long with Austin and I felt nothing. Ten seconds with Gavin and I had forgotten why I'd held myself away from boys for all these years.

He grabbed my shoulders and yanked me to him, crushing my face against his neck. I fit there as perfectly as I always had, but his bare skin was a jolt, a spark that zigzagged through my body. I wanted to lift my chin, let him search my face like he used to, and lean in with those tantalizing lips. I needed to look at him, all of him, see what had changed and what remained the same. I wanted to feel something again.

I felt a wave of emotion and held it in, but a small sound escaped, like a whimper.

"Corabelle."

The word washed over me like a wave of cool air. No one pronounced my name quite like Gavin, who'd grown up with it, who first said it with chubby toddler cheeks, who tossed it out as we ran down pathways as kids. And who'd said it so differently that one time, that first time, when we realized we were not going to be forever friends, but expand into so much more.

Cars passed by in the broken parking lots of the complex, shining lights on us. Gavin pulled me inside and closed the door. "You asked for me."

My throat was too tight to speak, but I nodded.

"I won't walk out on you again. Never again." He was lit only by the yellowish light of the entry, but still, his dark hair and strong features were visible, those same eyes I'd looked into and trusted as a girl.

When I didn't answer, he pulled me back against him, and for the space of several heartbeats, we just stood there. I calmed down in degrees, relieved to be held after so long. I had forgotten how comforting it was to rely on another person.

"Let's sit down," he said and led me to my sofa, a ratty bit of salvaged furniture covered in a bright rainbow blanket.

He didn't let go, but pulled me into his lap, cradling my knees up against him so that I sat sideways, curled against his chest. He breathed onto my hair and his heart thumped against my ear. I never ever wanted to move.

19

GAVIN

I was so afraid of scaring Corabelle away, I didn't even want to talk.

Her hair was chilly against my chest, like she'd just gotten out of the shower. She wore very little, just a tiny white tank top and silky shorts that showed so much leg, I had to clamp down every raging thought.

Everything competed for dominance. Relief that she asked for me. Worry about why. And the need to touch her, to connect with someone who hadn't been paid to be there.

I just knew it was that guy. He'd tried something on her. My heart started pounding. I pictured him on her, pinning her down, and her screaming and beating on his back.

I'd kill him. I'd break his scrawny neck.

"Did he hurt you?" I finally asked, already imagining my fist connecting with his pathetic little face.

Corabelle stiffened against me. "Who?"

"That asshole you were with earlier. Did he hurt you?"

She pinched the bridge of her nose, and I grasped her hand. "I'll take care of him. He won't go within ten miles of you again."

Corabelle shook her head. "No. No. He didn't hurt me. He just — he wasn't who I thought he was."

My relief was so intense that I exhaled in a big heavy rush. "Thank God."

"I — I haven't had any trouble like that." Her voice was so tenuous, so lost.

"You don't have to tell me anything," I said. "I'm just here for you." I hesitated. I'd been given this incredible opportunity. I couldn't blow it. "I meant what I said. I won't ever walk out on you again. Never."

With that, she pushed away from me and walked across the room. "It will never come to that."

I jumped up. "What do you mean?"

She waved her hand in the air. "I mean, I'm done with relationships for now. I can't do them. I won't."

"You sure seemed chummy with short stack."

"When did you get so bitter?"

"Maybe when everything went south, same as you?"

Corabelle turned her face to the wall. "I shouldn't have brought you here. I'm sorry."

Damn it. I was doing it all wrong. Bring it down. "I'm glad you did. I was dying to see you. I was so wrong the other day at your work. I said the wrong things. I even tried to badger Rainbow Brite to give me your number."

She turned her face to me, confused. "You mean Jenny? Yes, she told me." Then her face completely changed, morphing into rage. She stalked across the room and before I could fathom what she was about to do, she punched me in the ribs. "You jerk. You complete and utter asshole."

I grabbed her hand and stilled it against my chest. "I know. I shouldn't have called you that."

"Called me what?" She searched my face a minute. "Oh, right,

I'm easy."

"I'm sorry, Corabelle. I was so jealous. The thought that you were with him…"

She struggled with her hand a moment, then hit me on the arm with her other. I accepted the blow. She had every right to do it. "It's not that." Her eyes went totally dark. "You told Jenny about the baby!" She struggled against me, but I held on. "Why did you do that?"

"I was desperate. I had to get her to understand how important this was."

She tried to back away, but I kept her hand imprisoned. "I didn't want anyone here to know!" she said.

I jerked her back against me, my mouth against her hair. "I'm sorry. I didn't know what else to do."

Her breath was fast and hard, her shoulders jumping. I knew I was screwing up when I did it. Still, I was here. I couldn't regret it. Now I had a chance. She had to remember how good we were together. I had to remind her.

My hand on hers was trapped against her breast and I became acutely aware of her body, the softness beneath the back of my hand, the shampoo perfume of her wet hair. I went full mast immediately. I knew the moment she noticed because she let out a little gasp.

Corabelle tried to pull away again, but I kept her close. I couldn't bear to let her go, not yet. "Give me just a minute with you," I croaked out. "I won't do anything, but just let me have this moment."

She relaxed and her belly pressed against me. It took all the control I possessed not to push harder against her, to trail my hand down her back, to move back into that heat we felt in the dish room at her work. Remembering her reaction to me then made my cock jump. I glanced down at her, those soft breasts pressed against my chest. Her nipples poked into the white tank and I lost it completely, grinding against her, letting her hand go to cup her chin and raise her face to mine. My mouth felt so hot against her cool lips. I needed her, all of her, and held her so tight that I don't think either of us could breathe.

Her hand beat against me again, and I felt like I was that jerk boy I had been so angry about when I came in. I let her go and she spun away, putting distance between us.

"You can't do this," she choked out. "I called you here, but not for this."

I ran my hands through my hair, trying to cool down. "I know. I'm sorry."

"I just —" She covered her face with her hands. "I don't know."

The sofa cushions crushed beneath my weight as I sank down, trying to put my need on lockdown. Corabelle stood several feet away, back by the wall, but looking at her didn't help matters. Her hair was all scattered in a crazy knot. The tank clung to all her curves, her nipples still tantalizing beneath the thin fabric. The silky shorts v'd between her legs and I just wanted to race over there and part them, feel her, watch all the expressions come over her face as I pleasured her. I'd forgotten her feet, those little toes, decorated with pink nails.

I had to stop this.

"Tell me what you want me to do, and I'll do it." Except leave, I added silently. Please don't ask me to leave.

She sat on the floor, tucking her knees to her chin. "Just be here. Just keep it easy."

I leaned back on the sofa. "I can do that."

I caught her glancing at my crotch, and I willed it to behave. "Should we talk about astronomy?" I asked.

She nodded.

"I think Professor Blowhard has a pipe up his ass about having to teach nonmajors."

Corabelle almost smiled, I could see it.

"I'm sure it's more fun to teach students who aren't just there to goof around on the roof," she said. A piece of black hair had fallen from the tangle and she twirled it with her finger.

"I hope the next lab feels a little less like something you do at a kids' camp."

Corabelle shook her head. "Yeah, I'm thinking I may be a bit of an overachiever for this class."

"I bet you've got some perfect GPA."

She shrugged. "I've done all right. I need the grades to get into grad school."

I hated to think I'd lose her as soon as I found her. "Where are you thinking of going? Here?"

"Wherever I get accepted. I have a list."

"None of them UCSD?"

She turned her head. "You seem hopeful I'll stay."

"I'm hopeful you'll want to."

She looked at the floor. "I don't know what I want anymore."

The urge to crawl over to her was strong, but I forced myself to stay on the sofa. "I wonder if Crazy Charles has made good on his valedictory speech."

Corabelle smacked her hands against the carpet. "OH! That jerk! I forgot about him!"

"I never thought you'd forget the guy who stole the top spot from you." Corabelle had ended up salutatorian when a perfect tie on their grades meant the committee looked to their noncredit courses for a decision.

"Last I heard, he was at MIT," Corabelle said. "So he did well."

She seemed to be relaxing again.

"Remember when we were kids, and practiced teaching school?" I asked.

"I know where this is going." She kicked her legs out, and the sight of her thighs made my blood jump, but I stuffed it down.

I propped my feet on a scarred-up coffee table, hoping the position would hide anything that sprang up unexpectedly. "Charlie was always the student in the most trouble in our pretend classroom."

"Didn't we stick him in the corner? What did we use for him?"

"Your clown doll," I said.

"Yes! That was it. I seemed to enjoy giving him F's on all his essays."

"You were a heartless one."

Her smile was genuine and made her look so much like the old Corabelle. Our history seemed to fall away and we were almost like we'd been at the beginning of that terrible year, before anything went wrong. I wanted her so desperately, to talk to her while I held her close, to bring her around. I knew her. I knew everything about her. I could make her better, erase that sadness in her eyes, that panic that came over her so often.

Cool your jets, I told myself. One step at a time.

20

CORABELLE

I wasn't going to be able to resist him. I could already see it.

He sat on my sofa, his feet up on my coffee table, and everything about my difficult world suddenly seemed so simple. I could see he was on edge. He always had these explosive moments. But he cared, a lot, and I had always forgiven him because I knew where they came from, his father, that jerk who never thought Gavin did anything right.

But would he forgive me? I couldn't bear it if that anger was directed at me.

He talked about our old pretend school in my parents' sunroom, looking out over the yard and the fence that had a Gavin-sized gap going to the alley. Eventually my father had put in a gate to make it easier for him to come over. He had no idea that he would later be enabling our torrid nights, Gavin coming in my window as freely as the hot winds blew through New Mexico.

My belly burned and the heat rushed between my legs. I tried to remember the last time we'd been together, all the way together, my last time. Maybe a week before the baby was born. Only in the last day or two when something seemed off, cramps in my back and random contractions, did we stop.

I managed to answer when he asked questions, but my mind wasn't on the conversation anymore. I wanted to give him a shirt, so that I would stop looking at his chest. I'd been up against it twice already, and when he kissed me earlier, it had taken everything I had to get away.

But dang it, he made me mad. I was still so disgusted that our private story was out.

Gavin seemed to realize I'd quit paying attention and just watched me with those cool blue eyes.

I closed my own to cut off the visuals feeding my distraction, letting my head fall against the wall. Calling him had been a good thing. I felt in control again, less afraid of what had happened in the bathroom. Maybe now that the moment had passed I would be all right. I could send Gavin home, and we'd see each other in class on Monday, and fall into something easier than we'd endured so far. If I kept it light, then my secrets could stay tucked away. No more drama. No disaster or rejection or guilt.

His breath on my neck made me snap my eyes open.

"Is something wrong?" he asked.

"No! I'm fine. This is fine. It's good. Thank you." God, I was gushing.

He picked up my hand and bent each finger, one at a time. My heart sped up crazy fast. He first starting doing this when we were young and just experimenting with kissing and touching. He saw it in some movie and realized when he did it that it had an effect on me that worked even better than on the woman on the screen.

Later, when we were lovers, he'd do it when we were out in public, just to tease me, knowing it made me think of all the things it led to. Feeling it now, each finger getting its own moment of attention, everything flooded back. The innocence we knew as children and friends. The playful way we copied the grown-ups around us, acting like other couples, sometimes as a joke, and other times in perfect seriousness.

And of course, later, when we knew the baby was coming, and that we would marry, and life might be accelerated, but was still the path we planned to go down eventually.

I struggled to find a way to avoid that dangerous direction. "You did this at Finn's sonogram," I said. "You know, the big one when we found out if he was a boy or a girl." And if he was normal, I thought.

The sonogram had been fine, showing a healthy boy right on target for the dates they'd established before. We had no idea then that Finn would be born early and with a heart condition.

"That was a good day," Gavin said. He brought my hand to his lips and kissed each finger.

Heat flooded through me again, and I knew I was falling. "He was so beautiful."

"He was."

"Sometimes he doesn't seem real."

Gavin gripped my hand and held it to his cheek. "I feel that way a lot."

He did?

"You think about him? You had his picture." My chest still warmed over, even though I hadn't been ready when Gavin pulled it out in the stairwell.

"Pretty much every day." He let go of my fingers and stretched out on the floor, hands beneath his head.

I was both relieved and disappointed that he moved away. "But you — you can manage it. You don't get upset?"

He frowned. "Not much upsets me anymore."

"How does that work?" I felt like I was getting worse, not better, although until Gavin had come back, I had been in a manageable place.

"I burned it out of me with beer and work and everyday life."

"I can't do that. I can't watch TV for the baby commercials. And some stores are insufferable. There's this sign on campus —"

"I know the one."

"Tripped me up."

Gavin stared up at the ceiling. "Could you be pregnant? We can help." He looked over at me and his abs crunched together in a way I only knew from Hollister ads. "I know what it's for, but I want to paint the whole kiosk black."

"We never considered anything but keeping the baby, did we?"

"Nope. Hell, half the town was excited for us."

It was true. So many of our classmates married right out of high school anyway. Jumping the gun hadn't caused much of anyone so much as a blink.

"Remember how Old Man Wilkins brought over that ancient stool?" Gavin asked.

"It was so sweet. It had belonged to his little boy. I still have it."

Gavin sat up. "Really?"

"Sure. It's on the other end of the sofa."

Gavin stood fluidly, each muscle taut, and I tried not to think about him as anything but, well, like Austin, or lumberjack boy, or my coworkers — guys I'd come across and felt no temptation with whatsoever.

Who was I kidding?

He picked up the little green stool. "Do you have anything else from our old place?" he asked.

I pushed myself up, not nearly as gracefully as he had. "Just small things. The bedside table. The little hula-girl lamp."

"Hula girl!"

I had to smile. "Yes, the gift from the art teacher. She was always a little strange."

"You just say that because she loved my bad paintings of waterfalls better than your bad paintings of waterfalls. Can I see her?"

"Sure." I led him down the hallway to the bedroom, not realizing what a terrible idea it might be until I flipped on the light and saw the unmade bed, sheets strewn in every direction.

Gavin passed me and beelined for the lamp. "Turn off the overhead!"

I waited until he had his hand under the girl's skirt, then killed the main light. Gavin switched on hula girl and as she warmed up, her hips swayed gently back and forth.

He looked over at me, his face bathed in the greenish light. "I missed her!"

I could barely swallow then. Seeing him there, leaning over the lamp, we could be in any time, any place.

Gavin must have noticed I had changed. He walked back to me and tucked a loose strand of hair behind my ear, another familiar gesture that completed the sense that we had arrived in some other moment in our history. "This is good, really good. Don't you think?"

I nodded, not trusting my voice. This was going to happen. It had already begun.

21

GAVIN

Something had shifted in Corabelle. But it had been pushing and pulling all night, so I didn't trust it. She'd been in my arms by the door, and again on the sofa, and I'd screwed it up every single time. I turned away and sat on her bed, looking for something else from our past to comment on, something easy.

Hula girl swayed on her stand, keeping the light moving like a wave. Corabelle's room was simple, sparsely decorated, and all the pictures on the wall were of her family.

Then I saw it.

The frame held four images, two tall and two wide. The first picture was the sonogram, Finn's shape clear in white on black. The next was the first shot, one I had taken, right after he was born, red faced and covered in a white paste. The last two were after they hooked him to the ventilator, the blue tape covering his mouth.

So much for keeping it easy.

She saw me looking and sat on the bed next to me. I wondered why she hung them up if she didn't want anyone to know, and then I realized it was because no one came here. No one was in her room but her. She kept herself separate. Jenny said she only saw

Corabelle at work.

How alone we'd both been. I'd busied myself with work, and playing pool with Mario, and paying girls to keep me company. But we stayed away from attachments, from closeness. We were the same.

"I just had the one from the funeral," I said. "I didn't take anything with me when I left."

"I know. I thought you'd be back soon because you hadn't packed so much as a toothbrush." Her arm brushed against mine, but she didn't move away.

"I really thought I'd come back. It's just the farther I went, the harder it got to turn around."

The moment had arrived to tell her what I'd done, and why I'd stayed away. Just get it over with and see if she hated me or not, if she could forgive me. Maybe she would just say, get a reversal. Or maybe she'd take it so personally that the rift would tear us apart a second time.

But she laid her head on my shoulder and I couldn't breathe. Her fingers closed around my arm, and my blood rushed so hard, it was everything I could do not to pull her down on that bed, to love her mercilessly and without hesitation. Maybe we needed something stronger before we went down those dark paths. Maybe we could build again.

"Remember in the sunroom?" I couldn't say anything else, not trusting my voice to hold together.

"Which time? We were busy in there."

"The first time."

"Ah. Yes."

"Your parents thought it would be okay to leave us to go to that fire station fund-raiser," I said.

"We were only fifteen."

"Going on twenty."

Corabelle squeezed my arm. "They had no idea."

"What movie had done it this time?"

"*How to Lose a Guy in 10 Days.*"

"Yes, Kate Hudson. Hot."

Corabelle smacked my thigh.

"You did the same thing that night," I said, laughing.

"What was the scene that got us?"

"In the bathroom, when they finally decide they actually like each other. He takes off her shirt." I remembered that so clearly. As soon as I saw it, I wanted to do it with Corabelle. When the movie ended, we went into the sunroom, our together space since her parents were weird about me going in her bedroom now. We turned out the lights and talked for a while, then I stood up and dragged her with me.

"Raise your arms," I told her.

Corabelle had giggled. "What for?"

"Just do it."

The seriousness of my tone sobered her up. "Like in the movie?"

"Like that."

She looked up at me, dark haired where the actress was blond, but just as intense, just as sure, and lifted her arms in the air. I held on to the bottom of her shirt, barely able to breathe, and lifted it over her head.

We were young, and we fumbled, but Corabelle was already on the shot, so we had nothing to worry about except the how and the where. And once we began, there was no stopping us.

"You ever listen to that song anymore?" I asked her.

"I put the CD away with Finn's things after you left."

"You have it here?"

She hesitated. "Yes, but I can't open that box."

"Let me."

"It's under the bed. You'll know it." Her voice was unsteady.

I pulled away and knelt low, fumbling in the low light. But she was right. I remembered the box, given to us by the hospital just for the baby's things. A blanket. A little outfit. A candle. A handprint kit. We'd gone through it in the two days between his death and the funeral. The box had been put together by some volunteer group for families like us.

I didn't pull the box out, just lifted the lid a few inches. The CD was on top, and I was grateful, because just seeing the blanket was more than enough for me. "You got anything to play this on?"

"My laptop has a CD drive. Are you — are you sure we should?"

"I'd like to."

Corabelle moved to a backpack in the corner and tugged out her computer. She passed it to me, so I opened it up, waited for the chime, and opened the CD tray.

The first song of the soundtrack wasn't right, so I skipped down to "Feels Like Home." Hearing that crystal voice sent me back in time so fast that I half expected to look up and see that we were in the sunroom and Corabelle was holding her arms in the air. I realized she was wearing the same white tank from that scene, and I had to wonder about fate, timing, and what exactly the world had in mind when it signed us both up for the same class at the university we had once planned to go to before everything else happened, before life got so dark that it split us apart.

Before *I* split us apart.

The enormity of my regret crashed over me. I wanted to shut off the song, stop it all. I reached for the keyboard but Corabelle knew what I was doing and grabbed my wrist. "Let's just get through it. I know it's hard, but let's just tough it out."

The chorus tore through my heart. I was home. We were home. All we had to do was decide that this was where we belonged. She had to forgive me for leaving. Then she had to know what I had done, and forgive me all over again.

I pushed the laptop out of the way and moved closer to her. The mattress dipped and knocked us together. She fell on me, and I held on. The moment to tell her had come a second time, and I had to be man enough to say the words.

22

CORABELLE

I had to tell him what I'd done. The only way to move on with my life was through his forgiveness. I could start with what happened earlier that day with Austin, then back to New Mexico State and my arrest, and then the worst of all.

He was looking at me with those blue eyes, like I was the only thing in the world, just the way he had always done. I had forgotten what that could feel like. How important it was to be loved like that. How it could heal.

"Corabelle —"

"Gavin —"

We both stopped at the same time and just when I thought we'd both laugh, instead, we both almost sobbed, coming together in a crash, his arms tight around me and mine gripping him like a lifeline.

It was too much, my need of him overwhelming, how hard I ached. He shivered against me, and I could feel the emotion passing between us. For the first time in four long years, I thought — *I can be that girl I once was. I can have hope. I can find happiness.*

Gavin was home to me. Just like that night so many years ago,

I looked up at him with a mixture of anxiety and certainty, and just like then, just like in the movie, I raised my hands over my head to let him start the journey all over again.

He never took his eyes off mine, but his fingers grasped the bottom of the white tank — God, the same type of shirt as that scene, I realized — and tugged it up and off.

"Corabelle," he whispered, looking at me as if he'd never seen me before.

"I'm here."

He pulled me in, letting our skin have its own reunion. His chest was hard and almost hot to the touch. His heart hammered against mine. I wanted him to kiss me again, needed it more than I'd ever needed anything in my whole life. He took his time, running his fingers up the back of my neck and into my hair.

His mouth was achingly close, his nose bumping against mine. Everywhere we connected, I felt fire. His tongue brushed against my lips, and I parted for him.

At first his touch was so gentle that I barely knew we were kissing, the sensation featherlight. Then his hand on my neck pressed me into him and we were back, tasting each other and as close as we ever were.

I never wanted to do anything else but feel his arms around me, our skin touching, and his mouth crossing over mine, delving into me as though I could pour myself into him.

Every emotion I'd ever felt coursed through me, desire, need, joy, love, and even grief. We'd been through everything, through things people should never have to endure. No wonder we had fractured, blown apart. But we could fix it. We could get it back.

I wanted to be closer. I shifted on the bed, straddling his lap and locking my legs around his waist. The singer was right, I wanted to lose myself, fall into my one great love and just let everything disappear. He could do that. He'd been the only one who could ever do that.

His mouth never left mine as he kicked off his shoes. His fingers trailed across my spine, relearning every part of me. His thumbs made their way around, slipping into the curve below where our two chests smashed into each other.

Sensations splintered through me like lightning. I sucked in a breath and he moved, suddenly, like a panther, pushing me down on the bed. As soon as we were apart, he left my mouth to press kisses along my face and neck, dropping lower until he captured a nipple.

How could I have forgotten this, gone without? I arched against him, wanting more, needing him more than I thought possible. My hands went to his back, feeling each corded muscle, the angle from his chest down to his waist. He was so erect against me, pushing out against the silky shorts. I had never felt as bold as I did then, reaching for him, reminding myself of his length and breadth.

He sucked in a breath against my skin, his hands on my ribs. The song ended, so he reached around and closed the laptop, lifting it away from the bed and safely onto the floor. I could hear every rapid inhale, the silky sound of his palm running along my belly. He reached for the waist of my shorts, then hesitated, his gaze meeting mine. "Is this okay? Are you okay?"

The concern in those blue eyes sent another wave of emotion through me. He hadn't stopped caring. He never hated me, like I thought. He just succumbed to a terrible time, riddled with what-ifs. "Yes," I whispered.

He yanked on the shorts, bringing them to my knees, then dragging them the rest of the way off. My panties were simple, white cotton with an edge of lace. He ran a finger along the border against my skin, then followed some of the stretch marks across my belly. "I never knew about these," he said.

"They showed up later." I tried to cover them, but he pushed my hands away.

"They're beautiful." He began kissing each pale line, hip to stomach and back down again. "It's proof that Finn was once here."

Emotion welled up so hard that I didn't think I could contain it. Gavin continued to press his lips into my skin, but when his fingers began to slide the panties down, I forgot everything else, overwhelmed with physical sensations, gentle touch, and painful need.

Then I was naked below him, the only person who'd ever seen me like this. He spread my knees and pressed his face against the inside of my leg, pausing there, his mouth against my skin.

I could scarcely bear it. "Gavin, please," I managed to say.

His head lifted and I could see so much conflict there. Did he think it wasn't safe? That I could get pregnant again? "I'm still on the shot. I never stopped."

He closed his eyes and I knew he was thinking about how I was on it before, and it hadn't mattered. We'd been on the wrong side of every statistic. Less than a one-percent chance of getting pregnant. A heart condition that was one in four thousand.

His hands moved up my thighs, both thumbs resting against me, setting everything on fire.

"Some things just aren't in our control," he said. He spread me wide and his tongue flicked against me and then I couldn't think of anything as the world shattered.

I grabbed the sheets in handfuls. His hair tickled my belly and I zoomed into the next plane of pleasure so fast that I couldn't have stopped him if I wanted, his mouth so hot, the tremors in my body already taking me into the past, when we'd been like this constantly, greedy, feasting like the banquet would never end.

He worked every part, tongue and lips and fingers, and then

my body vibrated around him, and I let go of the sheets, my fears, the past and present, just rocketing into that shower of sparks.

Gavin knew just where to take it, and how to bring it down, pulling away gently, carefully, as my hips rested back against the bed. He pressed his face into my thigh, holding on to me, and I wondered if he would decide not to take this all the way, to spare the risk. And I couldn't bear it, I wanted it too, to see him lose control, to fall into me. I rolled over and got to my knees, tugging at his shorts, pulling everything down, boxers and all. I clutched at him, hot and throbbing between my fingers, making sure he couldn't let it go, couldn't resist.

I pushed him on his back, settling over him in a position that was so familiar. My hair was falling out of the pins and cascaded around his face. Before he could move or talk or do anything to stop me, I lowered myself down on him, sliding over him like slipping into cool sheets.

His fingers gripped my hips and I leaned down to kiss him, controlling the rhythm, taking his hands and pushing them over his head so that he was mine, control was mine, and I worked him, steady and deep.

Gavin's breathing sped up. I thought he was about to lose it when his arms broke free and he grabbed my waist, twisting me around and beneath him.

I gasped as he plunged into me, fierce and passionate, his face hovering over mine, the hula lamp undulating light against his hair. I was lost again, his hands on me, kneading all the soft parts and reaching between us. I didn't think I could go again but he led me there, rising up to meet him, and by the time he held still inside me, a long groan crashing over my ears, I was back, the world shattering around us, gasping for breath.

We came down in degrees, his body settling on mine, then shifting over to pull me against him. I never wanted to stop touching him, couldn't bear to think of him walking away again. I felt suddenly that it would happen, that we'd be forced apart, and this second loss would kill me. I tried to escape the grief, to revel in the moment, but I knew we had dark days ahead. Nothing between us had been easy for a long time.

"Shhh," he said, knowing as he always did when I was upset. "Just be here. Just be now."

I nodded against his shoulder. I could do that. I had to. Looking ahead or glancing behind were both too hard. We had right now. It had to be enough.

23

GAVIN

Corabelle needed to invest in some blackout curtains.

I crossed my arm over my eyes, trying to block the unrelenting sun. Corabelle's hair was draped all over my shoulder and chest. I was pretty sure it was the best feeling in the world. Okay, second best.

Her eyes were closed, her lips slightly parted. She breathed deep and even, like a kid. I wouldn't take this night for granted or assume it meant we were back together. I knew her moods could shift, and besides, I'd been a chickenshit. I could blow these good feelings sky high.

The clock behind her had giant red letters alerting me that I had 45 minutes to get out of bed and be at work. I didn't have a shirt. When Corabelle's text came through, I jumped on my bike without so much as a wallet.

Even so, I settled back down, relishing the moment. I'd showed up late more than once. I shouldn't push Bud, not after he'd moved me to mechanics, but damn it if I didn't want to stay right here a little longer.

Corabelle shifted, stretched, then her eyes flew open in alarm. She was about to jump out of bed when she seemed to realize where she was. "Oh!" she said. "That's right."

I understood her disorientation. I woke up several times in the night, not sure of the year, maybe back in high school and the little apartment we got so little use of. "You okay?" I asked.

She nodded, then twisted to look at the clock. "Holy crap!" She sat up. "I was supposed to be at work fifteen minutes ago." She jumped up and I had to admire how her boobs jiggled. She turned in circles and I got every view while she tried to figure out what to do first.

She tried running her fingers through her hair, to no avail. "I'm a mess!"

"Just call them. Tell them you're on your way."

Corabelle seemed only then to realize she was naked, and yanked the sheet off the bed, exposing me.

"Hey!"

"Sorry!" She was about to put it back when I waved her off.

"No, it's fine. This is highly entertaining."

She glared at me. "Then I'm not sorry for stealing your covers." She ran out of the room, and water started running on the other side of the wall.

I knew I should get up and find my clothes and get out of there. But I just couldn't, not yet. Corabelle's room was pretty sparse, just the bed, a table with the hula girl and a clock, and a stack of sideways crates that served as shelves. Looked like we'd both been living pretty close to the bone. My mind was already whirring, thinking that if we moved in together, I could probably support us, and maybe she could finish faster if she didn't have to work.

Then leave faster.

I rolled off the bed. She seemed okay this morning, but with

Corabelle, you could never tell. I picked up my boxers and shorts and headed for the hall. She'd left the bathroom door open and her silhouette behind the shower curtain made me want to go right in and join her.

But she was late, and remorse might hit her any moment. I had to play it careful.

The spray turned off and I leaned on the door frame as the curtain slid back. "Oh!" she said. "You're watching!"

"It's the best view I've had in a long time."

She wrapped up in one towel and snatched a second from a wire shelf for her hair. I noticed her phone in the corner on the floor and picked it up. "Leave this here?"

That panicked look came across her face again, and she snatched it from me. "Yes. Thank you." She passed me to head back to the bedroom, so I followed.

"Did you call work?"

"Not yet." She disappeared into a closet, a nice walk-in for such a small place.

I sat on the bed and shoved my legs into my boxers. I wondered if she'd keep the fast and furious pace until she took off, and we wouldn't get to do any sort of wrap-up on the night and what would happen next.

She came out in a pair of jeans and a simple blue T-shirt that was already wet on the shoulders. "I'm sorry I have to rush."

"I have to be at work too."

"Are you late? I didn't think to set an alarm."

"We had other things on our minds."

She blushed, shoving her feet into little pink tennis shoes. I finished dressing and searched around for my phone, which had slipped out of the shallow pocket when the shorts came off.

"Under the bed," she said.

I knelt down and saw it near the baby's box. I swallowed hard as I came back up. "Thanks. Can I call you?"

Corabelle pushed her hair out of her face. "I don't know. I have to think."

"No, don't think." I stepped toward her, but she moved away.

"It'll be okay. I just have to get used to this idea." She snatched a purse off the top of the crates. "I really have to go."

I followed her to the living room and picked up my keys from the table. She looked at me a moment. "Let me loan you a shirt."

I would have protested, but she ran down the hall, returning a minute later with a New Mexico State T-shirt that would have swallowed her now, but she'd gotten it back when she was pregnant with Finn.

My throat constricted as I took it from her. "I remember this."

"Yeah, it's a good one. Don't ruin it."

I pulled it over my head. "I guess this means I have to see you again to return it."

"You'll see me in class on Monday."

We headed for the door. After she locked it, I pulled her into my arms and didn't let her resist. She relaxed against me, her face against my chest.

"Corabelle, are we okay?"

She nodded.

I lifted her face. "Just one simple kiss?" I didn't wait for an answer but leaned in, just grazing her lips.

Her hands gripped me, and when I pulled back, she stepped away. "See you soon, Gavin."

She ran out to the parking lot and jumped into her car. I stood there, unmoving, as she backed out and drove away.

I turned back to her door. I hadn't imagined just a week ago that I'd be at Corabelle's home, and she would be back in my arms. I'd been given this amazing chance, and even if she seemed a little reluctant, I had hope that we could set everything right.

24

CORABELLE

Oh God oh God oh God. What had I done?

I pulled into an employee space a block away from Cool Beans, wondering if Gavin was still standing in front of my door. We could not do this. I could not tell him everything. Not now. It seemed like a way better idea to remember this one amazing night and just stop. No more.

I dashed down the sidewalk, worrying that Jason would be late as usual, but then remembered that Jenny was working that morning. She was pretty reliable.

The bells jingled as I ripped open the door. Jenny was waiting on an older couple getting plain coffee, judging by the mugs. I flashed her an apologetic look and raced behind the counter, stuffing my purse beneath the register and yanking out an apron.

Then I saw him.

Austin.

He pulled his headphones off and set them on the table, his usual one in the corner.

"He's been here since we opened," Jenny whispered. "Must have been some impression you made on him last night." She elbowed me. "You're one crazy chica."

The couple walked away from the counter, and I could see Austin heading toward me. "I can't talk to him!" I said, planning to scurry to the back.

Jenny grabbed my apron string. "Nuh-uh. He's been waiting for hours."

Austin leaned against the pastry case, a few feet away from Jenny. "Corabelle?" His eyes were full of misery.

God. What to say. I gave him a half-wave. "Hey."

"Are you okay? I've been so worried." His hands gripped the glass, the fingertips white from the pressure.

"I'm fine." I opened the back of the case and pretended to rearrange the danishes. "I just — that just wasn't my scene. I didn't mean to be dramatic."

Austin let go of the glass. "Okay. I didn't have your number or anything. I sent you e-mails."

I hadn't looked at any of that since yesterday. "I have a dumb phone, not a smart one. I didn't see them yet."

"Were you okay last night?"

I flashed through the evening. Gavin on my sofa, leaning over the hula girl, pulling me close, his face hovering over my body. "Yes! Yes. I was fine."

Austin stuck his hands in his pockets and looked away. "I guess this means you don't want to see me again?"

Jenny glanced at us, then moved as far away as she could, next to the window and the rows of plastic water cups.

I knew I couldn't see Austin anymore, even if I didn't intend to stick with Gavin. I had already succumbed. Austin hadn't kept me away, although I'm not sure anyone could have. I shook my head. "I don't think so."

He looked so dejected, his Adam's apple bobbing as he tried to swallow.

"It's not you," I said hurriedly. "I just can't be around — that."

I glanced at Jenny, who was certainly listening even though she was facing away. "That — that thing that was happening. It's a thing from my past. A problem."

Austin's eyes grew large. "Are you in recovery?"

"No! No. I mean, yes. Yes. That's it. I have to stay away. Even your stuff smells like it." It wasn't a total lie.

Austin backed away. "Okay, I get it. I can respect that. I wish it were different. I can't move, though. And Ben, he's a big-time toker. Not me, though." He held up his hands. "I can't afford it anyway."

I focused on the pastries, arranging and rearranging the same three bear claws. This was for the best. "Seems like we're stuck. I guess that's the way it has to be." Now, please, go, I thought.

Austin stepped forward again. "Wait, I think Steve is leaving. Maybe I could move to his room. His roommate's a girl, though. Would that freak you out?"

Dang, he was persistent. "I — uh, Austin, let's not push it. It's still going to be around. I don't want to — fall off the wagon." I hated saying it. I hadn't been hooked or anything, even back in the day. When it came time to quit, I quit. Besides, I was pretty sure weed wasn't addictive, but I didn't have a lot of contact with it, other than Katie.

He pressed his head against the curve of the glass case. "I guess this is it then."

"Seems like it. It was a nice day. I had a good time."

"Me too." Austin stared into the shelves, then turned away.

I let out a long sigh.

Jenny grabbed my arm and dragged me inside the back door. "What is going on?"

"Date ended badly."

"Did he put a move on you?"

"No, not at all. It just wasn't my thing."

Jenny pulled the door closed behind her. "Girl, you are going to talk."

I would have to give her something. "They were all doing drugs. I'm not into that."

"Oooooh." Jenny tugged on one of her pink ponytails. "Well, that makes sense." She opened the door a crack and peeked out. "Never would have figured such a goody-two-shoes-looking boy to be up in all that."

"We should probably head back out." I reached for the door.

"Not so fast." Jenny blocked the handle. "Why were you so late today?"

"I overslept."

"Not buying it. You never oversleep. Besides, you didn't return a single text last night OR this morning."

"I had my phone turned off."

Jenny narrowed her eyes. "Not buying that either. It was Gavin, wasn't it? You called him."

I fingered the strings of my apron. "We have a history."

"I knew it!" Jenny's whole face lit up. "You have that look of a girl who's been done right by her man."

My hands flew to my cheeks. "What do you mean?"

"I just can see it! I knew when I saw him pinning you on the counter that he'd be all up in your business in no time flat."

The front door jingled. "Someone's here. I'll handle them." I pushed past Jenny and this time she let me go, still chuckling. I felt like all my secrets had suddenly gotten chalked onto the menu. Well, not all of them. But enough.

25

GAVIN

Even if Bud had told me to toss tires all day, I wouldn't have cared. My feet barely touched the ground as I crossed the garage and clocked in. The other mechanics punched each other knowingly, and Randy shouted, "Looks like Gavin finally got something he didn't have to take out a loan for." I ignored their jeers. You'd think by the way they acted that nobody ever got laid around here.

Bud winked at me — was I wearing a damn sign on my back? As he handed me a clipboard and a set of keys to a Ford Explorer that needed a new belt, I realized I could never, ever bring Corabelle around here. Mario had found my preference for hookers hilarious and brag worthy, so he'd been talking about it ever since the night one of my regular girls showed up at the pool hall. Lorali. She made a show of stripping half-naked in the corner of the bar to get me to take her home. Which I had.

The story became legendary at the garage, and for a while, a grainy print of Mario's cell-phone snapshot of Lorali had been tacked up in the break room, her wearing only a tiny red bra and a matching thong with her denim skirt halfway down to her knees.

But this wasn't one of those secrets Corabelle ever had to know about. That was behind me, as of right now, and hell, if it meant I had to keep her out of the garage or find a new place to work, I'd do it. I had a feeling she wouldn't be too understanding, even if I could find a way to explain it.

I wanted to text her right away but figured waiting was better since she seemed a little torn up about what happened. She said she needed to get used to the idea. I'd give her some time.

The Explorer rolled easily into the bay. When I got out, Mario strutted by with a red oil rag tied around his chest and another making a triangle over his crotch. "Oh, Gavin!" he said in falsetto. "Oh oh oh, just another fiver and I'll scream loud enough to make your neighbors jealous!"

I shook my head and popped the hood of the Explorer. I unhooked the battery, still watching Mario in my peripheral vision. He pranced around, pulling off the rags like it was a scarf dance. I wanted to tell him this one was for real, but I didn't feel like sharing Corabelle. The whole night still seemed like a magic-carpet ride.

I moved on to the intake hose assembly, but Mario wouldn't let it ride, taking the rag and draping it over my head.

Bud crossed through the garage. "Boy, ain't you got something better to do than give Gavin a piss-poor burlesque show?"

Mario tossed the other rag at me and moved on toward the storage room, still laughing. "Sure thing, boss."

"You got a handle on this one?" Bud asked, leaning on the frame and peering into the motor.

"Easy job." I pushed the fat hose out of the way and reached down for the serpentine belt. "You got a 3/8 ratchet on you?"

Bud turned around and snatched the tool from the rolling chest stationed between the bays. "You seem to have this under control." He clapped me on the shoulder and left the garage.

I didn't realize I was tense until he moved out of sight and my shoulders dropped down half a mile. Bud still hadn't said anything about moving me up, just kept handing me keys rather than keeping me up front, taking oil changes and tire repair jobs.

Saturday was my late and long. I arrived after the early morning rush but hung out until the last car was off the lot. Still, we locked up at six, so I had plenty of time to go home and think about what I'd say to Corabelle when I called.

After two tune-ups, one belt tightening, and a brake job, I was ready to go home. I debated waiting until I was alone to call Corabelle proper, but I turned chicken, so I copped out by sending a text message instead.

Can I see you?

Waiting for a reply was agonizing, and I wished I'd just called. She might not see the message for hours, or she might not reply, ever. I raced home and checked again. Still nothing. After another ten minutes of painful waiting, I jumped in the shower.

I wasn't fully dry when I snatched the phone up again. She'd written back, and my stomach hit the floor.

I don't think so. Not yet. It's hard.

I wanted to throw the damn thing. I could go over there anyway, make her see me. I knew all the right buttons. I wanted to push every one. I'd just gotten started. We'd been crazy in high school, but last night. That was a whole 'nother level. Damn. I couldn't stand it.

The room was still littered with barbells and I considered another workout. But no, I should get out, do something. Mario had been an ass earlier, but shooting pool was better than hanging out here and waiting for Corabelle to change her mind.

A group of guys roared with laughter from the back corner as I tried to concentrate on getting the nine ball in the right corner pocket. My patience was wearing thin, and Mario watched me warily as he lifted a bottle to his lips. "Never saw a man so worked up over a piece like you are tonight," he said. "She raise her rates?"

The ribbing had gone on the whole night. My credit card must have been maxed out. I didn't get my two for the price of one. On and on. When this game ended, I intended to call it a night. I'd rather lie around obsessing about Corabelle than deal with this.

My game was off. I smacked the cue but got a whole lotta nothin'.

"Looks like somebody needs a stripper in his corner," Mario said.

I backed away from the table and perched on a stool, picking up my glass of beer, which had gotten warm. My fury was rising and everything in me tried to push it back down. This was the bullshit my dad had pulled, getting all worked up until BOOM, he was set off. What was this genetic thing that made me just like him, even though I hated it? Maybe I learned from the best.

Mario leaned over the table and I thought about what the night would be like with Corabelle here instead. She'd smile at me — I'd get her smiling again — and lean over the rack, a stick in her hand, face all screwed up in concentration. Her shirt would hang a little low, and her white bra would sort of glow from the light overhead, that sweet bit of cleavage just a shadow.

"Hey, Gavin, snap out of it!" Mario whacked me on the leg with his cue stick, and I caught myself just before I would have hurled my glass at him.

"I'm done here." I shoved my stick onto the wall rack.

"What? It's like nine o'clock! And I'm kicking your ass in the game."

"Not feeling it."

"It's some girl, isn't it? Not one of your hookers. A real girl."

"Right. Because the others aren't real girls."

Mario dropped his stick on the table. "You know what I mean."

I didn't feel like telling him anything. "I'm going to head out."

Two girls ran up to our table. "Are you leaving?" asked a blonde with the shortest skirt imaginable. "Can we have your balls?"

I could tell Mario was about to say something stupid, so I jetted through the crowd and toward the door. I had no interest in the women, or in Mario's fumbling attempt to chat them up.

"Gavin! Hold up!" Mario darted through the maze of tables and players. "Damn, she's got you wound up like a clock, whoever she is."

The sudden quiet and cool of the night air calmed me considerably. I headed for my Harley and threw a leg over.

"Man, you're like a different person tonight," Mario said, stuffing his hands in his jean pockets.

"It's nothing." I grappled for something to say to deflect the conversation and get me home. "Still haven't figured out why Bud moved me up to mechanics."

"You paid your dues, bro. You worried you can't cut it?"

"Nah. I can figure most things out, and I got the rest of you guys to ask." The gravel crunched beneath my boot.

Mario kicked at the curb. "I think you should call up one of your girls, for real, burn off a little steam."

My anger flared again, but Mario didn't know anything, so

instead of blowing up, I just kick-started the Harley and yelled over the motor, "Yeah, will do."

Tomorrow was Sunday. I didn't know Corabelle's work schedule, but I was betting that if she worked today, like I had, she didn't have to tomorrow. I'd figure something out, something so perfect she couldn't turn it down. I knew her. I could make her come around.

26

CORABELLE

The bed was a crazy reminder of what happened last night.

I sat on the corner, picking up the sheet I'd yanked off Gavin that morning. My legs were shaky after a crazy long walk through the valley, avoiding going home even after eight hours at work. I had the silly idea that Gavin would still be here on my porch, waiting, and I wasn't up for seeing him again yet. I didn't totally trust that he'd obey my text message to stay away.

But of course he wasn't. He had a life. And that life had not included me for four years.

I slid down to the floor and peeked beneath the bed at the baby's box. Other than packing and unpacking it when I'd come to San Diego, I hadn't looked at it in years. Gavin had gotten me to open it one more time, and I needed to put the CD back in it.

The soft blue fabric had faded a little, the stars and moons and teddy bears floating across the lid. As I brought it out, my eyes pricked with tears. No matter how much time passed, this wound didn't really seem to get any better.

I knew that on top of the baby's things were memories of my last days with Gavin. The box was pretty large, almost a milk crate, and we'd had so little to put in there for Finn. So when I moved from our apartment to a dorm room in New Mexico, I added other stuff I wanted most to save. There was more in a box at my parents' house, hidden in the bottom of my closet, but these were the most important.

I opened the lid and the baby's blanket peeked out, the layer between Finn's things on bottom and the scattered mementos of Gavin on top. I planned to just set the CD back on top, but the first item inside was a little scroll tied with silver ribbons. My nose ran as I slipped the ribbons off and unrolled the parchment paper.

Corabelle,

I know you said when we found out about the baby that we didn't have to get married, but I want to. I have wanted to marry you since we went to your Aunt Georgia's wedding and hid beneath the cake table when we were five, fingers sticky from sneaking frosting, always together, even when we were in trouble. Please say you'll marry me. I know you don't have to. I can only hope you'll want to. That you'll have me. And we three can be together for always.

All my love,
Gavin

The middle of the page was crumpled from when I first looked at it again, a few days after the funeral, when it was clear Gavin wasn't coming back. I wanted to destroy everything then, all the memories of Gavin, all the things for the baby. And I had wrecked some things. The beautiful little mobile we made out of hundreds of butterflies cut from card stock was gone. I'd torn it from the ceiling and ripped it apart, sending the colored wings flying all over the room.

And the photographs. God, the photographs. I'd torn them, shredded them, flung them wall to wall. The drawings of the sea and our little school, ones we'd done as kids that decorated the baby's room, all gone.

But I hadn't gotten rid of this, his proposal. In the box still rested the red velvet case that held my ring, a tiny blue stone on a silver band, as by then we knew Finn was a boy. I set the letter back in the box and picked up the case, popping it open. The ring was loose on my finger now that I was no longer puffy with baby weight. I held out my hand, trying to remember what it felt like to be secure in Gavin's love, to have never known any other way to live. I had zero doubts back then.

But he'd walked away. He'd said all these things to me, written them on paper, and still, he left. On the worst day. When I needed him the most.

I tore the ring off my finger and shoved it back in the velvet box. I didn't bother rolling up the scroll or putting the ribbons back on, just tossed everything back on top of the blanket and thrust the whole thing under the bed.

I was right to avoid Gavin. One night with him alone and look what happened! I was so stupid. So stupid.

I crawled up on my bed and buried my face into the pillow, annoyed when I could smell him on the fabric. I pushed it off the edge and curled up in a ball, all the lights still on, and decided to hold my breath.

The minute I started I knew it was different. Hardly any time had passed when my chest started heaving, trying to make me take in a breath, the way it used to be before I worked so hard for control, to stay calm, to slide into the blackness with acceptance and peace.

My lungs felt like they would explode, my whole body trying to make me breathe. I pressed my face into the sheets, but it didn't help, I rolled over and gulped in air. The tears came, streaming down my face in a hot rush. I needed this. I had to do it. I couldn't handle thinking. I wanted oblivion.

I jumped up for the lights, dousing the room in darkness. This time when I held my breath, I let the void come over me, no thinking, no impulses, and when my body resisted, I exhaled into it, floating into the perfect stillness. This time, when the blackness descended, hopefully I would just stay asleep.

I woke up to the sun blasting through the window. My body ached from all the walking yesterday and chafed from sleeping in my clothes. I was tempted to see if Gavin had written me again, but then, my phone had gone all night without charging and was probably dead.

Just as well.

I heard people talking outside my window, a low murmur as though there was a small crowd. People here mostly just came and went, although an occasional party spilled out of someone's door. The apartment buildings in this complex were small and placed between trees, a setup that always helped me feel like I wasn't quite so hemmed in by neighbors.

My bedroom window faced another building, so I wandered to the living room. The blinds were closed, so I carefully pushed a couple of the slats aside.

Unbelievable. I stepped back a minute to blink, then looked again.

In the trees outside my door, hundreds of colored paper butterflies hung from the branches. Their wings glittered in the sunlight, winking, the wires so thin as to almost be invisible, as though an entire flock of them had chosen this moment to breeze by my window.

I ran to the front door and wrenched it open so I could see it better. That's when I noticed the neighbors walking through the butterflies and touching their sparkling bodies.

"Isn't it beautiful?" An older woman I'd seen a few times walking to her car cupped a bright blue one in her palm.

A younger girl in a red beret saw me and smiled. "They lead to your door." She pointed behind her. "See, there's just a few up there, and then they get thicker as we get closer to you."

"Come see," said the first women, her silver hair sparkling as she gestured for me to walk up the sidewalk. I stepped out carefully in bare feet, avoiding the bits of bramble and fallen acorns on the path. I saw what they were talking about. As I arrived at the street and turned around, I could see a clever progression of the butterflies in color, depth, and density.

The young girl held one close to her face. "These are all hand cut." She glanced over at me. "Whoever did this for you spent a lot of time on it."

I moved up the path again. White butterflies with iridescent sparkle gave way to pale blues, then pinks and gentle yellows, moving to minty greens and lavenders that shifted to plum and fuchsia and deep red and sapphire. I caught a movement at the corner of the building and we all turned to it. Gavin stepped out, as beautiful as I'd ever seen him, fresh and combed and wearing a crisp button-down shirt loose over khaki shorts.

My breath caught and the women murmured their appreciation as he came toward me, holding out his hands with another butterfly, a lovely, opulent eggshell blue. "One more," he said and handed it to me by the slender wire. "For Finn."

He held my hand as we both lifted it to the branch closest to the door and tied it around the slender limb. The other women moved away as I brought my palms to my hot cheeks. "I don't know what to say."

"Say you'll spend the day with me." He backed away, giving me space.

The setting was like a fairy tale, Gavin, looking so much like he had in high school, the trees and morning sun striking the glittering butterflies. A breeze wafted through, shifting the strings and making the bits of color dance among the falling leaves. I nodded; what else could I do? Each of these moments were new wonders, memories I could hold on to. Even if it all fell apart later, we would have this.

27

GAVIN

The sand packed beneath our feet as Corabelle and I walked along the shore at La Jolla. She'd refused to ride my motorcycle over, which made me laugh, but I climbed into her car and let her drive us.

My fingers were cut up and sore from all the butterflies, but making them half the night had been bittersweet, remembering doing it years ago for Finn's crib. Corabelle had gotten the idea from some Etsy shop. I resisted, saying we should just buy a plastic one with a battery and music. But she had this vision for the nursery, all our hopes and dreams with the drawings we'd made of the sea.

So I dutifully cut butterflies from card stock, laying them out on newspaper to be spray-painted. Served me right to be making hundreds more years later, since I was pretty sure I grumbled and complained the whole time we did it the first time.

The wind whipped Corabelle's hair into a frenzy, and she fought it constantly, twisting it in her free hand, holding her shoes in the other. This was probably a good thing, as it kept me from reaching for her, which I knew was too much for the moment, despite the other night. She was distant and reluctant, and I had to tread carefully.

"Do you come down here much?" I asked her.

"Not this far. It's quiet."

We'd walked about half a mile from the parking lot, the umbrella rentals, and the beachgoers trying to get a last weekend of sun before it got any colder. Compared to New Mexico, the temperature was downright chilly, but I had gotten used to it. "I prefer to stay away from the crowds."

"You always did," she said.

Rocks rose to our right, brown and sparse and dotted with tide pools. The great expanse of the ocean spread to our left, blue and sparkling, occasional white crests breaking across the surface. Gulls swooped along the shore, their distinctive caw the only sound other than the roar of the waves. It seemed we were the only two people in the world.

Shouts broke the peace of the moment and we turned to the rocks, where a father and his two sons scrabbled along a path. "Wait for me!" the dad called. The boys were young, maybe seven and four. The little one tripped and skidded in a bit of sand. Before he could cry, the father had scooped him up. "Almost there, Champ, no tears."

I realized I had stopped walking, watching the man with the boy the age Finn would be now. Corabelle slipped her hand in mine, and I knew she was thinking the same thing. The threesome continued past us back the way we'd come and I forced myself to look ahead, not to turn and see them go. The missing part of our picture was very real and all my optimism that Corabelle and I would move on together began to crumble.

She leaned her head on my shoulder. "It is always that hard for you?"

"No. I normally don't pay any attention."

"Then it's me." She tried to pull away, but I gripped her hand hard. Her hair was completely wild, blowing like a black specter, a haunting image against the backdrop of the tumultuous sea.

"I'm glad it's you," I said. "I didn't know how numb I'd been until you came back."

She nodded, her expression lost in her hair.

"Here," I said. "I think I remember how this goes." I dropped my shoes and let go of her hand to gather up the wild mane. She turned into the wind so it all blew back and I separated it into three sections. I learned to make a braid when we were in middle school, after she left me one weekend for a slumber party with other girls. I felt lonely and betrayed and when I asked her why she chose the girls over me, no doubt with some pathetic sulky look on my face, she said they could fix each other's hair.

I stole one of my sister's dolls to practice this, working out the pattern. The dolls were easier than the real thing, though, as the layers and head shape made the lengths inconsistent, and I never quite knew what to do with the ends. But I wanted to learn. I wanted Corabelle to never find me lacking in any way.

My fingers felt fumbly and uncoordinated as I tugged her hair into a braid. When I got to the end, I told her, "Hold this," and reached for my boot, swiftly removing the lace. I tied her hair down, weaving the lace back and forth across the bottom half of the braid so that it wouldn't come out easily.

When I let go, she ran her fingers along its length. "Not too bad."

I scooped up all our shoes, lashing them together with the ends of the other lace, and didn't hesitate, but took her hand again. She accepted this, more relaxed than before. It wasn't until we resumed walking, this time with our feet in the water, that I realized we'd gotten past that hard moment together, and I felt sorrow for all the other times we could have shared those hardships instead of bearing them alone.

"So are you going to feed me or do I get to walk for hours on an empty stomach?" Corabelle asked. She looked so young with the braid, her face so innocent, a few stray tendrils curling along her forehead.

"We'll have to turn back to La Jolla for food," I said. "Ahead is Black's Beach and there's nothing there but naked sunbathers."

Her eyes grew wide. "I've heard about that beach. I've never been."

Just the idea of her there, her body laid out in the sand, made my blood start jumping. "Go with me and I'll be your slave forever."

"You're already my slave forever." She cracked the smallest smile, but still it was a smile.

"We'd get arrested. I couldn't possibly keep my hands off your delectable body." I pulled her toward me, letting the shoes drop again.

She didn't resist, tilting her head up so that I could kiss her. She tasted like sand and salt, and her cheek beneath my thumb was gritty. I pictured her skin drenched by the sun, and I could scarcely keep myself in check, pulling her in so tight that she fitted against me, my mouth feverish over hers, tongue sliding between her lips into her warm waiting mouth.

When our hips moved together, she broke away, gasping. "This is so hard," she said.

I pressed her face into my shoulder and just held her. "It doesn't have to be."

"I don't know what I want."

"I do. I know that I want you."

She shuddered against me. "The butterflies. I destroyed the mobile."

"That's okay."

"Tore it apart with my bare hands."

"I'm sure it's what you needed to do at the time." I stroked her head.

"I shouldn't have done that. It was Finn's."

"It's okay."

Her breaths were fast and shallow, like they had been in the stairwell that day. I started to worry about her fainting again, but she quieted down, slowing down her exhales. I just held on and waited for her to come back around. At last she looked back up at me. "Thank you for the new ones."

I kissed the top of her head. "You can thank me by getting naked on Black's Beach."

She half-smiled again and pulled away, punching me on the chest. "In your dreams. Besides, you'd pummel anybody who looked at me."

I snatched up the shoes. "True. They'd have to call it Blood Beach." I turned to lead her back to La Jolla and get her something to eat, but she stood staring at the waves. "You okay, Corabelle?"

She looked at me, her brown eyes so full of sorrow. "I don't know how to be happy."

My heart squeezed. "I think it can be a choice."

"But I'm trying to choose it."

"Here's what I think." I knelt and picked up a stick that had been washed ashore. "I can draw this line." The end of the stick cut through the smooth surface of sand between us. "On your side is grief." I pointed at her feet. "On my side is happiness."

I stood up and tossed the stick away. "Now you can step across it and not look back."

Corabelle kept looking at the line, the sharpness of it stark against the miles of smooth unbroken sand. "But I want to look back. I want to remember Finn."

"Crossing the line isn't about forgetting the people we love. It's about not letting our past sorrow steal our future joy."

She still didn't move. I knew this was hard for her. I crossed over years ago, not exactly into happiness, but at least away from the misery. Our lives were made up of hundreds of these lines. Choosing when to cross was different for each person. We each had our own timeline for letting go.

She looked up at me, and I held out my hand. Her eyes shifted to it, waiting there for her to accept what I offered, hovering between us like an unspoken promise. Then she reached for it, closed her fingers around mine, and took that first tremulous step, out of her old world, and across the line into mine.

28

CORABELLE

I was pretty sure I'd never had a hot dog as good as this one.

Gavin laughed at me, mustard topping his upper lip like a mustache. He reached over with a yellow fingertip and traced my upper lip. I felt something cold left behind, and ran my hand over my mouth. It came back yellow. "You have not grown up one bit, Gavin Mays!"

We sat on the beach at La Jolla, surrounded by people soaking up the sun. Nobody was venturing into the water, due to the chill. My butt was covered in sand and the hot dog was gritty, but something about stepping over that line must have worked because I couldn't stop laughing.

"You used to love it when I gave you a mustard mustache!" Gavin put on a goofy grin and rolled his eyes. "Mr. and Mrs. Mustardash!"

"When I was six!" I laughed and swiped his lip with a napkin, only succeeding in smearing it up to his nose. "I can't take you anywhere."

"You can take me to Black's Beach. We don't have to wear anything but our 'stach." He waggled his eyebrows at me.

Heat rose up from my belly, and I knew I'd be taking him into my bed again that night. I vibrated with need for him and already lamented wasting a day with my angst and indecision. Just going with it was so much easier, so much more natural.

He misunderstood my silence, running his hand along my arm. "I would never push you on this, Corabelle. I can wait for you to come back to me."

I stuck my hot dog back in the paper tray and crashed into him, knocking us both into the sand. I leaned over him, ignoring the stares of families around us. "I think I'm already done waiting."

He lifted his head, his mouth perilously close to my lips. "Then what the hell are we doing on this beach?" he whispered.

We snatched up our trash and dumped it into the nearest bin. Sand kicked up from our feet as we hightailed it back to my car. "You better drive fast!" Gavin insisted as we backed out of the parking space.

"I might run over small children!" I shouted, then realized I'd just made a reference to kids without feeling horrible inside. Gavin was right. We could choose to let go of the stranglehold our past had on us.

I careened through town, flooring it between lights as we headed back to my apartment. "God, remember that time the police pulled me over just a block away from my house?" I asked.

Gavin laughed. "The one time I thought it would be clever and sexy to unbutton your pants in the car."

My face burned just remembering. "I just knew he was going to ask me to get out, then my parents would come and see me both half-dressed and with the cops."

"What had you done?"

"I think a taillight was out or something."

"It certainly wasn't speeding."

I stomped on the gas. "You mean like this?"

He laughed. "You are one terrible driver." His hand snaked over to my thigh. "I think it was something like this, right?" He unsnapped my jeans.

Sparks shot through my body, and I eased off the gas, unable to drive irrationally if I couldn't focus on the road.

"Or was it more like this?" Gavin lowered the zipper and slid his thumb along the edge of my panties.

We came to a red light, and I was relieved, because I was afraid I'd start swerving if he did anything more. "Gavin, we're going to have a wreck."

"Then I better make the most of this traffic light." His palm flattened against my belly, and he reached farther down.

Now I couldn't think about anything but his fingers, slipping inside me, pressed tight inside the jeans. The light turned green and a car behind me honked. I jumped, startled, and Gavin chuckled. "I'll be good," he said, but he didn't remove his hand, just kept it still.

I stayed off the freeway, taking side streets since I didn't trust him not to distract me, even if he didn't intend to. His hand was hot against my skin. When we got to the next light, he started up again, a gentle pulse in just the right spot. My breathing grew faster. I wished it was dark so we could simply pull over somewhere, but the midafternoon sun was merciless and bright.

When I hit the gas again, his hand stilled, but the ache was so fierce I couldn't concentrate. "We're closer to my place," he said. "You can turn right here and it's two streets down."

I jerked the wheel and followed his directions to a set of aging apartments. I didn't relax until I'd pulled into a spot and killed the engine. "Can we go in now?" I asked, my body trembling all over.

"Not just yet." Gavin released his seat belt but left his hand in my pants. He couldn't unbuckle mine without pulling out, so he left it but turned toward me, letting his free hand trace my collarbone.

"I like it right here."

I shut my eyes to the open windshield and let the movements of his fingers send cascades of pleasure through me. I felt completely wanton, spreading my knees as he found the perfect placement, spiraling me up into showering sparks.

"I want to hear you, Corabelle. Talk to me."

We'd always had to be so quiet when he snuck in my window that when we finally got our own place, he always asked me to talk to him, to let him know what I was feeling with sounds.

I began with a whimper, the smallest noise. He began to work faster, deeper, and shifted his free hand down to my breast, tweaking the nipple. I forgot everything then, where we were, who might see, and my voice grew to an elongated "oh."

"That's my girl," Gavin said, and now the second hand aided the first, spreading me more open, and his fingers worked that perfect pattern until I hit a peak.

"Gavin!" I cried, then kept it going, "Oh my God, Gavin Gavin Gavin Gavin." I couldn't take any more, everything was swollen and writhing and painful with need until finally I was over the top and clutching his hands, keeping them still as the orgasm crashed through me, long and rhythmic. I didn't even know what sound I was making, just that it must have been loud, as Gavin covered my mouth with his, kissing me as I came down and back to reality.

We sat there a while, my hands on top of his, hiding my exposed belly as people passed by on the walkway through the complex. I closed my eyes again, not wanting to think about anybody knowing what we had done.

Gavin knew what I was thinking. "Nobody saw," he whispered. "You were amazing."

My mouth was dry. I swallowed and said, "I think you were the amazing one." He had skills now, beyond what he had done to me when we were teens. I tried to push away the thought of the girls he might have practiced on, but realized too that my responses were different, and he might be wondering the same thing. And there had been no one.

Don't let your past steal your future. It applied to both of us. Whoever they might have been or however many, they were the past. I was his future. He meant what he said, and he was willing to show it, to do whatever it took.

I opened my eyes, and Gavin was right there, looking at me with amusement. "You ready to face the world?" he asked.

I nodded. He withdrew from me and I buttoned back up. "I'm going to make you suffer for that," I told him.

He kissed me quickly on the cheek. "I look forward to my punishment."

We hustled from the car and he led me by the hand to where he lived. His home. I could look forward to another night in his arms, to revel in the company of someone who had known me as long as I'd been alive.

29

GAVIN

When Corabelle took her seat down the row from me in the lecture hall, it was the farthest apart we'd been since yesterday. I could barely stand being ten feet away, but it was comforting to lean forward and be able to see her, knowing she would smile back at me.

Her friend watched us come in, obviously anxious to get to Corabelle and find out what had happened. I hoped she got every scintillating detail and felt bad for not helping me sooner, although I guess I had to thank her for giving Corabelle my number in the first place.

The professor droned on about supernovas, the rock stars of stars. The lecture was sort of interesting for once, and somewhat related to geology, so I should have been listening, but Corabelle was too close and the memories of yesterday too fresh. I'd followed her into the shower that morning, and just thinking about all the places the soap suds had gathered on her body made parts of me wake up.

Corabelle was trying to pay attention, hunched over her iPad and tapping wildly, but every time I glanced at her, she looked at me, and we were like two little kids with a big secret, grinning like fools. I could scarcely stand it, dying for class to be over just so I could touch her in some small way. Maybe we could rechristen the stairwell with a completely different sort of memory than what it held for us now.

Everyone started to get out of their seats, and I realized I hadn't even noticed that the professor had stopped talking. I pushed past the students trying to walk in front of me and moved toward the middle of the row as Corabelle packed her bag. The pink girl headed straight for her too, eyes on me, and her brows shot up when I leaned down and kissed Corabelle on the forehead.

"So I guess you ended up not having any time to write me back all weekend." She pouted, her bright lips matching her hair.

"Sorry," Corabelle said. "We were all over the place."

"All over each other, I'm guessing." She crossed her arms over her neon green sweatshirt, one shoulder cut out to reveal an equally bright pink tank. That girl liked her color.

Corabelle didn't answer that, and I had to force myself to keep quiet and let them have their tiff. When she stood up, I took her hand.

"I get it," the girl said. "I get a little crazed over a new guy."

"I'll call you later on, okay?" Corabelle said.

"All right. I want details." She appraised me from my boots to my black T-shirt. "They're bound to be good."

"Let's go," I said, tugging Corabelle toward the door.

"You two lovebirds going up in the tilted house now or saving it for later?" the girl asked.

I turned around. "What are you talking about?"

"The assignment," Corabelle said. "The professor gave us a task to do in the house on the roof."

"Somebody was in la-la land," the girl said, and I really wished she'd just go away. "I have to put in an extra shift at Cool Beans, but you might want to get it done. They aren't open but a few hours a week."

About the last thing I wanted to do was waste what little time I had before heading to Bud's on homework, but Corabelle said, "That's a good idea."

When we got out in the hallway, instead of heading for the stairwell, she went for the elevator. Several others in the class were waiting outside it, and I could see we were going to have a lot of company. "What are we supposed to do up there?" I asked her.

"Measure the angle of a photograph on the wall against the true straight line from the center of the ceiling. There's apparently a chandelier that hangs properly."

"Can't we just get this off their website or something?" I asked.

Corabelle squeezed my hand. "It'll be fun."

I wanted to say, no, you naked on my sofa would be fun, but we were surrounded by students. I pulled her to the back of the group as the others squeezed onto the elevator. "Let's see if the rest of them can get through it first and then we'll go."

"Okay." She let me lead her down the hall and pull her around a corner that ended abruptly in a doorway to a lab with a biohazard sign and more security locks than Fort Knox.

I yanked her into my arms and kissed her thoroughly. I didn't stop until I felt better, less tense than I'd been having to sit away from her during class.

"Gavin," she said. "We do have to carry on with normal life."

I pulled her in close. "I don't want to."

She laughed. "You have that same whiny voice you got when you had to go home every night when I lived with my parents."

"Feels about the same too."

"You're killing me. I don't remember getting this sore before."

"We never had a break before."

She wrapped her arms around me and rested her head on my chest. I could have stayed there for hours, but the locks behind us began to turn, and we had to step out of our secret alcove to let a harried-looking student dash by.

"We should probably head up," Corabelle said.

I sighed. "Okay. I still think we can get the answer somewhere else."

"You didn't pay a lick of attention in class, did you?"

"How could I, when you were sitting so close, naked under all those clothes?"

Corabelle smiled, and once again I wanted to revel in it, seeing her happy again. I vowed never to do anything to take that smile from her. Maybe I could do a reversal on the vasectomy somewhere down the line without telling her. It would work. I would make it work. She didn't even have to know what I had done.

We punched the button to the elevator, and I was pleased to see it empty when it opened. I held her close as we ascended to the roof garden. The tilted house was part art experiment, part joke, depending on who you asked. It had been installed a year ago and made a big splash in the student papers. I hadn't paid much attention at the time, but you couldn't help but notice the little blue building if you looked up, hanging off the roof like it might fall with the slightest breeze.

"Have you been up here before?" Corabelle asked as the doors slid open.

"Nope."

"Good." We stepped out into the hall. A dozen or so students were waiting to get in to go down. I recognized a couple from the row in front of me. "27 degrees," a tall guy in a hipster fedora said.

"I got 28," countered a girl.

"It's 27," said another girl.

"I say let's go with 27 and head out," I said to Corabelle.

She shook her head and tugged on my arm, past the growing horde and through the glass doors.

The garden was still blooming, chaotic with flowers and bees, and a few straggling students who were all saying, "27 degrees, don't bother measuring" and moving back up the path.

We waited by a pair of Adirondack chairs for the rest of them to move through and walked up the steps to the house. Inside, a woman with a badge led an older couple around the small interior room. "Sorry about the crowd," she told them. "Sometimes professors require their students to come up here."

"What are those blue flowers by the door?" the woman asked, and the three of them stepped outside the house to look.

I pulled Corabelle into the corner by the fireplace, catching her as she stumbled into me. "This is very disorienting," she said.

The floor was slanted, and the walls were at opposite angles, the pictures hanging to complete the unsettling sense that you were the one off-center. Corabelle clutched my arm. "Are you feeling sick?"

"It's strange." My head couldn't quite wrap around the disconnect between the tilted floors and slanted walls and the way my body tried to hold itself.

"Look up at the chandelier," she said, still trying to find her footing.

I pulled her closer and examined the metal loops hanging from the apex of the ceiling. Seeing a straight line that matched what my brain said was up and down calmed the sensation that I was falling sideways.

"It's like finding true north," Corabelle said.

We still held on to each other as though we were lashed to a ship's mast in a storm, but she no longer seemed like she was going to fall. I knew if we looked anywhere else, to the sides, or down, or even straight ahead to the door, we'd lose our balance again. But as long as we focused on the right spot, the world was manageable.

The tour guide stepped through the door. "It's calming, isn't it? Some people actually feel sick inside here, like the last poor couple. But if you just stare at the chandelier, you find peace within your discomfort."

"Who built this?" Corabelle asked.

"It was installed by Do Ho Suh, an artist from Korea," the woman said. "He wanted others to feel the disorientation that he felt coming to a new country."

"It certainly works," Corabelle said. Now that she had looked away from the chandelier, she gripped me hard, already starting to sway. "Do you get used to it?"

"I only volunteer here once every two weeks, so I have to adjust all over again every time. After about half an hour, I can manage. Are you here for the assignment?"

"Yes," Corabelle said.

"The picture your professor wants you to measure is that one." She pointed to an image of a baby, allegedly one of the deans.

Corabelle tried to step toward it and stumbled into me. I managed to catch her, but my stomach began to turn. The angled walls seemed to be falling inward. I tried staring at the floor, but the position of my feet made the confusion in my brain hit a fever pitch.

I wanted out of there, back to normal ground, where I could control things again. Screw the assignment. "Come on, Corabelle," I said. "It looks like 27 degrees to me."

The guide looked displeased with us, and Corabelle almost protested. But when she turned to me, something in my face changed her mind. She just said, "Thank you" to the guide as I led her out.

Once we were back on a level surface, I expelled a huge breath. "Not my thing," I said. "Thanks for not being the usual you and insisting we do the assignment the right way."

"You were turning kind of green." She squeezed my arm.

I glanced back at the house. It seemed perfectly normal from the outside, well, other than the fact that it teetered on the edge of an eight-story building. Funny how something so ordinary could knock you sideways.

We reentered the hallway and waited for the elevator. "Can I make dinner for you tonight?"

"Since when do you cook?"

"I've got the internet. I can figure it out."

Corabelle harrumphed. "I've got to see this. When do you get off?"

The doors slid open and I pulled her close to me. "As soon as you get there." As the elevator closed, I lowered my mouth to hers.

30

CORABELLE

"Girlfriend, you have to SPILL."

Jenny hadn't let me so much as tie my Cool Beans apron before peppering me with questions about Gavin.

The shop was quiet midafternoon, just a few regulars. Austin was conspicuously missing. He probably decided to stop coming. Jenny perched on a stool in front of the counter covered with little table signs. She was switching the summer specials out for the fall coffees. I winced when I saw "Hot Pumpkin Spice," which Jason had threatened to re-nickname me with.

"About time we switched out the menu," I said.

Jenny pointed a finger at me. "No stalling. I want to know everything."

"We seem to have gotten back together, that's all." All sorts of torrid scenes flashed through my head, the car, the shower, on his weight bench. But I didn't need to share all that.

"Will you return to the dish room for a grand finale?"

I laughed. "I don't think so." Although I silently thought, *maybe*.

"Huh. Corabelle laughs." Jenny stuck another cardboard sign

into a metal frame. "Maybe this hunk boy isn't such a bad thing."

"We always used to be good together."

"Until he walked, right?" Jenny snatched up a handful of the table signs. She handed several to me, and I followed her out into the main room.

Jenny was always quick to the point. "He did. It was bad."

She set a frame down, cutting her eyes at me. "And you think he's changed his ways?"

I moved to the other tables, dropping the signs in the center of each one. "We're not teenagers anymore."

"Doesn't mean we grow up." Jenny pointed to her cotton-candy hair. "I mean, look at me. Who'd guess that I'm legal to drink?"

Anger started simmering. What did Jenny know about Gavin or how he might have changed? I smacked a couple more signs on the far tables.

"Don't start getting upset, Corabelle. I'm only worried about you. The whole time I've known you, you've been crazy cautious, ignoring anyone who glanced your way." She slid the last frame across the corner table, the one Austin used to sit at. "Now you're jumping in with both feet. Just strikes me as sudden."

She weaved through the chairs. "What do you really know about Gavin, as he is right now? People can change a lot in four years, especially after something like that."

I had changed too. Jenny didn't know that I was the one with everything to hide. But I'd crossed that line, just like Gavin told me to, and I wouldn't think about it anymore. It didn't matter now. My future would not be stolen.

"I don't know what I'm risking here, exactly," I said. Although I did. Another pregnancy. My heart. Another disaster.

"Okay. I get it. He's worth it." Jenny headed back to the counter as a family of four entered the shop. "I'll be here if it turns out he isn't."

Dang it. Now I was blue. I walked to the back room to check on how many beans were ground and what desserts might have been delivered for the evening shift. I didn't appreciate being dragged from my happy-cloud, but it had to happen sometime. Gavin and I had only been back together for a day. We hadn't exactly been put to any tests.

Gavin opened his apartment door. "Breathe the fantastic aroma of my cooking," he said.

I yanked the price tag off his immaculate oven mitt. "I have a feeling you're new at this."

"I'm hoping for beginner's luck."

I walked inside. The old smell of sweaty socks and gym equipment had been replaced with garlic and warm bread. "I stand corrected. Maybe you can cook."

The living room was mostly clear of workout gear, and a tablecloth covered the crates that he used as a coffee table. On it was a fat candle and two mismatched plates. "Wine for my lady?" Gavin asked, handing me a plastic stemmed cup filled with something red.

"You're outdoing yourself," I said.

"Not really. It's a frozen lasagna and store-bought garlic bread. But it's a start." He clinked his plastic cup against mine.

I sniffed. "Something might be burning."

He stuck his wine glass on the shelf of a listing bookcase and hurried to the kitchen. I tried not to giggle.

Gavin brought out a cookie sheet with a loaf of garlic bread, blackened on the edges. "We can eat the middle," he said.

"Absolutely." I moved out of his way as he set the tray on the coffee table.

"Let me check on the lasagna."

I followed him into the kitchen. He pulled the aluminum dish out of the oven. "Looks right," he said.

"Let me see." I picked up a spatula and poked the surface of the noodles. The edges were bubbly and soft, but the middle was still frozen solid.

"I wrecked it, didn't I?" he asked.

"You can put it back in."

"But the bread is done."

I laughed. "Don't worry. We can eat around the edges."

Gavin went for the plates, and I pushed through the layers to find the thawed parts. He had a microwave at least, so we could heat up the pieces if necessary.

"I'm not used to cooking anything more than leftover pizza," he said.

I plopped a lukewarm slice of lasagna onto one plate. "You did great."

He handed me the second plate. "You were always diplomatic."

"Just where you're concerned."

We returned to the living room. "Drink faster," Gavin said. "Then everything will taste perfect."

"Sounds like a plan." I lifted my glass. "To making the best of things."

Gavin picked up his cup. "To making the best of things."

The dinner reminded me of those two months we'd lived together, other than the wine, which made me feel light and loose before we'd finished eating. When Gavin leaned back on the sofa, drawing me into him, I let out a happy sigh. "We've got this now," he said. "It's going to be like it should have been."

My heart rebelled. "It will never be like that. Finn changed things."

"You're right," he said. "Of course. But we're here. We're together. We can go on now."

I wasn't sure if it was the wine, or the mention of the baby, but suddenly I felt like weeping. I turned my face into Gavin's shoulder, trying to bring back my happiness, to stay on his side of the line.

"Hey," he said. "I'm sorry. I didn't mean to act like he didn't exist."

I shook my head against his shirt. I didn't want to talk about it. I didn't want to talk at all. Instead I put my hands on either side of his face, holding him firmly, and kissed him. Gavin knew the places to go to make me forget. I could hate him for leaving, for taking away my escape. But I had him now, and I didn't have to do this alone any longer.

He lifted my legs and swung them across his lap. "You're wearing entirely too many clothes," he said.

"So, take care of it."

Gavin slid his arm beneath my knees and stood, lifting me with him. He'd always been strong, but now the workouts and mass of muscles eclipsed the body of the boy he'd been at eighteen. I held on to his neck as we moved down the hall to his bedroom, ready to revel in another night where I didn't have to think about anything but each moment as it came.

Sometime in the night I awoke with a pain in my side, like a stitch, but lower, in my abdomen near my hip. I crawled from the bed and padded to the bathroom, wincing at the light. On the birth control shot, I didn't bleed often, but sometimes it came lightly. I wiped carefully, grimacing at the tiny smear of pink. That wasn't typical.

I flushed the toilet paper, trying to calm my panic. Maybe Gavin should wear a condom, make doubly certain nothing happened. I had no idea when to expect cycles and wouldn't know if I got pregnant any more than I had the first time.

Remembering the positive test, just a week after the SAT and that period where I'd smoked more weed than a 1960s stoner, made my breath speed up out of habit. I gulped in air, trying to slow it down. I'd just drunk a half bottle of wine, and that was no better if I got pregnant and didn't know. I hadn't learned anything. I hadn't grown up one bit.

I knelt on the hard tile, trying to pull myself together. But my body was used to this, and as soon as my mind wandered, I realized I was holding my breath again and my vision dissolved into black and white.

I sucked in a fast breath. I didn't need to hit the floor here at Gavin's. I was done with that, totally finished. I had crossed the line, and I didn't need this anymore.

The bed squeaked. Gavin. He might come in here, see me. I scrambled to my feet, wavering when the sudden movement made the spots come. I turned on the water and splashed my face. Control. I had to get in control.

Gavin's head poked into the doorway. "You okay, baby?"

"Yes. All good." The towel was rough against my skin. "Time to teach you about fabric softener."

"That's an extra fifty cents at the laundromat." He wrapped his arm around my shoulders. "But I guess you're worth it."

I turned in to him, accepting the comfort of his arms. I'd bring up the subject of condoms tomorrow.

31

CORABELLE

The week settled into a pattern. On my late work nights, we stayed at Gavin's and he made dinner. On his late nights, we stayed at my apartment and I made something for him. We went to astronomy class together since it was our only class that day and we had time to get home and go to work separately. Tuesdays and Thursdays were my longer class days, and I stayed on campus since I was taking more coursework than him.

I started to recognize what he'd already seen that night of the ruined lasagna. We were back to where we were meant to be.

Friday morning, the astronomy professor gave us a star assignment to do over the weekend. "You will use the two pointer stars, Dubhe and Merak, to locate Polaris, the North Star," he said and leaned forward on his podium to stare at us intently, as if imparting some great truth. "You may think you know where the star is, but I trust you will find in this assignment that you do not yet know your place on this earth."

"He sounds like Dumbledore," the boy next to me said, and I clapped my hand over my mouth to avoid laughing out loud.

Gavin looked down the row at me, scowling, and I sat back to keep him from staring. He hadn't shown any jealousy back in high school, but he definitely seemed sensitive to it after the incident with Austin. I focused my attention back on the professor.

"You will use your hands and fingers according to this diagram." The professor laser-pointed to the screen. "Which you will find on the class website. You will use the altitude of Polaris above the horizon to determine your own location on this planet."

He killed the overhead. "If you have questions, see your TA. Good day, see you Monday."

Gavin headed straight for me, glaring at the guy in the next chair. He picked up my backpack from the floor. "Ready?"

"Just a minute," I said. "I need to pack that. Give it here."

My neighbor walked away and Gavin settled into his seat. "Maybe I can get the TA to move me next to you."

I ignored him and shoved my iPad in my bag. "You want to do this Polaris lab together this weekend?"

"Definitely. We should drive out of town a bit Saturday night and find a good place."

"Sure."

"You think you'll be ready for the bike? You'll love it, I promise."

I slung my backpack on my shoulder. "Okay."

"Perfect." He held out his elbow. "To your chariot?"

I slid my hand through his arm. "Lead the way."

"You two are just too cute," Jenny said, falling in beside us. "Set a date yet?"

I nudged her. "Don't be snarky."

"It's an honest question. I expect to be maid of honor. And Lumberjack can be my escort, since he was the one who got you both at the same star party." She dropped behind us as we headed for the stairwell. "When are we going to double date?"

"Whenever you want," I said.

"Oooh, I know!" Jenny said. "We should do the star thing together. He's the TA. We'll obviously get it right."

"Corabelle and I already have plans for that." Gavin held the door open for us.

"Party poopers," Jenny said. "Well, maybe something Sunday? We have to stay away from campus. Robert isn't supposed to fraternize with his students."

Gavin coughed. "I'm guessing there is a bit more than fraternizing going on."

Jenny laughed, a tinkling sound. "You bet there is. Ta-ta, you totes adorbs two." She dashed ahead of us. "I have to meet my lumberjack at an undisclosed location!"

"Don't do anything I wouldn't do!" I called after her.

She turned back. "I have a feeling that doesn't leave much out." Her pink hair streamed behind her as she raced out of the building.

I turned to Gavin. "So, your scowl could have peeled paint off the walls earlier," I said. "You're not seriously going to be upset every time I talk to some other guy."

Gavin's jaw started working and I squeezed his hand. "We've got this, right?"

He nodded.

"Shoot, I just remembered something." I stopped walking. "I have to pick up a book on reserve for my lit class. Do we have a minute?"

Gavin checked his watch. "Sure. Even if it takes a bit, I can call Bud."

We doubled back toward the looming Geisel Library. I had only been inside once, taking a cursory look at the Dr. Seuss memorabilia. Gavin walked along the clear cases of drawings and war posters as I collected my book. "Have you been on the top floor?" he asked when I came up beside him.

"Nope. Are there stacks up there?"

"Not many. I think they use it for storage. It's a mess. You want to see?"

I glanced at the clock. We still had a half-hour before we really needed to head to work. "Okay."

When we stepped out of the elevator, I saw what Gavin meant. Most of the library shelves were empty. Shrink-wrapped crates blocked some of the aisles. But the view through to the windows was unobstructed, and I wandered in a daze over to the giant panes of glass. "It's beautiful," I breathed.

"You can get a full panoramic of campus," Gavin said.

Students worked at small tables facing the windows. A sign above their heads read "Silent study area."

This would be an incredible place to write papers. The side facing the ocean was inspirational all on its own, even if partially blocked by other buildings, including the dorm where we had our star parties. Between the towering buildings, the vast white-blue of the Pacific expanded out forever like an empty canvas. Craggy bluffs bordered the shore, leading to houses, and eventually back to campus.

"This is interesting," Gavin said.

I turned around. He'd discovered a cache of huge crates among the empty stacks. These were upended to rest on their sides, forming a circle almost as tall as he was. I turned my head to read the black numbers spray-painted on the wood. Dewey decimal numbers, maybe. Between two of the crates was a gap filled in with the heavy-duty plastic that had been cut away.

He pushed aside the plastic and ducked in among the crates. At first I could see the top of his head, but then he disappeared.

"Gavin!" I whispered. "What are you doing?"

His hand snaked out from the opening. When I grasped it, he pulled me through.

"It was a trap," he said, his voice raspy and low. He pushed the plastic over the gap, obscuring the opening.

The crates surrounded us, but the empty space in the middle was plenty large enough to stand in. "What are we doing?" I asked.

He slid his hand beneath my shirt and moved up to cup a breast. "This." He lowered his head to kiss me.

My heart pounded, but I relaxed into his mouth. His free hand tugged the backpack off my shoulder to rest on the carpet. "Are you sure this is a good idea?" I asked.

"This is always a good idea." He unsnapped my jeans. "We'll see if you can control yourself enough to be quiet."

His hand slipped inside my panties and searched out the spot he was looking for. My mouth opened, but he closed his lips over mine before I could cry out. "Easy, girl," he said against me, his fingers spreading me so he could get better access. "How's this for a new challenge?"

I gripped his shoulders, breathing into his ear.

"That's it," he whispered. He grew frustrated trying to work inside the jeans, so he jerked them down past my hips. I leaned forward to bite his shoulder as sensations splintered through me.

He worked me carefully, using all the new knowledge he'd gained in the last few days. When I was writhing against him pretty hard, he withdrew, silencing my protest with a kiss.

His hands on my waist guided me in a circle to face away from him. He pushed on a crate to make sure it was heavy and steady. It tilted a little, but braced against one of the stacks. He moved my hands to grasp the corners of the box, and I heard the jingle of his belt.

Heat flashed through me. We were going to do this, here, in the library, with students a few yards away. Gavin steadied me with one hand on my hip and pushed me down a little with a firm press on the back. "Just a little more."

I bent over and felt him seeking me, getting the angle right, then he was in, and I clutched the crate, still worried we could tip all the empty stacks in a domino crash worthy of a sitcom. He held both my hips, rocking into me, and just the idea that we were here, doing this, made everything so much more intense.

He reached around, finding his favorite spot again, and even though I couldn't spread my legs in the jeans, he was close enough. I was soaring, up, the fluttering building into a cascade. He felt me start to go and thrust faster, harder, so that I totally forgot where we were. I pressed backward, taking him in deeper, and everything tightened at once, letting go in a quivering release that set him off immediately, emptying into me with a force I'd never felt in him.

He exhaled against my hair, and I shifted my weight so that I wasn't leaning on the crate, which had mercifully held. The image of it falling, and all the startled students seeing us, our jeans around our ankles, struck me as so hilarious that I started giggling.

"Uh-oh," Gavin said, pulling out and yanking up his jeans. "This isn't going to be one of those epic never-ending Corabelle giggle fits, is it?"

I had forgotten they existed. I couldn't even remember the last one. Before I got pregnant? Had I exploded into one at any point with Finn? I bent to pull up my pants but everything was so funny. Me, my butt in the air, holding on to a crate of books. Gavin, plowing into me, rustling the plastic. I held my belly, trying to stay silent, my laughter so intense that my ab muscles were starting to hurt.

Gavin bent and jerked up my pants, because I was doubling over, the giggles coming so fast now that there was no stopping them. I managed to grab my waistband and snap it closed, but still, images of us surrounded by downed crates, the loose plastic floating down in the aftermath, was just...so funny.

"How did I used to get you to stop?" Gavin asked, although he was on the cusp of cracking up himself.

I shook my head. "I…don't…remember…" I gasped for air. My stomach was aching. I tried to think of serious things like librarians and their stern expressions. The astronomy professor, leaning on his podium — no, that was even funnier. I burst into a fresh batch of giggles.

"Is somebody in there?" A voice outside the ring of crates made me clap my hand over my mouth.

"Now we've done it," Gavin whispered, but he was already laughing.

The plastic began rustling. "You should come out now."

Gavin put his finger over his lips.

I was heaving with effort and trying to stop, sucking air in. I should have been appalled, worried, but no, I couldn't bring it down.

A head peeked through the gap, a guy not much older than us with square black glasses. "I knew it!"

Gavin held up his hands. "We're busted."

The face disappeared and resumed as just a voice. "I'm the TA in charge of the graduate study area up here. This is a silent study floor."

"We're coming," Gavin said. He turned back to me and handed me my backpack. "You ready for the great escape?" he whispered. "I'll go left, you go right, and we'll meet in the stairwell."

I nodded, only just now able to get my giggles under control.

"I'll go first, distract him, then you bolt."

"Got it."

Gavin pushed through the plastic. "Hey there. I don't think we were making any noise."

"You're not supposed to be in there."

I waited a second, not sure when to leave.

"What's in these crates anyway?" Gavin asked, and I could tell he'd moved away from the opening.

I took a deep breath, then pushed on the plastic and wormed my way out. As soon as I was free of the crates, I took off to the right, barreling along the interior wall that held the elevator shaft and stairwell. I didn't look back, not even when the TA said, "Hey!"

I saw the exit sign and snatched at the door. I went down one flight, then looked up, waiting.

Gavin burst through it and said, "Go!"

I began running down the stairs, holding on to the rail. Gavin caught up. "Let's not go to the bottom, in case he's waiting there for us. We'll kill time on one of the middle floors."

We leaped out at the fourth floor, a busy area with full stacks and tons of students. Once we were safely away from the elevator and stairwell, we collapsed at a study desk.

"That was nuts," I said.

"That was awesome!" Gavin's smile was as wide as his face. "We never were troublemakers in high school. We have to make up for our well-spent youth."

I swallowed, trying not to wreck the moment. I'd done enough bad stuff for both of us. All three of us, I amended.

"Hey." Gavin reached over and squeezed my arm. "I'm sorry. I didn't think about how worried you'd be about getting in trouble."

"No, no, it's fine. It was fun." I faked a smile. "I just had forgotten about the giggle spells. It's been too long."

"I'll say."

"How long do you think we should wait?"

Gavin checked his phone. "It's 10:30. I'm guessing he'll go to the ground floor, wait a couple minutes, then he'll have to get back to his duties."

"When do you have to be at work?"

"11, but it's not a big deal. I'll call Bud if we get stuck. Meanwhile," he reached for my hand, "I'll just sit here and gaze at you lecherously."

I felt a trickle in my jeans and realized that once again we'd gone without a condom. Might as well bring it up now. "So. I was thinking."

"About doing me again in the elevator?"

I smiled. "Maybe. But also about how the shot failed us before."

His expression sobered.

"So maybe we should do something extra?" My fingers gripped his. "Like condoms?"

He let go and sat back. "You think it will happen again?"

"Statistics seem to indicate that if you have a hormone birth control failure, you have a higher incidence of another. I might not be a good fit for it."

His face was looking angrier as I talked, and I couldn't understand it.

"You want to keep me at risk? You want it to happen again?" I stood up, ready to walk away.

Gavin jumped from his chair. "No! No. Of course not. I just don't think it will happen again."

"But it might. Are condoms that big of a deal?" A couple of students were looking at us, so I sat back down.

I could see him relent. "No, no they aren't. I'll buy some." He walked around the desk and bent down to wrap his arms around me. "I'll do whatever you ask on this."

My shoulders relaxed. We would be all right. Surely lightning wouldn't strike twice.

32

CORABELLE

The Harley's engine was so loud I could barely hear myself think as Gavin handed me an extra helmet. "I'm not so sure about this!" I yelled.

"You'll love it!" he shouted.

"It looks like a red bowling ball!"

Gavin laughed. "You'll rock the look."

I stuck the helmet on my head. "Now what?"

"Get on behind me." He pointed to a footrest. "Your feet go here."

I held on to his shoulders as I threw a leg over the seat. He revved the motor and I could feel the vibrations in my girl parts. "Hey, this is like a sex toy!" I said in his ear.

"Now you're getting it."

I found the footrests and clasped my arms around his waist. "Aren't there any seat belts on this thing?"

"I'm all you've got," he said, and he backed us away from the curb in front of my apartment.

The butterflies still twinkled in the trees. I got a notice from the management yesterday that they had to come down, but I'd ignored it. I kept Finn's blue butterfly inside the house for safekeeping, but the others would stay. The apartments were cheap. The overworked maintenance guy would probably be too busy to take them down. I couldn't imagine Lorna, the stuffy and perpetually stiletto-heeled office manager, sinking into the damp ground to yank them out of the trees herself.

We lurched forward, and I screamed in Gavin's ear. I could feel his laughter in his ribs, even though the motor drowned out the sound. When we paused at the exit to the complex, he turned his head. "You'll be fine."

Maybe. So far we'd only been going five miles per hour. I wasn't sure I could hang on at sixty.

We jetted onto the street, and I screamed again. I felt like I might rocket off the bike at any moment.

Thankfully, we hit a red light almost immediately. "I don't think I can do this," I said.

"Sure you can. Just relax into it. Sink into me a little rather than being so stiff."

He took off more carefully this time. I tried to be like Jell-O, and fitting loosely against Gavin seemed to help. I could sense when he was about to lean one direction or the other and could move with him. The ride became less bumpy.

We swung onto the highway, and I tried to stay relaxed as we merged into traffic and really got going fast. I could see so much, every direction, unlike the fragmented view through windowpanes in a car. I could smell the ocean as we rode along the harbor. The air was exhilarating, flowing around my neck and tossing my ponytail. Okay, I was getting it. I could see the appeal.

We exited to go east on I-8 toward the mountains. The drive would take a half-hour just to clear civilization. Gavin had packed some sandwiches. It would be a good evening, even if we never got around to the assignment.

As the minutes passed, random body parts began to get tired of their position, and I would adjust. First my neck, then my foot, vibrating on the rest. Eventually I found the right place to fit, and I could just hang on, my head against Gavin's back, and watch the landscape change from city to suburbs to open road.

We slowed down past Alpine, and he turned off the freeway onto a dirt trail.

"I don't think this is a real road!" I said.

"I know!" he yelled. "That makes it better!"

We followed the path for another mile through scrub brush and dirt, until we were in the foothills. The going got slower, as the road was bumpy. I thought my guts were going to get jarred right out of my body.

Finally Gavin turned onto another path. Cars couldn't come here. We hadn't seen anyone for miles and I didn't expect we would.

Gavin revved up a hillside until the path broke down into nothing but rocks and dirt. When he killed the engine, I realized my ears were ringing.

"We can walk it from here," he said. "Just make sure we have the flashlight for getting back."

I tried to lift my leg from the bike, but it wouldn't quite go, stiff and locked into position. Gavin laughed and slid his hand beneath my thigh to give me a boost. I managed to swing back over, my muscles protesting. "I hope you didn't have any wild ideas for that flat up there, because I can barely move."

"We'll start with a full body massage," Gavin said. He tugged off his helmet and hung it on the handlebars. "We should have a good view here."

"I'll say." I handed him my bowling-ball helmet. "I can't even imagine how far it is to electricity, much less lights that would interfere with the stars."

Gavin unpacked the leather satchel with water and sandwiches and the folder with our assignment. He handed these to me and untied a blanket from the other side.

"Flashlight?" I asked.

"Right." He dug around in a little box attached behind the seat. "Got it."

We tramped across the parched earth that crunched with dried grass punctuated with tumbleweeds. "Looks like a good place to leave a body," I said.

He laughed. "You might want to learn to ride the bike before you bump me off in the middle of nowhere."

"Point taken."

We scrambled up an embankment to a plateau, which was only a few yards wide but plenty big enough to spread a blanket and our meager things. The wind whipped in random bursts. I tucked the folder beneath the edge of the blanket to keep it safe and laid the food on a corner. "Now we just wait for dark?"

"Time for that body massage," Gavin said and sat next to me, pulling me between his legs.

His hands worked the muscles of my shoulders, and I relaxed into him. The sun burned yellow on the horizon, just taking its first tentative dip behind a set of hills to the west. The ocean was long gone from our view, but the rolling landscape, barren and edged in scrubby trees and rock, offered a different brand of beautiful.

"We should have brought a camera," I said.

"I can snap a shot with my phone," Gavin said. "Crappy though it is."

"Mine won't take decent pictures at all. It's too old," I said.

He tugged his phone from a pocket. "First the sunset," he said, snapping an image of the sun's rays just starting to striate over the hills. Then he flipped the phone around. "And now us." He laid his head against mine and took the shot.

Gavin turned the phone around. The picture was only of our chins and chests. "Fail!" I said, laughing.

"One more." He held the phone out, angling it up a bit more. "I'm not practiced at selfies."

"Me neither," I said. "I'm not even on any of those social-media sites."

"I know. I looked," Gavin said.

I swallowed. I hadn't wanted to be found, not by Gavin or anybody from my past. But now life was settling in again, back on track. Gavin snapped the shot, our happy faces backed by mountain and sky. It was the sort of thing you would post to your friends, but I didn't do that. I couldn't afford to be discovered, to be shared, to leave a trail. I had to live solely in the here and now.

33

GAVIN

I stared at the picture of Corabelle and me for a minute, trying to remember the last time we had an image together. We'd missed prom. I'd skipped graduation. It must have been some random shot. I didn't have much of anything from those days, not even a snapshot of us. Just the picture of Finn from the funeral.

"So we're on a plateau, right?" Corabelle asked.

"Well, that would be a compliment to this little chink in the mountains." I stretched out on the blanket, hands beneath my head. A few stars were already emerging in the twilight.

"So, Mr. Geology Major, tell me what it is then. A mesa?"

"Not really big enough to qualify for that either."

Corabelle settled next to me. "So what created this little flat space?"

"Same as the mountains, tectonic shifts in the mantle. Pushed the ground upward."

"But what makes it flat?"

I swiveled my head to take in the landscape around us. "Probably wind and erosion. We're in the path of a natural tunnel, so it wore down faster than the hills around us. Although it could have been formed this way from the start, when the ground goes straight up while being pushed. Sedimentary rock tends to split."

"Huh." She laid her head on my shoulder, and I wanted to hold on to the moment forever.

"So, Gavin?" she asked.

"Yup."

"What are you going to do with a degree in geology?"

I chuckled. "You mean if I ever manage to finish?"

"How many hours do you have?"

"About sixty."

She sat up. "That's all? Four years to get sixty hours?"

"I work full-time. I couldn't take a full load."

Corabelle settled back down. "Wow. You'll be in San Diego for another four years easy, at that rate."

I didn't know what she was thinking, but it sounded like she was making plans around me. "I can transfer, if you want to go somewhere else."

She got very still, and I wondered if I assumed too much. Only a week had passed — a very good week, and with crazy moments. I smiled to myself remembering the race down the library stairwell yesterday. We were good together. I couldn't help but think we were back to our old plan. "Corabelle, you tell me what you want."

Her face pressed into my shirt. I reached for her ponytail and twirled it in my fingers.

"I want to go back in time," she said.

"And do what? Figure out which night got us Finn and not do it?"

She didn't answer, so I stared up at the sky, growing darker to reveal more of the stars. I wouldn't mind a trip to the past, at least to the funeral. "I wouldn't go away," I said.

She lifted her head. "What?"

"The funeral. If I could go back in time, I'd stay. I would be there for you." And not go to Mexico, I added to myself. That was worse.

"I don't know what all I would change," Corabelle said. "There are so many things."

"Like what?"

She got still again, so I waited. The North Star was visible among the others, bright and almost twinkling.

"I can't say I wouldn't want Finn. That wouldn't be right," she said. "He had his little life."

Until I signed it away. My whole body tensed, but I forced it to relax again. No point going there.

She wanted to talk about him. I could do that, for her. "I was so panicked when you told me your water broke. But you did great."

"I wasn't screaming like the lady in the next room."

"Man, she had some lungs."

Corabelle turned onto her back. "You got to see him first."

"I was closer to that end."

She punched me in the ribs. "I didn't want you to look."

"My kid was going to come out. It's not like I hadn't seen those parts before!"

"But they were all gooey and bloody."

"True. I wasn't thinking of licking them or anything."

She smacked me again. "Gavin!"

"He slid out pretty easy, really."

"Easy for you to say."

"Well, it looked easy. His little head started to pop out, then everything sort of stopped for a second. I was a little confused, because he was all white."

"It's called vernix."

"It was not what I expected. I almost dropped the camera. He looked like a snow baby."

"I didn't really get to see that."

"They cleaned him off pretty quick, got the worst of it."

"They took him away so fast."

Because he was sick, I thought, but didn't say it. Corabelle turned in to me again, her head on my chest, rising and falling with my every breath.

I knew the doctors were tense about it. They were supposed to let Corabelle hold the baby, but instead they got him cleaned up and into a plastic bed right away. We only got a few minutes with him before they rolled him down to the NICU.

I stayed with her a little while, so she wouldn't feel deserted, but when her parents came in, I took off down the hall to see when we would get him back. I didn't know how anything worked. We hadn't even finished birthing classes when she went into labor. The doctor on call wasn't ours and said we should probably go to a bigger hospital, but then the baby just started coming.

At first the nurse at the window didn't want to let me into the NICU. They didn't know who I was and Finn had Corabelle's last name taped to his bed. Apparently I was supposed to have some wristband.

Finally one of the nurses recognized me and let me through. I wanted to go over to him right away, but she made me stand at a sink and scrub my hands and arms and even use a little pick under my fingernails before I could go into the area where the beds were.

I couldn't even see him. He was surrounded by doctors and nurses. When I finally got a glimpse, I could only see his little hat, a stretchy thing with white and blue stripes. He hadn't cried, I realized. Babies were supposed to cry when they were born.

The nurse who let me in made a space for me in the circle around the plastic crib and tried to explain what they were doing as they attached disks and put something down his throat. But I couldn't follow her, and I couldn't stay calm. Finn looked terrible, things stuck to his head and a giant tube taped to his mouth. The sounds of the machine were awful, like a helicopter flying.

The nurse gave me a card with his weight and measurements to take back to Corabelle. Despite my horror at everything, I didn't want to leave. The NICU was strewn with rocking chairs between the plastic incubators. This row was completely empty, so I sat in one to wait.

I heard a lot of words I didn't know. I could tell they were worried about oxygen levels and his heart. When several of the doctors moved away and I could see Finn again, terror washed over me. He wasn't pink like before. He was gray. Was he dying right there?

I jumped up and grabbed one of the nurses in pink scrubs. "This is my son. What is happening to him?"

Another woman, this one with a doctor badge, took my shoulder and pulled me out of the way. Another team arrived and began working frenetically, packing up the machines like they were going to move him. "We'll have a meeting with you and the baby's mother shortly."

"But I'm standing here now!"

She barely even looked at me, checking things off some damn piece of paper. "We are taking him to do some more tests, mainly pictures of his heart and lungs. I can't give you a conclusive answer to what the baby is facing right now, but I promise you, we will come down and talk to you as soon as we can."

I wanted to snatch the folder from her. "Finn! His name is Finn! Why are you putting tubes on him?"

"His first Apgar scores were low, at four, and now Finn has dropped to a three."

"What the hell is that?"

"It's a measure of the health of a newborn baby. Ten is the highest." She glanced over at the team, who were now moving the bed out of the room. "Was anything wrong at any of the sonograms?"

I ran my hands through my hair, panic rising fast. "No, he was always healthy, always fine. Until he came early."

She nodded and flipped through the chart again. "Go see to the mother. We'll be there soon." She gave me a smile, like that would be reassuring, and said, "Try not to worry." Then she tugged her phone out of her pocket, clicked on something, and walked away.

"Her name is Corabelle," I tried to say, but the doctor was already gone.

I stood rooted to the floor, unable to move. On the other aisle, a few women sat by more plastic beds. One of them looked at me sympathetically, and I couldn't stand it.

The pink-scrubs nurse came back in. "Mr. Mays? Let's go back to your room. There isn't anything you can do for Finn here."

"How long will he be gone?"

"Probably a while."

"Is he going to die?"

She led me back to the sliding doors. "We're going to do everything we can."

I was kicked out. The hallway morphed into a horrifying wall of mirrors, every room decorated with pink or blue ribbons announcing the birth of happy, healthy babies. Mine could be fighting for his life right now, dying, or dead, and I wouldn't even know.

I gripped the front of my shirt, so overwhelmed with fear that I thought I was having a heart attack. My chest was tight and I could barely breathe. I leaned against the wall. Corabelle was probably all snug in her bed, happy and waiting for them to bring Finn back. What would I tell her?

My lungs sucked in air and I forced myself to be calm. She was going to need me, and I couldn't let her down.

Corabelle had known the minute I walked back into her room that something was wrong. "Where's Finn?"

I sat on the edge of the bed. "They've taken him for some tests."

"What kind of tests?" Corabelle's dad asked.

"Pictures of his heart and lungs. He's having some trouble with his oxygen levels, I think."

"I'm going to go see what is going on," he said.

"You need some sort of wristband to get into the NICU." I held up my empty arm.

"I'll get that taken care of." He strode from the room.

Maybe they would take him more seriously than a teenage boy. Corabelle was sobbing in a way I'd never seen her do, great heaving gulps.

"Oh, baby," her mom said, "it's the hormones. After I had you I cried for hours a day. It'll get better."

I wasn't so sure. The sides of the bed kept me from crawling in next to her like I wanted, so I just perched on the end, my hand on her ankle. "They asked about the sonogram. There wasn't anything wrong, was there? I don't remember it."

"We just had two," Corabelle said, clutching the tissue her mom handed her. "They didn't say anything about a problem. They said he was fine."

The wait was excruciating. Corabelle cried herself to sleep. I moved to a chair in the corner. Her mother sat on the foam sofa that converted to a bed. Her father returned after a while, shaking his head. "I couldn't get anything out of anybody, other than I can't see him right now." He glanced over at me. "I had to tell them you two were married. Otherwise Gavin doesn't have any part in this. I didn't know that."

I swallowed and glanced at Corabelle. She hadn't been wearing her ring when we left for the hospital, so she didn't have it now.

Her father sat on the sofa. "We just have to wait."

Corabelle's mother buried her face against his shoulder. "I should have been in here when he was born," she said. "We should have gotten here faster."

"That wouldn't have made a difference," her father said.

"But I would have gotten to see him!" She brought a handkerchief to her nose. "What if something happens?"

"You'll get to see him." He put his arm around her, and I envied his ability to pull her close. Corabelle seemed so far away.

A nurse came in and Corabelle's dad and I both stood up.

"I'm here to check on Mom," she said.

"What about the baby?" I asked.

She frowned. "He's in the NICU."

"They took him out."

"I'll see what I can find out." She wrapped a blood pressure cuff around Corabelle's arm. As it inflated, Corabelle stirred.

"Where's Finn?" she asked.

The woman waited for the machine to beep. "I'm going to find out just as soon as we check this." She placed a gadget in Corabelle's ear. "You're looking good. Any pain?"

Corabelle shook her head. "I just want to know about Finn."

The nurse hustled out, but she didn't return that hour, or the next. I finally wrestled with the hospital bed and lowered the side so I could get close to Corabelle.

"It's almost midnight," Corabelle's dad said. "I don't think we'll get any news tonight."

"I don't want to go home," her mother said.

"We'll see where we are in the morning," he said firmly. "We'll be back first thing."

Her mother leaned in to kiss Corabelle on the forehead. "Stay strong, honey." She squeezed my arm. "Take care of her."

When they were gone, Corabelle started sobbing again. "Why won't they tell us anything? This is horrible."

"I'm going back to the NICU. They have to know something."

She clutched my hand, and I wished I'd gone before her parents left. I'd be leaving her alone. "Kiss him for me," she said.

I nodded, but based on how they acted earlier, I wasn't going to get within touching distance.

When I got back to the NICU entrance, the stern woman had been replaced by a friendlier-looking nurse. "I'm Finn Rotheford's father," I said.

"Do you have your things together?"

I washed over with fear. "What do you mean?"

She glanced the clock. "They should be transferring you to El Paso as soon as the ambulance is prepped."

"No one told us." My head started pounding, my heart trying to explode. "Why are we going there?"

"They have an NICU better able to handle your baby's needs."

I slammed my hands against the window. "Nobody has told us what those needs are!"

"Let me see who is available." She picked up a phone and spoke into it so quietly I couldn't hear. "I've paged the doctor to your room. You can meet him there."

I raced down the hallway, but when I arrived, several people were already there.

"Gavin?" Corabelle cried. "They're moving Finn!"

"I know!"

A tall man with buzzed gray hair held out his hand. "I'm Dr. Fletcher. I'm coordinating the transfer of your baby to a unit in El Paso."

"Why are we going there?"

The doctor perched on a stool at Corabelle's feet. "Your baby has a very serious condition called hypoplastic left heart syndrome.

We first suspected a heart problem when we listened to his heart tones right after birth. The attending obstetrician was on top of it, which was why Finn was taken so quickly to be checked. The first few hours are very important."

I moved to Corabelle's side to hold her hand, for her or for me, I wasn't sure. She wasn't crying right then, just listening, her brown eyes wide and full of fear.

"We did some imaging of Finn's heart and confirmed the defect. Unfortunately, this hospital is not prepared to manage the care of a baby in this condition. He'll need a heart specialist and a surgeon, possibly within the next 24 hours."

Corabelle sobbed then, and I gripped her hand hard. "What will happen?" I asked.

"He'll be assessed on his ability to withstand the surgery. Then you will be given choices about going forward with the surgery or choosing palliative care."

"You mean watching him die?" Corabelle's voice was strained and choked.

"The team there is very good. They will do everything they can."

"Why haven't we already gone?" Corabelle asked. "Finn's been here for hours."

The doctor glanced at one of the nurses. "We had to stabilize him to survive the trip. He's in very critical condition."

"Oh my God," Corabelle said. "He could die any minute?"

"His heart is not very strong. The left side is barely functional. We've left the ductus arteriosus open, a vessel that connects the two parts of the heart, one that normally closes at birth. This way we can keep Finn's heart working until surgery. But it will have to happen within a few days."

"Or what?" I asked.

"He'll eventually go into cardiac arrest. But that is the same risk if we do close it. This gives us time to work on his heart."

My blood was pounding in my ears so hard that I wasn't sure I could hear anymore. I looked at Corabelle, ghostly white against her pillow. She took several rapid breaths, then sat up and threw her legs over the side of the bed. "I have to get dressed."

"You can't leave yet. You just had the baby!" I said.

"I'm not staying here while they take Finn away!" She limped to the sofa, where her duffel bag waited, and started jerking clothes out of it.

"Can she do that? Can she go?"

The doctor looked at the nurses. "When will she get discharged?"

"Tomorrow at the earliest. Possibly another day," one said. "She's only six hours postpartum."

Corabelle whirled around. "I'm walking out of here whether you sign a paper or not."

The doctor nodded. "Did everything go normally for her?"

The nurse picked up her chart. "I didn't attend, but everything here looks clear."

"Let her go. Inform her OB."

Tears streaked Corabelle's face. "Thank you." She turned to me. "Help me dress."

Another nurse came in. "They are ready to transfer."

"Never mind," Corabelle said. She stuck her feet in her shoes. "I'm going like this." She shoved her bag at me. "I'm riding with the baby."

"Get her a wheelchair," the doctor said. "Take her down."

Once we got to the hospital, Corabelle started checking out books and making sure she understood every term. We were given a room at the Ronald McDonald House, and she printed out internet searches, peppering the doctors with questions whenever anyone made rounds.

Finn was enclosed in a clear incubator. We could snake our hands through round openings on the side and touch his hands and head wherever the wires weren't taped. Corabelle kept a vigil, standing by him as much as she could, or sitting in one of the rockers that seemed to be a staple in NICU wards.

The room was never silent, but whirred and buzzed with alarms and machines. On the first day, I thought I would go mad with it, but eventually I learned to cope. We had nothing to do but this, no school, no job, just be there for Finn, to sit in the ward, watch them run the tests or wheel him out when he had to be assessed on some other floor.

The journey had been hard on him, and at the new hospital we saw the nurses come over to him when he had something called apnea, where he stopped breathing. Apparently during one of the nights we weren't there, they had to do CPR to restart his heart. We were waiting for some definitive word, and we talked to so many doctors, from normal baby doctors to heart specialists. It seemed every time they made a decision, something would happen to Finn, and they would want to assess him again.

Corabelle's mom tried to convince us to go home for prom, to try to enjoy a night out. Corabelle had a fit. "How can you even suggest that, when Finn is so ill?"

The last time we saw the neonatologist, on the morning of prom, he said the surgeon would be meeting with us. "Why hasn't he already had surgery?" Corabelle demanded, shoving a printout in the man's face. "Five days is the recommended maximum to keep the ductus open. It's been seven!"

I could see what Corabelle couldn't. The man's face was a mask of professionalism, of detachment. They'd given up on Finn, but they hadn't told us yet. I couldn't bring myself to say this to Corabelle, even though I knew.

Her phone had been blowing up with messages all day.

Everyone seemed to think that since Finn was okay all week, he'd be okay for the night. Several of Corabelle's friends sided with her mother, telling her to get back home and attend her prom.

"They don't get it." Corabelle threw her phone in her purse. "We can't go dance and laugh and have our pictures made. This is our whole life." She pressed on her swollen breasts. "Besides, I can't exactly pump milk in the middle of the crowning of the king and queen."

I sat on the floor of the NICU, leaning back against the seat of her rocking chair, her knees on either side of my shoulders. My arms wound around her legs. I didn't know how anybody did this long-term, just waited. Corabelle had talked to some of the other mothers, but their babies were all doing well, growing and getting better. She couldn't bear it any more than seeing the curtains get wrapped around a family and a bed, rolled along a track to hide their tragedy from the other occupants of the ward. Two babies had died in the week we'd been there, and both times Corabelle had sobbed half the night.

Our favorite NICU nurse, Angilee, came and got us for the last meeting with the doctors, her face somber. Unlike the other times, when they talked to us in the ward or the hallways or the waiting rooms, this time we were led to a conference room with a large table and rolling chairs.

A nurse brought in a cart with a computer on it inside the room. Inside was one of the NICU doctors who talked to us every day, plus two other new ones, a man and a woman. They stood when we walked in.

My senses immediately went on alert. This was too formal. Something bad was about to go down. At the last minute another woman rushed in, dressed in regular clothes.

I don't remember everything they said. They showed us an MRI of Finn's brain they'd done during the night. They talked about lack of oxygen and mental activity, about what sort of life he might lead even with surgery.

Corabelle demanded to know why surgery hadn't happened yet, more force in her voice than I'd ever seen. I remember staring at the image of a brain, all strange colors like they'd dyed it with Kool-Aid. Then Corabelle was standing up, shouting, and I pulled on her, tried to bring her down. "They want us to take out the tubes," she said to me. "Don't just sit there and let them take out the tubes."

One of the doctors turned to me. "Finn is almost completely dependent on the ventilator now. Instead of growing stronger for surgery, he's weakened. There really isn't any hope for a recovery."

"So you get to decide?" I asked. "You make the choice about whether he lives or dies?"

The doctor looked over at the others. "It's come down to how long this will go on."

"But you're supposed to fix his heart," Corabelle said, her face doused in tears. "You were supposed to do surgery."

"It's a complex surgery," one of the other doctors said. "We don't think the prognosis in this case is good enough to attempt it."

"So you're saying no?" Corabelle said. "Is that what you're saying? No surgery? No chance?"

The woman spoke up then. "No decision of this magnitude is ever made by one person."

Corabelle sagged in her chair, dropping her head to the table.

The first doctor stood. "I'm very sorry for your loss," he said.

I wanted to punch him. It hadn't even happened yet. Finn was still in there, breathing along with a machine, his heartbeats still registering on the monitors. He wasn't lost. He was in there.

Corabelle ran from the room, back to the NICU. I wanted to follow her but the woman in regular clothes stopped me. "We have forms to be taken care of," she said.

"What sort of forms?" I demanded.

The doctors filed out as she spread papers out on the table. "This is just to initiate measures to make the baby comfortable."

"Comfortable how?"

"We're shifting into a different kind of care now," she said quietly.

"What if we don't agree? What if we want another opinion?"

"Finn has been assessed by several doctors. But if you'd like to have a meeting with the hospital ethics committee, it can be scheduled."

I sank back down in the chair. "Who are you again?"

"I'm Alice, the social worker."

"So you see this sort of thing all the time?"

"This is part of my job, yes."

"If Finn was your baby, would you do this?"

She sat in the chair next to me. "It's hard to let go. Only you as Finn's family can decide when you're ready, when you feel you've exhausted all your options."

"But they won't do the surgery."

She set down the pen. "They don't feel it would be successful, and it is a difficult, painful, long surgery."

I held my head in my hands, staring at the sheets of paper. Finn would be cut open, his heart sliced up, and all for nothing. That's what they were saying.

I snatched up the pen, scrawling my name everywhere there was a flag. They'd already prepared all of this before the meeting, so anything we said wouldn't have changed what happened. Even so, her words nagged at me. *Only you as Finn's family can decide.*

When the woman finally picked up the papers, I hurried after Corabelle. She was in the NICU, leaning over Finn's bed, stroking his head. "We didn't get much parenting in, did we?"

I came up behind her and put my arms around her waist. "We

crammed in all we could."

Finn's chest rose and fell with the ventilator. I'd never gotten used to the sound, a choppy mechanical wheeze. A nurse arrived and shot something into his IV. "We're giving him a stronger medication. He'll rest very peacefully now." I had no idea what she was talking about, but not long after that, I could see he had changed, his arms flatter against the bed, his legs very still. He was more than asleep now. He was out.

"What did they do to him?" Corabelle asked. She picked up his limp hand.

I knew they had sedated him, and that this was the beginning. "You should call your parents now," I said. "They should be here."

Corabelle fumbled with her phone. I knew I should probably call my mother, but I couldn't bring myself to do it. She might bring my father, and I didn't want him there.

The staff didn't allow calls in the NICU, other than in emergencies, so Corabelle left the ward. I was alone with Finn, seeing the same things Corabelle had seen. He already seemed gone. The machine continued its helicopter sound. I tried to picture him somewhere else, asleep in the crib at home, the butterfly mobile fluttering above his head. He was healthy and fine, and if I wanted to, I could pick him up, stick him on my shoulder, and carry him around with me, warm and breathing and curled into my neck. I'd never held him. No one had. I wasn't sure any of us would.

A nurse walked by, and I reached out to stop her. "So what happens now?"

"What do you mean?"

I could see she didn't know what had been decided earlier that day. "When they turn all of this off." I gestured vaguely at all the machinery.

Her eyes grew wide. "Let me get someone who is updated on Finn." She stroke briskly away.

The nurse Angilee popped around the corner. "I'm so sorry, Gavin. Finn is such a beautiful little boy. You two can decide what time we remove the ventilator. We usually do it around eight in the evening, as that is a quiet time here. Does that give your family time to be here? Or do you want another time?"

I tried to answer her, but my mouth had gone completely dry. "I will ask Corabelle if eight works."

She took my hand, her dark fingers surrounding mine. Her braids were tied together in an intricate weave, like a halo on her head. "Do you want to have Finn baptized?"

"I don't know," I croaked out. "I need to ask Corabelle. Our families aren't very religious."

She squeezed my hand. "Let me know. We have a chaplain here. I'll just need some notice to make sure he can fit it in sometime today."

"So what happens?"

"Well, first we'll seat Corabelle in a chair, and then we'll take off the monitor wires so we can move Finn out of the bed." She pointed to the disks on his chest. "He'll still be on the ventilator." She let go of me and moved around the machines to point out the thick air tubes that led to his mouth.

"This we can move with him, and we'll untape it. When you both are ready, we'll take it out."

I gripped the edge of the bed. "Will he die right away?"

"Not usually. He'll breathe a little on his own for a little while. But he won't be pumping enough oxygen."

"He's going to suffocate?"

Angilee came back around and rubbed my back. "We will not let Finn be in any pain whatsoever."

"He's sedated, isn't he?"

"He has been since he was given the ventilator, for his safety."

"But it's more now."

She hesitated. "Yes."

"He doesn't feel anything?"

"Nothing at all."

So he really was already gone. Anything we said to him, any touch we did. I had made that choice. I had signed the paper and now it was too late to even say good-bye.

"He's still with us, Gavin. He's still here." She pulled a clipboard from the shelf above the machine and wrote his statistics on it.

"How long will it take, once he's off?"

"That's up to Finn. He'll decide when he's done."

Corabelle came back, her eyes all red. "Mom wants him baptized. Can we do that?"

"Absolutely," Angilee said. "Come here, child." She wrapped Corabelle into a deep hug. "Is she going to ask her minister or should I get the chaplain here?"

"I guess someone here."

"I'll call him. He'll come talk to you about it." She pulled away from Corabelle and looked into her face. "So much to bear for someone so young."

Corabelle started crying again, and Angilee walked her over to me. "I'll be back. Someone will be with you pretty much from now until it's time."

Corabelle looked over to me. "When is it time?"

"Eight o'clock, unless we want to change it."

She whipped around to look at the clock. "Eight more hours! Eight more hours!" Her legs seemed to give out, and I helped her to the rocking chair. "What can we do in eight hours?"

I didn't have an answer for her.

"I have to read him a storybook!" Corabelle said, popping back out of the chair. "And sing him a nursery rhyme." She walked up to the enclosed crib. "I have to teach him 'Twinkle, Twinkle, Little

Star.'" She looked up at me, and I knew I'd be haunted by her expression for a long time as she said, "We're never going to take him to Disney World, are we?"

I stood next to her, wishing I were anywhere but there, but at the same time, that I would never have to leave.

34

CORABELLE

Gavin was awfully quiet on the rock as we lay beneath the stars. I nudged him finally. "Do you want a sandwich?" I asked him.

The half moon let out so little light that he was only a shadow in the almost complete blackness. "Maybe in a minute." His voice sounded off.

"You okay?"

He didn't answer, which I took to mean he wasn't. "What is getting you?" I asked.

"Just remembering that last day."

"The funeral?"

"No. With Finn."

"Oh."

"Remember Angilee, the nurse?"

"She was good," I managed to get out.

"Once things got started, she didn't leave us for a minute."

"She must have worked past her shift."

"I think so."

"She got us that crazy chaplain."

His belly moved beneath my hand, a gentle laugh. "He was

something."

"God bless this holy child! Alleluia!" I mimicked the animated speech of the minister, who'd made Finn's baptism seem like a tent revival.

We both laughed halfheartedly. My mom had wanted the baptism, and I was glad we did it. We got pictures of him and could celebrate his one little life event. Mom brought a white lace bib to put over his chest and the wires, and a little satin hat.

For once I never wanted a prayer to end. The chaplain had arrived at 7:30, and I knew that as soon as the baptism ended, they'd start the process of disconnecting Finn. As the chaplain went on and on about suffering and salvation, I kept my eyes on the baby. He seemed so relaxed, so perfect, like a doll waiting for someone to pick him up to play.

Everyone murmured, "Amen," and I snapped my head up to check the clock, the mental countdown still running. Ten more minutes with Finn.

The chaplain signed a certificate and gave it to my mom. He shook everyone's hands, and I took my turn absently, unwilling to look away from Finn's face.

Another nurse arrived, and Angilee began pulling the curtain around our space, closing off the view from the rest of the NICU. My belly started heaving, but I was too dehydrated to cry anymore. I finally understood what people meant when they said they didn't have any tears left.

As the rest of the ward disappeared, the noises inside seemed louder, the endless ch-ch-ch sound of the ventilator. I couldn't see the clock anymore.

"Corabelle, you sit here in the rocker," Angilee said. "It's time to hold your baby."

I sank into the chair that had become so familiar to me that my body practically molded itself to it, a wooden frame softened with blue cushions tied to the base and the back.

The other nurse flipped several switches and the screen over Finn's bed went dark. "Just the monitors," she said. Through the curtains, I could hear the faint sounds of matching beeps of babies who were still being watched, babies who would one day go home.

Gavin stood behind me, hands on my shoulders. I wasn't sure it was fair that I got to hold Finn. What if he died instantly? I looked up at him and tried to speak, but my throat was too dry. He gazed down at me with understanding, seemingly more worried about my welfare than that of Finn. I just accepted it and waited.

The nurses carefully removed the little discs on his chest. Finn didn't flinch or move at all. He was so sedated. I wasn't sure he'd even hear anything I had to say, or if he was even vaguely aware of anything I'd done that day — wash his little head with no-rinse shampoo, read him *Goodnight Moon*. I tried twice to sing "Twinkle, Twinkle," but I couldn't get past the first line.

Eventually they got him down to just the ventilator going into his mouth, the tubes snaking from a complicated connector up to a machine above. Angilee rolled a cart closer to me, holding the tubes in her hand. The other nurse picked Finn up from the bed and wrapped him in a blue blanket.

My parents stood somewhere behind me, but I hadn't looked at them since the baptism ended. I heard my mom give a little whimpering cry, but I refused to let it set me off. I didn't want to weep the entire time I held my baby, the only time I held him. That didn't seem fair. There should be something happy in his life.

The nurse walked to me slowly, letting the tubes shift. Angilee kept them aloft. When they lowered Finn to my lap, I didn't know exactly how to hold him. He wasn't like the practice dolls from class, but warm and soft. The nurse laid his head in the bend of my elbow, and I adjusted naturally, lifting that arm slightly and bringing my free hand under his back.

"Perfect," the nurse said and arranged the ventilator so that the hoses weren't bent or crimped.

Finn was so much lighter than I'd imagined. He was four pounds at birth, but then he lost some, then he swelled with water weight the last day or two. He had downy hair at his crown, and his little ears lay perfectly flat.

Gavin came around and knelt beside me, cupping his palm at the top of Finn's head. "He has your nose," he said.

"I think it's yours," I said.

My dad came around and snapped a picture of us, but we didn't look up, or smile, or try to make this a normal image. There was no way to make anything that was happening seem normal.

"Can I have a turn?" my mom asked, and I looked up at the nurse.

"Of course," she said and looked to me. "You want to give everyone a chance before we go on?"

I nodded. More time. I wanted all the clocks to stop, for this moment to last as long as possible, even though the pain was excruciating, a tightness in my chest and throat, my head pounding, my jaw aching from trying not to cry. Still, I would take it to keep looking at Finn.

I lifted him a little, and the nurse took him back. Mom and I traded places, and she sat with him for a minute, rocking and humming some little song I remembered from when I was small. After a moment she started sobbing super hard, and the nurse took Finn. My dad sat with him a moment, and then we all looked at Gavin.

At first he shook his head, but my distressed expression must have changed his mind, because he sat in the chair. Of all the moments that were hard, seeing him there, his dark head bent over Finn's, was the one I thought might break me. I felt light, like I could float, and only when my vision started to go gray did I realize

I had to pull myself together. I breathed in several rapid deep inhales and forced myself to calm.

The nurse took the baby from Gavin and said to me, "Corabelle, it's time."

Gavin moved out of the way, and I took my place back in the rocker. I accepted Finn, letting his little bottom rest in my lap. The nurse slipped a pillow under him to steady us and bent over him. "First I'll just remove the adhesive."

She used a bit of damp cotton that smelled sharply of chemicals to loosen the sticky tape. Finn's mouth was red and misshapen beneath it. She pressed a wet cloth to it, surrounding the tube.

I couldn't breathe. The only lifeline for Finn was loose and ready to come out. I wanted to look around the room, to remember everything, but I couldn't tear my gaze from his face. My shoulder ached but I ignored it, keeping him still, fearful of moving and removing the tube by accident.

The nurse took the cloth away, and his mouth was soft again, pink rather than red. She looked up at Angilee, who nodded. "I'm going to take it out now," the nurse said and pulled the tube away.

Angilee whisked away the hosing, and I looked down at Finn for the first time without anything blocking my view. My mother whimpered beside me, and Gavin squeezed my shoulder. For the longest time, Finn didn't move at all, then his belly moved out violently, and he sucked in a breath.

The nurse placed the disc of a stethoscope on his chest in several places. "Heart tones are still there." She glanced up at Angilee. "Let's get her a wheelchair."

"Where is she going?" Gavin asked.

"We have a private room for you," the nurse said.

I couldn't stop looking at Finn. I touched his nose and lips and ears and chin. I pushed the blanket aside to run my fingers down his little chest and belly, places that had always been a mass of wire and adhesive.

"Let's move you into this." Angilee guided me from the rocker to the wheelchair. "You all can come."

Dad clicked images as we moved through the ward. I didn't take my eyes off Finn. His belly still moved a little, not as violently as before, and this reassured me. I imagined that somehow they were wrong, completely wrong, and that he'd keep breathing, start growing, and soon we'd be in our car and speeding home to put him in his crib.

Angilee pushed me out of the NICU and down a short hall. The other nurse opened the door, revealing a room with a normal bed like you'd find at home, covered in a soft blue bedspread. A normal sofa rested against the far wall, and a table held plates beneath silver covers, like at a hotel.

Angilee pushed the wheelchair over to the bed. "You can sit wherever you like," she said.

I stood and turned to the bed, then realized I couldn't easily get on it while holding the baby. "Gavin, take him for a second." I passed him over, thinking this might have been the most natural thing in the world, handing the baby to his father, if it had been any other time.

I crawled across the bed to sit against the headboard. "Okay, I'm ready for him back."

Gavin returned him to my arms and climbed on the bed next to me.

Angilee lifted a red remote from a side table. "Call us if you need us," she said. "We'll check in every fifteen minutes or so."

My parents settled on the sofa. "I guess it's just a matter of time now," my dad said.

I laid my hand on Finn's belly, feeling that motion, noticing that the space between the breaths had already grown longer. Gavin put his hand on top of mine, and for a moment, we could have been any new parents, looking down at our son, marveling at how he was made, how he breathed, how sweetly he slept.

I wished that he would open his eyes, just once. But he hadn't, and wouldn't.

His belly gurgled and I had to smile, but when the brief happier feeling passed, grief overwhelmed me so fast that I couldn't hold the tears back. My body had found more, an ocean of them, and I leaned back so they wouldn't fall on Finn's face.

His belly stopped moving, and I panicked, thinking it was already over. I wanted to call the nurses, tell them to resuscitate him. My head clanged with alarm bells, warnings to help him, to do something. Gavin squeezed my arm and said, "Take it easy," and I realized I was breathing very fast, as if I could somehow make the baby accept my oxygen.

Guilt crashed over me. This had to be my fault. I hadn't told anyone what I had done in those early days, before I knew I was pregnant. Maybe it would have mattered. Maybe the doctors would have done something differently. My baby was dying for my sins, as if I'd blown the smoke straight into his lungs.

Finally his belly rose again. I forced myself to calm, to stay in the moment. I couldn't do anything about the past.

"Let's give the kids some privacy," my dad said. As much as I might want my own mother there, I felt relieved that he would let us be alone, to have just a little time to have Finn all to ourselves.

Mom started to protest, but Dad took her hands and lifted her to standing. She came over to us and kissed Finn's head. "I love you, baby boy," she said before covering her face with her handkerchief again.

When they were gone, I laid my head on Gavin's shoulder. "Is there something we should say to him?" I asked. "Maybe something easy?"

"Anything you want."

"We love you, Finn. We wish you could stay with us." I picked up his little hand and extended the fingers topped by tiny fragile fingernails. "Daddy would have been happy to teach you how to clean a carburetor."

"Except that cars have fuel injectors now," Gavin said. "Mommy wasn't good at cars."

I tried to laugh, but it caught in my throat. "Well, by the time you were grown, it might have been hover cars."

"You still would have to have been home by midnight," he said, then kissed my ear. "We know all the trouble you can get into after midnight."

I pulled him higher, closer to my shoulder, so I could lay my cheek on his head.

The nurse came in, silently. "Just a quick check."

I couldn't believe it had already been fifteen minutes.

I turned Finn a little, and she laid the stethoscope on his chest.

"It's a long time between breaths now," I said.

She nodded. "He still has heart tones."

"How much time?" I asked.

"Every baby is different," she said. "But probably before the next time I check."

"Will we know? Will something happen?" Gavin asked.

"Probably not. It's a lot like he's asleep." She patted me on the shoulder. "Just let us know if you need us."

When she left, I curled into Gavin. He put his arms around us so that we wrapped Finn up between us. I held my breath as long as I could, waiting for Finn's belly to rise, but I couldn't make it. I took in another long breath and waited again. Still nothing.

My chest started heaving and Gavin held me tighter. We waited for the next breath, but it didn't come. I wondered what death really was, when you stopped breathing, or the silence of the heart? I had thought it would be so definitive, and that I would know.

"His face has changed," Gavin said.

I looked at him, the tiny nose, the gentle mouth still pink around the edges from the tape. And I saw what Gavin meant. His jaw was loose now, his mouth open.

I yanked him tight against my shoulder, tighter than you should hold a baby. I would not let him go, they could not take him from me. Deep inside my body a wail began, a low sound, completely outside my control. He was gone. He was gone. My baby Finn was really gone.

Gavin clutched at me, and we supported each other on the bed, rocking back and forth, the three of us. I don't know how long we did that, but eventually a nurse came back in and tiptoed back out without disturbing us.

When I couldn't sit up any longer, my own body giving out, I slid down on the bed, curling Finn's body into my chest. Gavin lay down with me, and we stayed that way until a doctor came in, one we didn't know, and checked Finn's heart. "He's gone," he said, but by then, I already knew, had already ached and cried, and I couldn't do anymore. He glanced at the clock. "Time of death, 9:03."

He laid a hand on the baby. "You can stay here with him as long as you want, overnight if you choose. Nurses will check on you. You will not be rushed."

So we settled back on the bed, the three of us, and even though I didn't sleep, we let the night fall over us, quiet and deep.

35

GAVIN

The rough surface of the rock bit into my shoulders. "Corabelle?" I nudged her, still lying across my chest. I thought maybe she'd fallen asleep.

She sat up and swiped at her eyes. "What do you think it is about stargazing that makes us think of Finn?"

I stared up into the night sky, showered with dots of light in a way you never could see in the city. "The infinite. The unknown. The Lion King and the souls of all the kings that came before."

Corabelle nudged me halfheartedly. "I never was able to finish singing 'Twinkle, Twinkle, Little Star' to him."

I wrapped my arm around her shoulders and squeezed. "That's all right."

I thought of all the paths our lives could have taken. The one if Finn had never existed. The one if he hadn't died. The one if I hadn't left after the funeral. And this new one, if Corabelle hadn't come to UC San Diego and signed up for astronomy.

The North Star stood out, brighter than the others. It was definitely easier when you were out here to believe that some great cosmic something was guiding our fate.

"Your stomach just rumbled in my ear," Corabelle said.

"Then feed me, wench!" It was an old joke born of too many pirate movies.

She smacked my ribs, but still sat up and felt around for the bag. "Where's that flashlight?"

"Not sure. It's darker than I figured."

We both felt around the edges of the blanket until our hands crossed paths. We both stopped, grasping each other. "I'd kiss you but I'm very likely to miss," I said.

She leaned into me, and now I could navigate the shadow of her, face and hair and arms and waist. My lips found hers and she sighed, sinking into me.

Her mouth was an oasis in the dry air; her tongue made me forget all the grief I'd felt thinking of Finn.

She pulled away with a broken laugh. "Why do I have a feeling I'm going to have bruised knees tomorrow?"

I pulled her down onto the blanket. "Because you are."

The night was cool, almost cold, so I pulled the blanket around us as I exposed each part of her to the autumn air. I laid my head against the skin of her chest, listening to her heartbeat, still seeing the monitors in my mind, a little jagged line across the screen that told us Finn was with us.

I made my way down to her bare belly, where he'd been, tucked away for seven months. We hadn't known that this was the best of times, him kicking inside her, none of us having any clue that we should have celebrated every day.

I kissed my way along her hip bone, bringing the jeans down with me. Corabelle sighed and lifted her hips, and I delved into her, feeling her shiver, listening to her sounds, and once again thanked the stars for bringing her back to me.

36

CORABELLE

A buzzing noise startled me awake later that night, after we'd finally left the rock to go home. I rubbed my eyes and looked first at Gavin, sprawled across his bed. Then the clock, which read one in the morning.

The noise was persistent, the sound of a cell-phone text message, one after the other.

For some reason I just knew it was Jenny, and Lumberjack had ditched her somewhere, and she needed help. I scrambled across the floor and dug through our clothes, trying to find my phone.

The light of a screen showed through a bit of fabric and I snatched it up.

But when I saw the image, I dropped it again.

I tried to breathe, suddenly feeling like I might hyperventilate. It was probably some mistake. Some porn bot or a friend making a joke.

I lifted the phone again, Gavin's phone, and swiped it to get past the preview and into the actual message. The image was still there, a naked woman sprawled on a bed, legs wide, fingers spreading herself open.

Below it, the message said, "Miss you, Gavin baby. I need a booty call."

I meant to set the phone down and crawl right back into bed. If this woman missed him, that means he wasn't seeing her anymore. So it was fine. He'd delete the messages in the morning, probably relieved I hadn't seen them. As I tried to bury the phone back in the clothes, another message popped up. "I dumped Jerry. Pimp free, like you said! Give me a shout. I'm good for a freebie."

I washed cold. Who was this girl? I glanced up at the bed. Gavin was still out. I knew I shouldn't read any more, but I remembered Jenny at the coffee shop saying, "What do you really know about Gavin, as he is now?"

I scrolled through the messages that woke me up. Her name was Candy, of course. She asked where he'd been lately. Then, "I learned a little rope bondage just for you. Tie up those strong arms."

When he didn't respond, she'd sent the picture.

Maybe it was a joke, maybe the picture was random. Maybe this was a friend. I set the phone down, unwilling to spy any more.

But then I thought — is he being careful? We were using condoms now, but we hadn't been. What if he had been with a prostitute?

I picked the phone up again and clicked on Candy's name to bring up their entire history. It went back a year. Meetups. Him telling her to ditch Jerry. Him worried because she had a black eye. Lots and lots of sexting. Him writing her, asking if she was available that night.

But nothing about ordinary things, dates, or movies, or normal conversation. In one she warned him Jerry was forcing her to up her rate to $125.

I wanted to put the phone down, but then I saw another name that looked suspicious. Lolly. I clicked on her. She also sent images of herself, large heaving breasts, pulling aside her panties. He was not as close to this one, as all their communication was businesslike. Locations. Times.

I closed the phone. What had he done? I sorted through the clothes, my chest heaving, fat tears dripping off my nose. I wasn't going to blame him for what he'd done. That was his past. But he wasn't the person I thought he was. He'd become somebody else, someone I wasn't sure I could live with.

My shirt was on backwards and chafed my neck with the tag, but I didn't care. I had to get out. My keys jingled as I crept to the door, and Gavin shifted on the bed. Afraid he would wake, I tore through the house, wrenching open the door, and hurtling across the pathways to the parking lot. Thankfully I had met him here before we left and had my car. As it started up, I saw him come out his door, wrapped in a sheet. He was shouting, but I couldn't hear him and backed out of the spot.

He would come after me, I knew, so I couldn't go home, not right away. I'd find some place to wait out the night.

Jenny's face was sympathetic when she opened her door close to noon. I had texted her hourly starting at nine, but apparently she'd been busy with Lumberjack and hadn't checked.

She yanked me into a hug. "Corabelle, you look like death. Come in here."

Color exploded throughout her tiny apartment, pink sofa, yellow chairs, big swaths of silk fabric hanging from the center of the ceiling like a circus tent. "Wow, Jenny."

She whirled around the living room. "Like it? I never want to see anything dull."

"You achieved that." I realized I had not been in anyone's apartment the whole year I had lived in San Diego, not until I walked into Gavin's. When had I become a hermit? I sat down on the vivid sofa, pushing a sequin pillow aside.

She sank into one of the furry side chairs, plucking at the baby-chick fuzz. "So, you want to tell me what happened?"

I shook my head.

"Oookay. Well, let's do girly things." She popped out of her seat. "I'll get the nail polish."

I felt too exhausted for aiming colored lacquer at my nails, and when she disappeared, I dropped my head to the arm of the sofa. The images from Gavin's phone wouldn't leave me. Every time I closed my eyes, I saw the glowing round boobs of Lolly, the sprawled body of Candy. No wonder Gavin could send me spiraling so fast. He'd been learning from the best.

I wanted a doctor. VD tests. An antiseptic. Definitely a scalding shower.

I could hear Jenny opening and closing drawers. The need for blackness overwhelmed me. I wanted comfort, an escape from my own head. I knew I shouldn't do it, as Jenny could come back any minute, but still, I held my breath, relaxing into the cushions, exhaling slowly to avoid my lungs forcing me to breathe. If I did it right, I'd be out, then asleep, and life would be so much more manageable.

Even with my eyes closed, the colored spots danced in front of me. My chest fought with me for a moment, then I started to go, slipping into oblivion.

It seemed only minutes passed before sounds woke me up, but the Hello Kitty clock on the wall read five o'clock. Something clanged in the kitchen, followed by Jenny's "Dang it!"

Sequins imprinted my face. I'd fallen onto a sparkly pillow. I rubbed my fingers along the indentations on my cheek. My hair stuck up every direction, tangled into a mat.

Jenny's head poked around the wall that divided the room. "Sleepyhead! I'm trying to make food. Somewhat successfully."

I stood up but my legs wobbled, so I sat back down again. We'd spent too much time on that rock last night, and done too many things. The back of my shoulder blades were chafed. Well, that was over.

Something inside me wanted to escape, a wail, like a ghost's lament. I should talk to Gavin, get it all out. But I just couldn't. Even if all that was past, I couldn't made peace with it, not now at least. Maybe eventually. I tried placing the image of Gavin with those paid women next to the one of him in high school, so sweet and clean-cut. It wouldn't go. I felt like I had been with his evil twin, or a black-sheep brother.

Jenny sat next to me. "You ready to talk about it yet?"

She seemed so much like a doll, what had Gavin called her? Rainbow Brite. Her hair was extra pink, like she'd just recolored it, falling into a perfect set of bangs across her brow and straight down to her shoulders. Her eyebrows were always an exclamation, thin and rounded, as though she was permanently surprised.

"I'll take that as a no," she said, since I hadn't moved or spoken. "Come over here and eat something." She took my arm and led me over to a tiny table with two chairs. "I made some eggs and toast."

The surface was painted with bright flowers. I traced the outlines of roses and tulips. When my fingers came across a butterfly, the wail filled me again, but I kept it inside, closing off any way for it to escape.

Jenny set a lime-green plate in front of me, prettily arranged with fluffy eggs and two triangles of toast. She placed the fork in my hand, closing my fingers around the silver handle. "I will feed you if you don't eat it yourself."

I slid the tines into a puff of egg and lifted it to my mouth. I swallowed and my stomach rebelled, flooding me with nausea. Jenny still watched me, so I picked up the toast and bit off a corner. At last she seemed satisfied and sat across the table.

"So I'm guessing this has to do with muscle man. Let me guess. He's sticking more than one blowhole."

I almost choked on the bread.

Jenny hopped up and fetched the orange juice she'd forgotten on the counter. "Here, drink." She handed me the cup. "Man-meat like your ex always have girls on the side."

If she only knew. I wished I had a delete button for my memory so that I could erase those images. Candy. Lolly. Couldn't they have something more original? Maybe those were Gavin's nicknames.

My stomach heaved, and I knew if I swallowed one more bite, it would come right back up.

"Okay," Jenny said. "I can see we're at DEFCON Five. When I see that boy in class tomorrow, I'm going to kick his muscled ass. AFTER I've filled his motorcycle with Karo syrup."

"Don't," I choked out. "Don't talk to him."

"She speaks." Jenny leaned forward on the table. "She speaks only to defend the asshole who got her so upset in the first place."

I stuck a fork in another bite of egg and shoved it in my mouth so I wouldn't have to answer. It didn't want to go down, but I forced it. I had to get a grip.

Jenny pushed up from the chair and paced in little circles. "Why aren't there any nice guys? Sweet normal guys who open doors and buy you dinner and don't have a room full of drugs or bonus women on nights and weekends?"

"I don't think he was seeing someone else," I said. I was settling back into something more akin to numb than grief, a comfortable place, nice and familiar.

She sat down again. "So what happened? Is he stalking your apartment?"

"I don't know. After I left his place, I knew he'd follow me home."

"I'm sorry I didn't get your message sooner."

"It's okay. I just hung out at Angel's Coffee Bar. It's 24 hours." Talking helped my stomach settle.

"You going to tell me what he did?"

"He didn't do anything to me. I just found out some things."

Jenny propped her chin on her hand. "I'm listening."

"I just have to decide if I can live with it. I don't want him around while I decide."

She popped up out of her chair. "Fair enough. Let's color those nails."

When she disappeared into another room, I carried the plate into the kitchen. I was stuck getting a manicure, but this would be an opportunity to ask Jenny a favor. I needed her to take notes for me in astronomy until I was up for seeing Gavin again. For the first time in my entire life, I was going to skip class.

37

GAVIN

I knew exactly how Corabelle felt four years ago after the funeral. Lost. Confused. More worried than mad, although I could see how anger might figure into it.

She hadn't answered any text messages or phone calls. She hadn't been at home. She didn't work Sundays, I knew, but I went to Cool Beans anyway. Some guy with dreadlocks was super interested in why I asked for her, but I didn't tell him anything.

I spent most of Sunday in a funk. I figured when I saw the image of Candy on my phone that this was what got to her. I should have done something to block all those girls. But even after wrangling with the cell service for an hour, I couldn't figure out how to do anything but mute the calls. I wanted to change my number, but Corabelle had it too. I couldn't do anything about that now.

I should have lived my life differently. I should have accounted for the possibility of a second chance. All my mistakes lined up in front of me and no matter how I pummeled them, they didn't fall.

Monday morning I put on the khakis and shirt Corabelle liked and rode over to campus, nervous as hell. She might not speak to me. She might punch me. I would take anything she dished out. I deserved it. But I had to make her see that those women were the past. Once I got her back, I had nothing to do with them, and I wouldn't. I didn't even want them. I hadn't even thought of them. The pictures embarrassed me now.

I paused in our stairwell and gripped the rail. You didn't find someone you loved and lost a long time ago just to lose them again. I refused to believe it. I wouldn't let that happen.

The stairs blurred beneath my feet as I hurried to class. I searched for Corabelle, but her seat was empty. So was her friend Jenny's on the other end.

I plunked down to wait, suddenly wondering if Corabelle would show at all.

The room filled up and the professor took his spot at the podium. At the last moment, Jenny dashed in and sat down. The TA Robert tried not to look at her, but I could see his hidden smile. If I couldn't get anything from her, and I was betting I wouldn't, he might be my way in.

I couldn't pay attention to a damn thing during the lecture. At the end, I wished I had, because I could have offered my notes to Corabelle. But she probably wasn't paying any attention to my messages. Shit.

Jenny took off like a pink streak after class. I tried to push my way into the hall in time to follow, but she'd already gone down one stairwell or the other, and I had no idea how to catch her. I turned back to the room to get something out of Robert.

Robert shoved a folder in his backpack as I strode up. The blond TA, Amy, looked up expectantly, and I debated which one to approach. Hell, they were together.

"Corabelle wasn't here," I said to them both.

Amy looked away, annoyed. Robert shrugged. "Mondays. People skip." He turned away.

I grabbed his arm. "How many classes can she miss before it affects her grade?"

"Two," Amy said. "I'll e-mail her if she misses another one."

"What about the star parties?"

Robert tried to take off again, but I kept a grip on him.

"She has to make up all of those. You can't miss." Amy clutched her folder to her chest and turned away.

Robert looked down at my arm. "Dude, you going to let go?"

When Amy was halfway to the door, I said, "Jenny wanted to double date with us."

He jerked his arm from me. "I'm sure your winning personality works with the ladies." He tilted his head in the direction of Amy. "But you're acting like Asshole #1 to me."

"Did you talk to Jenny yesterday?" I was desperate. "Was Corabelle with her?"

Robert leaned against the podium. The room had emptied out. "So you alpha males can screw it up too. Good to know."

My rage was building. "Did you talk to Jenny or not?"

"I'm not allowed to fraternize with students."

"Cut the bullshit. The way I see it, I've got a number on you." I knew I was putting on my don't-fuck-with-me face, the one that always made people in Mexico move to the other side of the street, but I didn't have time for clever conversation. "So tell me if Corabelle is with Jenny."

"Of course she is. I didn't go over there last night. She's apparently strung out completely." Robert looked disgusted. "You have no idea how to treat a woman."

"And you're Romeo. Right."

Robert rocked back on his heels. "I have a way with the ladies."

"Where does Jenny live?"

"Not going to tell you that."

I didn't have any more time for his bullshit. I grabbed a fistful of his T-shirt. "Fuck your job. I'm going to fuck up your pretty Romeo face if you don't tell me where Corabelle is."

I had to give him credit. He didn't lose his cool whatsoever. "The thing about you over-testosteroned alpha males," he said, laying his hands on my shoulders. "You just don't get that aggression won't get you anywhere with the nice girls. They go for the underdogs every time. So take a piece of my face. It'll just get me more sympathy, and you will be further from your goal."

Shit. I let go of his shirt and pushed him away. Little fucker was right. I backed off and stormed across the room.

"Hey, Thor."

I turned around. "My name's Gavin."

"Right. Thor. I'll tell you this. Don't bother with Amy's star party Wednesday. Corabelle won't be there."

"What do you mean? Amy said Corabelle had to go."

"She already switched to mine. And I have no intention of letting you up there. Unless of course you want to get suspended. I might enjoy seeing that." He smirked, like he had won the round.

I smashed my fists into the door, making it open so fast it rebounded against the wall outside. Corabelle meant more to me than this school. If I got suspended, I got suspended.

38

GAVIN

I purposefully went to my own star party with Amy on Wednesday to stay on everyone's good side. We had to map the moon, which was almost full. The morning lecture had been about the lunar surface, and I'd forced myself to focus even though Corabelle's empty seat distracted me. She probably had convinced the TAs to mark her present and I'd never see her again.

No, I would. I would show up to Thursday's star party, whether '90s boy wanted me there or not. Corabelle had to listen to me. She had to hear me out.

Work had been pure misery all day Thursday, but the rest of the crew gave me space. No one teased me about dropping wrenches or tossing boxes around. Bud hadn't even moved me to throwing tires despite the very real risk that I'd break something rather than fix it.

I checked on Corabelle's apartment every time I was out. There were never any lights on. The butterflies were thinning out, but I didn't think she was taking them down. A few had fallen, and others were probably pilfered by neighbors.

Everyone at Cool Beans had to be protecting her. Twice I'd

gone up there, but nobody would admit that they had seen her. No sign of her car either, but Jenny could be dropping her off. I couldn't imagine Corabelle skipping work too. I wanted to crash into the dish room to see if she were hiding, but I hadn't done it. If I didn't see her tonight, that was my plan, though. To go in that back room and refuse to leave until I saw her.

As much as I wanted to storm the steps to the star party on the roof, I decided a kinder, gentler approach would serve me better. A few students milled around the base of the dorm where we held the labs. I took the elevator to the top floor, then crossed the hall to the stairs that led to the roof exit. A few other students were heading up, and I mixed in with them, hoping to stall the moment when Robert spotted me. I wanted to get Corabelle alone. To explain.

I knew I was done for when Amy stood at the doorway, checking everyone off as they passed through. They had never done that before. Still, I was committed, so I headed up behind the others, thinking maybe I could somehow push by while Amy searched for names.

My heart was hammering like I was about to head into a street fight, and this pissed me off. This was Corabelle, and a couple TAs. I could get past Amy.

She looked right into my face. "Gavin, what are you doing?"

"You're here for me, aren't you?"

A couple of the other students turned around at my tone.

"Robert has your assignment," Amy said to them. "Go on out."

I pressed against the wall and let the others pass. Amy no longer made a show of checking them off.

"I'm going out there," I said.

Amy stood in front of the door. "This is serious, Gavin. It's stalking. We're prepared to write you up to the dean."

Like I gave a shit about that. "Do what you have to do."

She held out her hand. "Gavin, you know I don't want to do that. Can't you two settle this outside of class? Not involve us?"

"I've been trying that. She won't listen to me."

Amy waited for a couple more students to cross between us and go out onto the roof. "She's really upset. I don't know what happened between you two but —"

"A baby."

"What?" she sputtered, her eyes sparking.

"We had a baby. We were going to get married. Then the baby — Finn — died. There's way more here than I can explain in two minutes, but I have to see her. She's naturally very reluctant, but I want that chance to help her through this."

I knew I was saying too much to Amy, to everybody. But I didn't want to hide all of this anymore. If we didn't talk about it, who would?

Amy clutched her clipboard to her chest. "Five minutes, Gavin. And if I see her upset, I'm calling campus security."

"Works for me." I shoved through the door. Robert stood in the cone of light, handing papers out to the students who had been before me. He never even glanced my way, probably not expecting me to get by Amy.

Corabelle sat on the ledge where I'd been at the first party, gazing up at the moon. Lines of undergrads snaked from the two telescopes, and I cut through them to get to her. Jenny was peering through the eyepiece, so I didn't have to worry about her trying to stop me for the moment. Everyone thought they were safe.

Corabelle saw me and jumped up. "What are you doing here?"

"I had to see you."

Corabelle grabbed my hand and pulled me around to the far corner in the dark. "They will write a disciplinary report if they see you!" she whispered.

"Too late. I negotiated five minutes with you."

Corabelle dropped my hand. "You knew I didn't want to see you. I have skipped class — twice! I haven't gone home or answered your texts. I had to share my personal business with everyone just to keep you away."

I spread out my hands. "Why? Am I that horrible now?"

She squeezed her eyes shut. "No."

"Is this about my phone?"

She pinched the bridge of her nose and shook her head. "Yes. No. I don't know. Seeing those pictures was just a dose of reality. I needed to clear my head. You were already planning our future together."

"I want to plan our future together."

"But I don't know anything about you."

I reached for her hand and tugged it away from her face. "You do too know me. You've known me since I could say my first words."

"I didn't know you had a taste for…" She trailed off.

"Prostitutes. Yes. I've been with a few. But not now. Not anymore."

She turned away and headed for a ledge. I thought for a terrible second that she intended to jump the rail, but as I ran for her, she just sat down.

I knelt in front of her. "Corabelle, I just had to stay away from normal girls. I had broken the heart of the only girl who mattered to me, and I didn't want to be in a relationship, maybe never."

"Those girls are girls too."

"Yes, but they were pros. Company. Paid company. They were…" I didn't know how to say it. I couldn't say I was with them because of her. I didn't know how to lay bare what they were to me.

"What were they, Gavin? And God knows how well you protected yourself."

I swallowed. "I always wore protection. And I took tests every so often, just to be sure. I just didn't want ties. Expectations. I didn't want emotion in it."

"She said you tried to get her away from her pimp. That sounds like emotion."

Damn. She'd read a lot of the messages. I had to make her understand. "I hate pimps," I said. "I didn't like them beating up on these girls. It's common decency, and I wanted them to get out."

She got quiet, and I hoped I'd made some headway.

"What else do I not know?" she asked quietly.

"Nothing!" I said, then cut myself off. Of course there wasn't nothing. There was the big huge something. Once more, the moment had come to tell her. I tried to make myself say it. To just blurt it out. But she talked first.

"I'm going to the doctor tomorrow," she said. "The one on campus."

"You that worried I gave you something?"

She glared at me a moment, then sighed. "Yes and no. Yes, I want that checked. But also, I have not been well."

My belly flipped. "What do you mean, not well?" I remembered her in the stairwell, almost fainting, and again, when I first went to her apartment, how she'd been so weak and shaky. If something happened to her, I couldn't stand it.

"I've been sick. I can't eat."

"You're going through a lot."

She nodded. "That's probably all it is. But it's how it started last time."

"How what started?"

She hesitated. "With Finn."

My face burned like a bomb had exploded. Corabelle thought she was pregnant. She couldn't possibly be. I had to tell her. I had to calm that fear in her, the one that blazed in her eyes.

"Did you take a test?"

"Several, all negative. But still. I just feel off. So I'm going." She stood up. "I'll let you know how that goes."

I jumped in front of her. "Let me go with you."

She shook her head. "No. I don't want you there. I need to talk to him myself."

"Will you tell me what time?"

"No, you'll just camp out there. I'm asking you to please let me be." She pushed on my chest. "And please don't come to my work anymore, or drive by my apartment."

"You knew about that?"

"I know you."

I couldn't let her go so easily. "On one condition."

She turned her face up to me, pale in the moonlight, ashen, and I could see why she thought she was sick. "What condition?"

I leaned in and kissed her, gently, just grazing her lips. I couldn't let her forget what we were, what drove us together, what made us work. When she didn't pull away, I touched her face, my thumb on her cheek, and parted her lips with my tongue.

She stayed with me, so I drove the kiss harder, deeper, pulling her tight against me. When she found out she wasn't pregnant, and hadn't been exposed to anything, I wanted her to remember this, and to want it back, and to seek me out. I had to put everything I felt into the kiss.

Corabelle made a sound, a terrible sad sound deep in her throat, and I knew she got my message. She pulled away and pressed her forehead against my chest. "Let me go, Gavin."

I gripped her even tighter. "I can't do that."

"You have to."

"Tell me when I can talk to you about the doctor."

"Tomorrow night."

"Can I come over?"

"No. I will text you."

"Then can I come over?"

She looked up at me, anguished in ways I didn't understand, maybe ways I'd never understood. "I have to go now." She pulled away and I released her this time. I turned to watch her go around to the other side of the roof, back to the light and the class, and disappear from view.

The moon glowed from its resting place in the sky, almost but not quite full. It looked forlorn, a piece of it shaved off, and I knew that as each day passed, it would get smaller and smaller, until it disappeared into the black.

39

CORABELLE

The walkway to the Student Health Center wasn't any different from all the other concrete paths that crisscrossed campus, but this one felt like a bridge to hell. My leaden feet dragged as I approached the glass door, and when my sweaty hand slipped on the metal handle, I wasn't sure I wanted to know anything after all.

The receptionist gave me a form to fill out, and I sat in a brown-cushioned chair against the wall. A few other students waited in the small room. A sniffling freshman looked to be wearing her pajamas. A couple impatient guys in rugby outfits looked around, tapping their legs and shifting constantly. A panicked woman in her late twenties picked at the bottom of her marine-blue sweater, creating a pile of fuzz.

I brought a book to study, but instead I pulled out my phone and scrolled through all the messages Gavin had sent me since I ran from his apartment almost a week ago. He wrote me throughout each day, short encouraging lines like "I hope your lit class keeps you awake today," or "Don't let the morning coffee rush get to you." He wished me good night every evening. In between, he sometimes asked if he could see me, or said he missed me. I hadn't responded to any, even the one this morning that said, "I'm thinking of you as you see the doctor."

I felt like holding him at arm's length was the best course for the moment. It gave me the ability to function, when otherwise I could easily succumb to embarrassing crying jags or fits of fury that we'd come to this dysfunctional part of our lives.

Today would probably be the last astronomy class I could skip. I'd taken my two free days, and I purposefully scheduled this appointment during class so I would have a doctor's note. Robert and Amy seemed on my side, but I knew the professor himself could step in. Then I would have screwed up my grade over Gavin after all.

Jenny's notes were pretty abysmal, but I could get by with her random bursts of typing that at least helped me peg what part of the book to study. I wasn't worried about my grade. The class was one of the easiest courses I'd ever taken.

I am fine, I told myself for the hundredth time since I'd started skipping. I just wanted this appointment over, to know I hadn't made any huge mistakes, and then I could start fresh again. Whether or not Gavin played a role in my future wasn't something I had to decide right this minute.

Unless, of course, I was pregnant.

I placed my hand on my belly, wishing I could tell. The stick test that morning had been negative again, and since the last unprotected encounter was a week ago, I was close to being out of the woods. I was no more ready for the consequences of my actions than I had been at eighteen.

A nurse opened the side door. "Corabelle?"

I shoved the phone in my backpack and stood up. The woman in pink scrubs smiled, her hair an intricate weave of thick braids that instantly made me think of Angilee from the NICU. Same wide friendly eyes, dark skin, and powerful frame, the sort of person that made you think of a warrior princess.

"So tell me what's going on," the nurse said as we walked down the hall.

"I'm here for a VD screening and a pregnancy test."

The woman nodded. "Let's get your weight and blood pressure." She led me into a small room that held only a scale and a seat with a cuff.

When we finished there, she pointed to a bathroom. "Urine sample. Write your name on the cup and leave it on the little ledge by the window."

I knew the drill and left the cup in front of a frosted window that didn't lead outside, but to another room. As I opened the door to the hall, someone on the other side slid the window open and collected my cup with a latex-gloved hand.

The nurse caught up with me and brought me to an exam room, and the sight of stirrups made my heart palpitate. I sucked in a breath and steadied myself with a hand on the end of the cushioned table.

"You all right, Corabelle?" The nurse set down her clipboard and took my arm. "Let's get you lying down."

She helped me up on the table. "You'll have to undress from the waist down and cover yourself with this paper sheet," she said. "But don't do it until you're sure you're doing all right. Do doctor offices always make you this anxious?"

I shook my head. She turned back to the forms I'd filled out. "Okay, so I see you have been pregnant before." She paused. "So your baby is how old now, four?"

My throat closed up completely.

"Corabelle, you okay?"

Tears escaped from the corners of my eyes and slid down to the paper pillow. "He died."

"Bless your heart, child. When did that happen?"

"When he was seven days old."

Her warm hand squeezed my arm. "I'll check your test myself. Do you know the date of your last menstrual period?"

"I'm on the shot. It's been a while."

"When did you get your last shot?"

"Two months ago."

"Did you do it here?"

"No, I wasn't a student yet."

"The doctor will take a look." She gave me one more squeeze and headed for the door. "Take your time getting up and changing. He's slow as molasses anyway."

I stared at the ceiling when she left, reading a breast self-exam poster that had been taped there. One corner was peeling, and a patient was bound to get a surprise when it finally fell. Maybe I'd point it out when the nurse came back. Imagining the paper floating down, drifting side to side, helped distract me. I wiped my face and sat up, easing off the table to undress.

I'd gotten this far. I would make it the rest of the way. At least the walls weren't lined with pictures of babies, like at my old ob/gyn back in New Mexico. When I went for my postpartum checkup, just a week after Finn died, I couldn't bear to look at the collages of smiling mothers and red-faced infants. My mom had come with me, and she tried to block my view, but both of us sobbed pretty continuously until the exam was over. I think I was supposed to go back again later, but I never did, switching to Planned Parenthood for my shots since they didn't have all the trappings of happy motherhood anywhere in their office space.

A rapid knock at the door made me startle. I jumped back on the table, snatching up the paper sheet.

"Everybody indecent?" the man asked.

I arranged the crinkly sheet around me. "Yes, I'm pretty indecent."

He entered the room, followed by the Angilee lookalike. "I'm Dr. Alpern. I'll be making you uncomfortable today."

I managed a smile. I'd imagined someone stern and disapproving, lecturing me about unprotected sex.

"I'm very sorry to hear about your baby," he said. "Was there a problem during labor?"

"He was eight weeks early. He had a heart defect." I sucked in air, trying to make sure I breathed, but the next words still came out as a gasp. "They didn't operate."

The doctor nodded. "Well, your urine test was negative, but we'll do a blood test to be sure. How long since you had unprotected sex?"

"A week."

"So it could still come up. You can keep testing at home, but let's take a look. Lie back for me and scoot to the edge."

I fell back on the pillow and wriggled down to the end. The doctor aimed a light between my legs, and the nurse handed him something in a plastic wrapper. I focused again on the illustrated hand cupping the wide-nippled breast on the poster.

"Going in. Take a deep breath," the doctor said.

I tried to relax. Still, the metal against my skin made me tense again.

"Just a little swab," he said. "And another little bit of pressure."

I felt something bump me inside, then he withdrew the speculum. I exhaled, not sure if I'd breathed even once while he was in there.

"I don't see anything that worries me," he said, pulling off his gloves. "No redness. No bumps. And no discoloration of the cervix that might indicate a pregnancy." He reached for my hand and I grasped it so he could pull me to a sitting position.

He perched on the stool. "You can come back in a week for a

follow-up blood test if you still feel concern, but the home tests are pretty accurate. Did you have a reason to think you might be pregnant?"

"I was on the shot last time I got pregnant."

"You want to try something else? There's the patch, IUDs, and diaphragms."

"I hadn't had sex for four years, so I hadn't worried about it."

He nodded, and I figured he was thinking — you picked a real winner to break your fast if you need VD screening.

"The shot is pretty good normally, but if it failed once, then there's reason for doubt. You want to try an IUD?"

"Maybe," I said. "We did add condoms."

"Condoms aren't a bad idea." He nodded at the nurse, who promptly left the room. "So, Missy said you were pretty distraught when you came in. You want to talk about it?"

"I hadn't been around stirrups in a while. Might be a bit of post-traumatic stress involved."

"Makes sense. But you know what happened to the baby was not your fault."

I couldn't meet his gaze. He had no idea.

"It's natural to think something you did caused a problem in the baby. But I assure you, it didn't."

Something cracked in me. If I couldn't tell Gavin, if I had crossed the line in the sand with him, I could still tell his man. Maybe saying the words out loud, dispersing them into the air, would release the poison.

"I smoked pot when I was pregnant."

He nodded again, no different from the gesture he'd made all along. "The whole pregnancy?"

"No, just before I found out."

"How far along were you when you stopped?"

"Seven weeks. I didn't know until then, not until I had real symptoms, since I hardly ever bled anyway."

"Smoking anything — pot or legal cigarettes — can harm the baby's lungs, but doing it that early isn't going to cause a heart defect. What did he have? Do you remember?"

"Hypoplastic left heart syndrome."

"I've never done a neonatal rotation, but I do know that heart problems are usually genetic. Did you talk to the hospital doctors about this at the time?"

I shook my head. "I didn't tell anyone. I've never told anyone."

"All these years?"

"No." My voice had lost its force, so it came out as barely a whisper.

I teetered, the room swirling, and the doctor steadied me by my shoulder. "Slow down, Corabelle. Take a deep breath in through your nose, and exhale it through your mouth."

I realized I was breathing fast. I brought it down, forcing myself to be calm.

He let me go, waited to see if I was steady, and said, "We have a speaker who comes to campus every year who talks about suicide."

"I've never been suicidal," I choked out.

"But it's her story. She lost a baby when she was seventeen. He was born and lived a few hours." He snapped his fingers. "I think she was here last night. I wonder if she's still in San Diego." He stood up. "I'm going to ask the nurses. I think you could benefit from meeting her."

I didn't want to talk to some stranger about our dead babies, but I nodded.

"I'll see what I can find out." He stood up. "Are you doing okay in school? Is this anxiety affecting your work? I can refer you to the mental health clinic. In fact, I'll write it up. You can decide if you want to use it."

"But I'm doing fine." A lie, and we both knew it.

"You are. You really are. I'll send Missy back in. We'll have the lab results back in a couple days, but I think you're fine."

He strode out, but I didn't move for a while, trying to pull myself together. When the nurse returned, I still wasn't dressed.

"So I found Tina," she said. "She's heading to the airport tonight. We were thinking —" she held on to my arm like she did before —"that maybe you could drive her out there. Give you a chance to talk. Do you have a car? Could you do that?"

My brain screamed no, but Missy looked at me with so much earnest concern that I couldn't say it.

"Okay." I didn't think I'd talk about anything important, but I could take her. Sure. Why not? If she once was suicidal, maybe there was someone out there who had a story worse than mine.

40

CORABELLE

Tina wasn't anything like I expected. She waited in the lobby of the hotel, flipping through a magazine full of glossy images of nature photographs. Missy had told me I'd know her by her tiny pigtails, coming off either side of her head like a little girl's.

She wore a short denim skirt, frayed at the bottom, and a crazy set of over-the-knee stockings with blue and black stripes. A couple mismatched suitcases sat by her legs. Her face was pixieish, and she lounged with her feet on a coffee table like she owned the place. By looking at her, you wouldn't think for a minute that anything ever got to her, but as I approached, the red jagged scars up her wrists peeked out from her sweater sleeves, which were pushed up due to the oven-roasting heat that blasted across the lobby.

I came up behind her. "Tina?"

She looked up, her gray eyes merry, but still, I could see the sadness in the corners, lines around the edges from harder days. "You must be my ride."

"I am. I'm Corabelle." I stood awkwardly behind the sofa as she gathered up her suitcases. "I can carry one of those."

"I'm good," she said. "I travel light."

We exited to the parking lot. "It's still blistering hot in Texas," she said. "I'm almost sad to be wrapping up this tour and going back."

"You in college there?"

"I'm done, actually, but I haven't found a job yet, so I kept my speaking tour going while I figure things out."

So this girl was older than me? I opened the trunk of my car for her bags, studying her. Her petite frame didn't seem sturdy enough to hoist even her smallish suitcase, but like most of us with baggage under our belt, she was tougher than she looked. "When did you graduate?" I asked.

"Just last spring." She walked around to the side door. "Finished out my internship at an art gallery over the summer, but nothing permanent has turned up."

We got inside the car. "What sort of art do you do?"

"Digital photographic manipulation. I was a black-and-white snob for the longest time, but I had to change my attitude if I wanted to get a job. I have worked for some photographers, but removing zits wasn't my thing for the long haul."

We headed out of the parking lot. "What is your thing?"

"Well, on the art side, I create fantastical images, mainly of night-sky scenes with mythical creatures, like Pegasus. Sometimes angels, if I'm feeling sentimental."

I gripped the steering wheel a little tighter, wondering if the doctor's office had told her to bring up the subject of our shared history.

"I could stick my work all over the web and sell a print here and there, but I was getting nowhere."

"What do you want to do?"

Tina settled back in her seat. "I'd love to find a sugar daddy so I could live in a mansion with a huge room full of windows and every art supply in the world, with a high-end New York gallery waiting breathlessly for my newest work."

I laughed. "I think there are dating sites to help with that."

"Don't think I haven't looked. Those millionaire types want eye candy, and these puppies take up negative space." She pointed at her chest. "Besides, I only had money for tuition or silicone. Couldn't have both."

We pulled onto the freeway and immediately got waylaid by Friday afternoon traffic. "When's your flight?" I asked.

"Not for two hours. We'll be fine. The airport's not far, right?"

"No, right on the water. If the freeway stays too jacked up, I'll take side streets."

"You must love living by the ocean," Tina said.

I swallowed hard, remembering the images Gavin and I used to draw of our school by the sea. "Growing up in New Mexico, I can definitely appreciate it."

"When did you move to California?"

"Just last year. I had to wait to be eligible for in-state tuition benefits, then I started up again."

"Ah, so this is your second college."

"Yes, I did three years at New Mexico State."

She turned to me, her pigtail smashing into the headrest. "That's unusual, leaving with only a year to go."

I shrugged. "School with a view."

We sat in silence, the knot of traffic easing forward only a few yards at a time.

"I could live here," Tina said. "This is my third time to come to UC San Diego. It's a cool campus."

"I've liked it."

"What do you study?"

"Literature."

Tina shuddered. "I'm not much for reading dead white guys."

I laughed. "It gets more diversified after high school."

"It was all so dramatic. Heathcliff. Romeo. Gatsby. Fools for love, the whole lot of them."

"You're not dating anyone then?"

"Ha!" Tina said in disgust. "My high school boyfriend ditched me in the hospital when I was in labor. By the time it was all over, premature birth, baby dying, hospital stay, go home, he'd moved out!"

My knuckles were white with my death grip on the leather wheel. "I imagine that would put you off men."

"Not right away, actually. I tried my damnedest to find a man to knock me up again."

I whipped my head around to look at her. "Really?"

"Hell yeah. I got kicked out of the pregnant-teen school and sent back to a horrid public one. Misery. They called me baby killer. When they weren't calling me a slut."

"Wow. I didn't have it nearly that bad."

"I kinda draw the foul," she said. "I was always pretty out there."

"Everyone was really nice to us. We got an apartment and everyone furnished it for us. Our whole town seemed to chip in."

She hesitated and I realized I had brought up my own pregnancy.

"Big town, small town," Tina said. "Houston wasn't kind."

The cars inched forward, and it looked like we might loosen up, but then the brake lights all lit up again. I leaned back in the seat. "I'll bail at the next exit."

"So what was your baby's name?" Tina asked.

"Finn."

"We called mine Peanut." She flipped her purse around and showed me a picture on a key chain tied to the strap. "I guess I never gave him a proper name. He was always just Peanut."

"They do sort of look like that in those early sonograms."

"Exactly. He lived for three hours."

My stomach turned. "Finn lived for seven days."

"Seven days. I can't imagine. They didn't try to save Peanut. He was too early. We just waited for his heart to stop."

My eyes burned. I was sitting right next to someone who had been through exactly what I'd been through. "We did too. We had to shut off the ventilators. He had a heart defect, and they wouldn't fix it."

"Hell of a thing, isn't it?" Tina said. "You think modern medicine knows everything but then these babies come, and they can't save them."

"I agree there." I pictured the doctors in the conference room, telling me they wouldn't operate. I'd never forget that scene, seared into my memory like a scar.

"Is that why you left school?" she asked. "The baby?"

"No. That was three years later."

"But it's related, isn't it? I find that everything goes back to the baby. Do you?"

I had to swallow hard to reply. "Yes, it was related. I — I punched my professor."

Tina's eyebrows shot up. "You did what?"

"I hit her."

"Oh my God. Why?"

"She was pregnant."

"Jesus!"

The explanation tumbled out. "She was smoking pot behind the building. I didn't even mean to really hit her. I was trying to knock the stupid joint out of her mouth." I was glad traffic had stopped because I didn't think I could navigate anymore. My vision was gray, and my head pounded with my hammering heart, thundering like a stampede.

"I assume you got arrested and expelled."

"They suggested I leave, but they didn't put it in my permanent record, at least not the parts I've seen. I had to do community service. I had to apologize."

"Shit, Corabelle. Why did her smoking get to you so bad? I mean, stupid women do it all the time."

I pictured the line in the sand and the waves crashing at my feet. I didn't answer.

"Sorry, too personal. I get it," Tina said.

"No, no. I mean, yeah. I just…" I stopped.

"So I'm guessing you feel some sort of guilt. That's natural. But you know, women smoke crack and their babies don't die."

"I smoked pot."

"I'm sure you're not the only pregnant woman to do it. Obviously your professor did."

"Finn had a heart defect."

"Did anyone say it was caused by the pot?"

"No."

"Then let it go. All the way. Otherwise you'll end up with some beauty marks like these." She held up her wrists.

I'd do anything to shift the conversation away from me. "So what happened there?"

"Oh, hell, I don't know. I mean, I do this circuit, and I say a lot of things about life getting better, and feeling suicidal isn't a failure, just a condition, one to treat and fight, not to fall prey to." She tugged her sweater sleeves over her arms. "But honestly, I did it just because I felt like I should be scarred. This big thing had happened. My baby had died, and my boyfriend had ditched me. Those things should leave a mark."

"So you made the mark yourself."

"Yes. I didn't realize at the time that these marks weren't the ones to worry about. It's the one in here." She drew an "x" over her heart. "I sabotage my own happiness a lot. It's obvious from looking at me. It's why my talks work. I swear half the people leave thinking, 'Hell, I'm not half as fucked up as her.' Whatever works."

"So you don't date?"

She shook her head. "Nope. I'll screw anything with a functioning dick. But they are out the door before the clock strikes one."

"I haven't dated either, not since Gavin left me." I paused. "Except, he's here. In San Diego. We ran into each other."

"Did you know he was here?"

"No. He walked out of the funeral and I never saw him again."

"Holy shit. I thought ditching me in the hospital was bad."

"That's pretty bad."

She laughed. "We sure can pick them, can't we? So have you talked to him?"

"He's hell-bent on us getting back together."

Tina frowned. "You going to do it?"

"I was. I have been. But then, God. He's different. I'm not sure it's a good idea."

"Did he blame you? Back then, I mean. Is that why he left?"

"He didn't know I smoked pot."

Her eyes grew wide, taking up so much of her doll-like face that she looked like one of those caricatures that artists draw of people at theme parks. "Does he now?"

I shook my head. "I can't tell him now."

"But how can you be with him if you don't? It's screwing you up, plain as day. Can you carry that secret to your grave? Should you?"

The exit was coming up and I started fighting my way over. Anger started to build. Who did she think she was, lecturing me about this? "We're nearly there," I said. "You should make the flight if security isn't long."

Tina reached over to touch my arm. "I'm sorry, Corabelle. I

don't mean to upset you. I've been in all the bad places. I remember when the blood started coming out of my arms, thinking, 'Yes, this is the right thing. I can be with my baby and no one can take him away again.' I'm not sure we ever fully recover from thinking that way. It's like we always have a last resort that's way way beyond what other people consider."

We pulled up to a red light. The signs for the airport loomed ahead. "Gavin drew a line in the sand and said we should just step over it, and let the past be the past."

"I think that's a good philosophy, if you can do it. I have the bad habit of dredging up the muck, over and over again, ad infinitum." She tugged on her stockings where they were curling at her knees. "I should stop wearing these now that I'm a proper grown-up."

"They're cute on you."

"I wore them when I was pregnant. They're like a basketball player's lucky socks. Sometimes I think a bit of Peanut is in them, since I sweated like a pig when he was cooking."

The light turned green. "We're here. I'll just pull up wherever I can find curb space. It's pretty crazy here."

"That's good. Thank you, Corabelle. I know you were probably coerced into doing this for your own good. I hope I didn't piss you off forever."

I shook my head. "Maybe you're right. Maybe I have to own up to the past after all."

"Each of us has to find our own way. I'm hoping to figure it out before I kick the bucket for real."

I had to focus for a while, dodging taxis and cars pulling out. A red truck left a gap near one of the terminals and I whipped into it.

We ducked out of the car and into the mayhem of honking cars and a stern security man blowing his whistle and smacking his hands on car hoods, making them move along. "No waiting!" he shouted. "Circle back around."

I popped the trunk so Tina could grab her bags. "Thanks again. Good luck," she said and passed me a business card. "Feel free to look me up if you need something. Not like I'm doing anything anyway."

The security guy started eyeing us, so she entered the fray heading into the terminal. I jumped back into my car and fought my way out of the curb lane.

Only after I'd gotten away from the melee and into the calm of the cars leaving the airport at a leisurely pace did I realize what had just happened. Tina had undone all of Gavin's work to make me let go of the past. If I wanted to keep him, I had to tell him what I had done.

41

GAVIN

A lone couple walked along the ocean's edge, kicking into the spray, sending water droplets flying. I banged my shoes together, knocking out the sand, wondering where Corabelle and Jenny might be. Jenny had texted me over an hour ago, simply saying, "Meet us at the end of the path between campus and the shore."

Pretty much everyone who went to UCSD knew how to access the path that cut through a swanky neighborhood and led out to the sea. Usually it was pretty busy here, being the easiest access for students living in the dorms, but the day had dawned chilly, and the winds had been howling all day. Not beach weather by any stretch.

A few seagulls circled, then flapped away as a cluster of loud teen boys jostled each other on the path through the brush, then turned to walk along the beach.

"Tell me again how she called out your name, 'Arnold, Arnold!'" A guy in a Chargers jersey shoved his friend, presumably Arnold, so hard that he stumbled into the foam.

"Damn it, now I'm wet. Asshole." Arnold leaped back onto the packed sand. "I'm totally going to interrupt your next hookup."

"You'll be waiting a long time for your revenge, my friend, a long time," said a third guy. Then their conversation was lost to distance and the crash of the waves.

Bud hadn't said a word when I took off early to meet Jenny and Corabelle. He seemed to know that if he protested, I would quit. I figured Corabelle had found out that she wasn't pregnant and was either going to blow me off or give me a friend speech. Those seemed like the only two possibilities if Jenny was coming along.

I stared at the waves and the blue-gray of the Pacific. The sand crunched behind me, and Jenny plunked down next to me, kicking her green-spandexed legs out in front of her. She looked like Kermit the frog, a fat green coat creating a bulbous torso over the spindly tights. Her hair was tied in a single pink ponytail.

"So here's the rules," she said. "I stay, but I go over there." She pointed at a rock near the edge of the underbrush. "You make her cry, you die. You get upset, you die. You do anything but show her love and understanding and unconditional lifelong groveling, you die. Are we clear?"

The girl knew how to make a point. "Clear."

She scrambled back up, and over my head she said, "Man-meat's all yours."

I turned to Corabelle, standing slightly behind me. Once again I thought of a fragile doll, sad and beautiful, every feature perfectly detailed on her face.

"Would you rather walk?" I asked.

She shook her head and sat beside me. Her arms were crossed tightly over her midsection as she huddled in an olive wool coat. Her hands were bare, pink, and looked cold. I wanted to hold them, to warm them up, but I suppressed the urge to reach for her.

"How did the doctor visit go?"

She shrugged. "I don't have the blood work back, but he seemed to think I was fine."

"Good. Do you feel better?"

"I guess so."

The seagulls returned, circling over the water in front of us. She seemed content to just sit without talking, but my anxiety rose. I wanted this bad part over, so we could get back to where we'd been.

"Corabelle, I'm sorry you found out about — the other girls, the paid girls, the way you did. I should have told you."

She drew her knees up to her chin and wrapped her arms around her legs. "That would have been an awkward conversation."

"It was past, so I left it in the past. But I should have known they'd write me eventually. It's their business."

"A business," she repeated, and I realized I was screwing up.

"I'll change my number. They won't bother me anymore. I don't want them anymore. I want you."

Her dark eyes watched me with measured calm. "You sure about that? You sure there isn't something I could do or say to change your mind?"

"No way." I gave up on resisting and moved closer, putting my arm around her shoulders.

She closed her eyes a moment. "I got arrested in New Mexico. That's why I left school."

A wave of shock coursed through me, but I kept my voice steady. "What happened?"

"I hit my professor. She was pregnant."

Damn. I squeezed her shoulders. Had she been jealous? Bitter? Regret washed away the shock. I should have been there. "Did they expel you?"

"No. I had a really good relationship with the university since I worked in the main office. They let me leave quietly."

I wanted to ask her why she'd done it, but just held on to her. She would say what she needed to say.

Corabelle looked out over the water. "She was smoking a joint behind a building on campus. I knocked it out of her mouth."

Now this made sense. "You were protecting her baby."

"Yes, but —" She silenced, her eyes following the flight of the gulls.

I waited, flirting with the idea of bringing up the line in the sand again. But that speech was self-serving. I didn't want to tell her my past, but clearly she needed to tell me hers.

"I blew up because I felt like I knew the consequences of smoking pot. People say — doctors say — it's not related, but it's hard to separate what you've done with the end result when you know you shouldn't have done it."

My arm loosened its grip on her shoulders. "Are you saying you smoked pot? With Finn?" I washed cold. When? How? I knew her so well. It wasn't possible.

"Katie thought it would help me on the SAT. I had no idea I was pregnant."

I felt Jenny's eyes on me. I kept my arm on Corabelle, trying to hold in my disbelief, my shock, my anger. I kept my voice even and steady. "So you were doing drugs while you carried my baby."

She was shaking so hard now that I could feel the movement through her coat. I withdrew my arm. "You never told me you were smoking pot. I thought we shared everything back then."

Something sparked in her, an electric charge so palpable that I could almost feel it flash through her body. "You know what, this is never going to work." She stood up. "We're both way more fucked up than we knew."

I scrambled up after her. "Obviously. You never told me any of this. Not even when he was in the hospital. Did you at least tell the doctors? Maybe they could have done something!"

"They were never going to do anything!" Corabelle's voice raised to a shriek, and out of the corner of my eye, I could see Jenny heading for us.

"You don't know that!" I dragged my hands through my hair. "Thank God I can't have kids anymore. This is way too fucked up."

Her face bloomed red. "What are you talking about?"

Now I had her attention. I loomed over her, my fury peaking so hard I could barely see her through the haze. "I had a vasectomy. So no more of my kids can get fucked up."

"Okay, that's enough." Jenny pushed at me, trying to put space between me and Corabelle, but I didn't budge.

"Why did you do that?" Corabelle's doll features contorted into something so tragic, it almost made me calm down, but hell no. She'd fucked up big time. The biggest way possible.

My fists clenched. "Because I always thought it was my fault Finn died. Because I would have been a crappy father, just like mine was. Because I signed to shut off the machines — lied even, to sign to shut them off, since we weren't married."

Jenny gave up on trying to move me and clutched Corabelle instead. "Come on, let's go," she said.

But I wasn't done. Not by a long shot. Hell, all this guilt and I wasn't the one guilty. "All these years I've been fucked up over this, and it was always YOU." My body leaned toward her, and suddenly my father flashed before me, the same pose, and now Corabelle was the young version of me, cowed, bending down to escape.

Corabelle sank back into the sand like a paper lantern collapsing. Jenny let go of her and whirled around to me. "That's enough, Gavin. Stop it now!" Her voice was a shriek. She snatched at my arm and dragged with everything she had. This time I let her take me away. I had to back off this. I had to regroup. But this was way beyond what I expected to hear from Corabelle.

Smaller birds scattered from an abandoned picnic as Jenny jerked me along the shore. "What the hell is wrong with you?" she asked. "She's trying to come clean! What happened to your unconditional love and acceptance, asshole?"

"Our kid is dead," I said, feeling the freeze come off my words.

"She didn't kill it," Jenny said. "Every doctor said it was not related."

"Then why the hell is she bringing it up?" I ran my hands through my hair and glanced down the beach. Corabelle was still huddled in the sand, rocking back and forth. I'd never seen her like that. Instantly, I wanted to go back and gather her up, hold her close, kiss it away. Damn it.

"She needed to get it out. It's what's kept her so screwed up for so long. This was the only way to fix things. The only way she could actually be with you."

Shit.

"She hurt just as much as you over that baby, probably more. So get back there and fix this." Jenny grabbed my face and made me look into her eyes. "I really couldn't give a rat's ass if she ends up with you. I don't think you're that great. But it's what she wants. And I'm helping her get what she wants."

Corabelle wanted me back. Or she had. I'd told her about the vasectomy now. We were done with secrets. I shook off Jenny's hands and we turned back to Corabelle. She was gone.

"Where is she?" I asked.

"Oh my God," Jenny said and pointed at the water.

Corabelle was heading out to sea.

42

CORABELLE

I couldn't stop thinking about what Tina said in the car yesterday, about that moment after she slashed her wrists and realized she might die.

Yes, this is the right thing. I can be with my baby and no one can take him away again.

When I stood up, I felt no hesitation whatsoever. I walked straight into the waves, shivering against the chill as the water covered my feet, soaking through my suede boots, and rising up beyond my shins, then my knees.

I stepped off some sort of ocean shelf, and the water rose to my waist. My coat soaked through and became heavier, pulling me down.

I held my breath in my most familiar way, still walking, picturing Finn in his little isolette, the disks on his chest and the ventilator going into his mouth. An oscillator, I remembered suddenly. They'd put him on the oscillator at the end, when he had too many apnea episodes. That's when he stopped moving around, medically paralyzed. Lost. When they decided not to operate.

Because he couldn't breathe.

I wouldn't breathe either.

The water crossed my neck and I saw the familiar spots fill my vision. I thought I heard Gavin's voice, but maybe it was Finn's. Maybe where he was now, he could talk, no tube in his throat. He'd never cried. I'd never heard his voice. But he'd sound like his dad.

Gavin had taken away all our choices. No more babies. No more babies with me. Life without Gavin hadn't worked. Life without Finn wasn't worth it.

My lungs began to heave, but I was already under by then. I tried to relax into the darkness, like I had in the bathtub, but the water wasn't warm, freezing cold instead, and the chill kept forcing me to gasp. I bobbed to the surface, and my body took a breath. Damn it. It wouldn't work. I couldn't do it.

I turned in the water, fighting against the coat. Jenny was on the shore, her mouth open, screaming. Gavin was nowhere, gone now, gone for good. I held my breath and exhaled, sinking below the surface of the water. Maybe it would work this time.

My boots touched bottom and I stood at the foot of the world, descending into hell, except everything was so cold. My lungs began to burn, throbbing with the need for air. I found another small bit to exhale, and relaxed into it. I began to curve in upon myself, drawing up my knees like a fetus, like Finn. I would get to see Finn.

The earth shifted around me, cradling my body in its watery embrace. I moved through the waves, one with the ocean, and now I felt no pain whatsoever.

Until a bright light seared through my eyelids. Air shocked my senses and I was brutally cold.

"Help me get her out!" a voice said, and I realized it was Gavin. I tried to open my eyes, but they didn't obey. My lungs hurt, pain beyond any measure I had known.

My head clunked against something hard, and now my body

heaved upward. Strong arms turned me on my side and I felt an eruption within me, the ocean spewing from my chest and out my mouth and nose.

"Call 911 just in case," Gavin said.

"I already did."

I began to recognize my various body parts, hair on my face, layered with sand. My cheek, gritty and half buried. My bare feet, painfully cold. My entire midsection quaked, heavy with the coat.

"She's breathing now," Gavin said.

I opened my eyes, but the light blasted through my head, and I had to close them again.

"Corabelle?" Gavin's voice made me think of some other time, some other memory. He was ten years old and his face was pressed against my window screen.

I crawled out of bed and walked over, my sleepiness dissolving at the distress I could hear.

"Corabelle?" he asked again.

"What's wrong?" I asked.

"Can I come in here?"

I glanced back at my open door and hurried across the room to close it. When I came back, he'd pried the screen off.

"Did something happen?" I asked.

He didn't answer, but when his face turned, the moonlight revealed a red welt across his cheek. I laid my palm against it. "What did he do?"

"I deserved it. I forgot to close the garage. The dog got out and dug up Mom's flowers." He pressed his hand over mine. "I got away from him."

"We should tell somebody," I said. "He shouldn't do that."

"Just let me stay here," he said. "He won't come for me over here."

I led him over to my bed and we sat down. "Did he hit your

sister?"

Gavin shook his head. "He says it's wrong to hit a girl."

I gathered him in my arms and put my head on his shoulder. "I want you to live with me."

"Me too," he said.

"Promise me we'll do that. Live together."

He squeezed me. "We will. I promise."

The sand had gotten in my teeth, making my mouth taste like dirt. I tried to spit it out.

"I think she's okay," Gavin said.

"EMS is coming," Jenny said.

Something moved under my head, soft and warm. I tried opening my eyes again and this time they accepted the sun. I saw nothing but green. Jenny's coat.

"Corabelle? Can you say something?" Jenny's face was inches from mine, black mascara streaking down her cheeks.

"You look terrible," I said.

She managed to laugh and cry at the same time. "You look worse." She glanced behind me.

"Was it Gavin?" I asked.

She nodded.

I shifted onto my back. Gavin leaned over me, water dripping off his face. "You scared me there for a minute."

"Just for a minute?"

He smiled, but his eyes were still full of fear. "If a minute lasts sixty-seven years."

"I think I'm going to need some help," I said. "Real help."

He closed his hands over mine. "We'll get it for you. We'll figure this out."

We. He still said *we*.

Footsteps approached at a run. "Is this her?" a loud voice asked.

"She's conscious now," Gavin said.

"How long was she in?"

"A few minutes."

Two men lifted me onto a stretcher, forcing me to let go of Gavin's hand.

"Do you know her?" one of the medics asked.

Gavin looked down at me. "She's the mother of my son."

"Then you can come with us."

One of the medics flashed a light in my eyes. "Can you tell us your name, miss?"

"Corabelle," I said.

The medic nodded at the other, and suddenly I was moving. Jenny held her coat, rooted to the sand, growing smaller as we rushed down the beach. Gavin kept up.

We got to the ambulance, and the medics paused while one opened the door. Something fluttered next to my head, and I turned to it. A monarch butterfly fought against the wind, sailing forward, then getting pushed back again. The next gale sent it straight into Gavin's chest.

Gavin stared down at the butterfly, flapping against his wet jacket.

"It's Finn, isn't it?" I asked.

"Has to be."

The butterfly paused for another moment, showing off its black and orange wings, then flew back into the wind. The medics lifted me into the ambulance and started peeling off my coat. "Blankets behind you," one said to Gavin. "You might want to get your coat off too."

He took my temperature. "You're very lucky. Not everybody who gets sucked into the Pacific wearing something like this comes back out breathing. People don't realize how a coat can weigh you down. How did you end up in there?"

I glanced up at Gavin and decided not to answer. I could tell a social worker, or not. Take the doctor's mental health clinic referral, or not. Those were decisions for another time. Gavin had said we'd figure it out. We'd saved each other time and time again. I had faith that whenever one of us needed rescue, the other would always be there.

THE END

Also by Deanna Roy

Stella & Dane: Stella is ready to blow out of her honky tonk town when a hot stranger rolls in on a Harley, leading to a dangerous romance that upsets the locals and sparks a tragedy that will change everyone's lives. (New Adult Romance)

Baby Dust. Abandoned by friends and haunted by what they've lost, five women forge friendships to survive the death of their babies. (Women's Fiction)

About Deanna Roy

Deanna is a passionate advocate for women who have miscarried. She founded the web site www.pregnancyloss.info in 1998 after the loss of her first baby and continues to run both online and in-person support groups for women who have endured this impossible loss. Find her on Facebook, Twitter, and Goodreads.

Learn more about the author at
www.deannaroy.com

Your review on Amazon is appreciated—it makes a huge difference to authors when readers provide their reactions to a work.

Acknowledgements

So many people have been instrumental along my baby loss journey, the founding of www.pregnancyloss.info, the writing of my first book *Baby Dust*, and now, this book *Forever Innocent*. It would be hard to list them all.

Some standouts:

My husband **Kurt**, who saw me through some really dark moments this last year when we learned we would not be able to have children. This is the book, baby! Let's raise that adoption money!

Chrissie and Kristin — I swear I'm going to fly around the world and meet you two. You are my TEAM, and I know somewhere, those babies of ours are cooking up trouble on some heavenly playground.

Robyn Bear. You are a spectacular example of turning tragedy into a life's work. Because of you, millions of women light candles on October 15. I can't believe I finally got to meet you, and you were as amazing as I always knew you to be online.

Mimi Strong. If I ever sell more than five copies of this book, I'm going to owe it to you! You are my role model, and Canada is on my fly-around-the-world agenda!

Dr. Marco Uribe. You know, I adore how I can go in for two icky surgeries this year, and still, all we talk about are the women on my web site, and you're scribbling notes to me about new diagnosis and treatments to tell them about in case their doctors haven't thought of it. Seriously — the day in 1995 that the receptionist set me up with an appointment with you instead of the doctor I asked for is one of the luckier days of my life. Of all the faces that have changed in these almost twenty years (even husbands!), yours has remained the same. I am grateful.

Jamie and Annie and the Face to Face Austin support group. Your stories always remind me of how important it is to keep up this work, even though my own body parts aren't functioning anymore. Know that I keep all of your babies very close to my heart.

My best friend and author **John J Asher**. Your writing inspires me, your friendship and daily pep talks keep me going. You are a treasure. Catfish Parlour should set aside a booth just for us!

Always, love to the **Austin Java Writing Company**. Wine, writing time, and friendship. All the things that make the perfect group.

My critique buddies **Darrell Bryant** and **Melanie Typaldos**. You read my work and help make it better even when it's a genre you'd never ever read otherwise.

Two amazing **NICU nurses Stacie SB and Audrey W**. Thank you for reading the medical sections of the book and keeping me straight.

I want to send out love and light to **all the babies I've photographed in NICUs**, and whose lives I documented, either to your happy release home, or to the peaceful end. You live in my heart.

In Memory of These Babies

- Gabriel Daniel Kemper ~ 2012
- Corabelle Victoria ~ 2012
- Bo Ortiz ~ 2012
- Rory Dick ~ 2012
- Aaron Christopher Miner ~ 2010
- Keira Marie Jurofcik ~ 2006
- Wesley Kennedy ~ 2001
- Melody Antonia ~ 1996
- Joshua Antony ~ 2005
- Sophie Angharad ~ 2006
- Christian ~ 2004
- Meredith ~ 2005
- Baby Boo G ~ 2004
- Baby Gummy N ~ 2011
- Baby Bear N ~ 2012
- Cara Jace ~ 2012
- Baby Marenic ~ 2010
- George Frederick
- Louis Marenic ~ 2012
- Baby Angel High ~ 2012
- AnaLeigh Grace Allin ~ 2012
- AmyLee Nicole Allin ~ 2013
- Hunter Louis Fratangeli ~ 2009
- Gabrielle Katherine ~ 2013
- Baby Angel Woehler ~ 2013
- Baby Angel 2 Woehler ~ 2013
- Baby Angel Hayleigh Sue ~ 2011
- Angel Marie Oliver ~ 2002
- Devan Michael Oliver ~ 2006
- Jeremiah Logan Oliver ~ 2007
- Taylor April Hall ~ 2012
- Tobiah Jesse Hall ~ 2012
- Rylie Kerby ~ 2013
- Rylan Kerby ~ 2013
- Jamison Nathan Monse-Perez ~ 2012
- Gabriel Lee Mousel ~ 2011
- Madeline LeAnne Teitsort ~ 2012
- M M Beurkens-Bakker ~ 2012
- Kaylise Campbell ~ 2011
- Kailena Campbell ~ 2011
- Kinston McLendon ~ 2011
- John Anthony Perlicki, Jr. ~ 2011
- Hope ~ 2011
- Saphire ~ 2009
- Katie-Jayde Scott ~ 2011
- Connor Scott ~ 2009
- Morton babies ~ 1989 x 2, 1990 x 2, 1991, 2004
- Ali baby ~ 2011
- Adrian Angel Couture ~ 1997
- Taylor Angel Couture ~ 1999
- Jake Burmeister ~ 2012
- Baby Esparza Castaneda ~ 2012
- Coralie ~ 2011
- 5 Villegas Sweet Angels ~ 2010-2012
- Charlie Suffolk ~ 2003
- The Cloke Triplets: Cadyn Joseph, Adalyn Grace, and Mikayla Michelle ~ 2011
- Elkins twins angels ~ 2008
- Abigail Bethany ~ 2011
- Baby Hammett ~ 2012
- Bentlee Talon Avery ~ 2012
- Reeselyn Kazuko Okuda ~ 2011
- 4 Renshaw angel babies 2004-2012
- Anna Tornes ~ 2012
- Ashton Paul Alvarez ~ 1995
- Jayden Lee Beale ~ 2008
- Angel Baby Andrews
- Mary Catherine Fassler ~ 2004
- Genevieve Clark ~ 2010
- Angel Baby Kozera ~ 2011
- Erin Maya Thompson ~ 2011
- Payslie Elva Deges ~ 2011
- Baby Angel Smart ~ 2012
- Taylor Sharitt ~ 2009
- Danny Bowser ~ 2013
- 5 Ash Mahmood Angels ~ 2009-2012
- Barcenas Baby Angel Boy #1 ~ 2010
- Barcenas Baby Angel Girl #2 ~ 2010
- Barcenas Baby Angel Boy #3 ~ 2011
- Yaretzi Estephania Barcenas ~ 2012
- The 6 Bear Babies ~ 1997-1999
- Rio Carmichael ~ 2012
- Aeden Archer Adriano ~ 2012
- Shaniyah Elaine Kendrix ~ 2009
- Kharisma Dawn Campbell ~ 2013
- Chibby Ferguson ~ 2012
- Sweet baby boy Kolton Anderson ~ 2013
- Samuel David Givan ~ 2010
- Lillian Carell Givan ~ 2011
- Olivia Dawn Givan ~ 2013
- Baby Castillo ~ 2012
- Baby Sawyer ~ 2012
- Baby Angel Rayborn #1 ~ 2012
- Baby Angel Rayborn #2 ~ 2012
- Baby Angel Rayborn #3 ~ 2012
- Joy Clemensen ~ 2002
- Briley Bennett ~ 2012
- Lillian Marie Rains ~ 2003
- Estella Noel Rains ~ 2007
- Linkin Wes Rains ~ 2008
- Adley Rose Miller ~ 2011
- Angel Baby Shaw-Mobbs ~ 2012
- Elijah Enoch ~ 2010
- Elijah John ~ 2008
- Charlotte Lillian ~ 2010
- Xaviar John ~ 2013
- Naomi Esther K. ~ 2011
- Gabriel Kelley ~ 2012
- William Scott Smith ~ 2011
- Emmanuella Pirie ~ 2012
- Angel Mary Blanchette ~ 1971

Forever Innocent

- Amanda Bailey Summers ~ 2013
- Reagan Skye Summers ~ 2013
- Calvin Abbott ~ 2002
- Little Angel ~ 2005
- Little Cougar ~ 2005
- Angel baby Harris ~ 2013
- Bretton-Elijah Lucas Roberts ~ 1996
- Ciara-Rose Kennedi Roberts ~ 1998
- 6 precious & tiny Roberts babies ~ 1988-2010
- Baby Angel Saenz ~ 2013
- Keira Marie Jurofcik ~ 2006
- Daniel Joaquin Gonzales ~ 2010
- Madelyn Lorene Crabtree ~ 2010
- Adam Ray ~ 2010
- Faith Ann Ray ~ 2011
- William Stimpel the 5th ~ 2012
- Baby Maze ~ 2013
- Matix James ~ 2011
- Niko Joseph Moores ~ 2013
- Jaxson Christopher Sanchez ~ 2011
- Baby Amilia Mary-ann Barber ~ 2011
- Preston James Skilbeck ~ 2006
- Brayden B. Buntemeyer ~ 2011
- Scarlett C. ~ 2013
- Elijah John ~ 2008
- Valerie Raeann ~ 2008
- Dylan Joseph Bernard ~ 2001
- Emily Claire Alton ~ 2008
- Matthew Ryan Shipman ~ 1996
- Baby Hunter ~ 2013
- Karissa Tarkington ~ 2013
- Angel Baby K ~ 2008
- Amy Heather Mandelbaum ~ 1977
- Ethan Thomas Ford ~ 2013
- Luis Bolivar ~ 2011
- Becca Bolivar ~ 2011
- Kylee Raelynn Marie ~ 2010
- Jaimee-Rose. C ~ 2012
- Dayton Asher Standridge ~ 2012
- Brynnleigh Erin Clary ~ 2011
- Charlie Stanley Iewer ~ 2006
- Soleil Jolie Ramirez ~ 2008
- Kylee Raelynn Marie ~ 2010
- Sawyer Joshua Murphy ~ 2013
- Giselle Genevieve Holliday-Bruton~2013
- Mollie Christina ~ 2004
- Amira Justina-Marie Hites ~ 2010
- Chaos David-Michael Hites ~ 2011
- Nicholas Gordon Thomas Farr ~ 2010
- Xoe-Lei Clementine Steele ~ 2012
- Amy Marie Shepherd ~ 2000
- Baby Stephen ~ 2013
- Landon James Cherrone ~ 2012
- Lily J. Carpenter ~ 2004
- Angel Walker ~ 2005
- Kyndall Jones ~ 2013
- Justice Michael Harrison ~ 2011
- Baby Harrison ~ 2011
- Babies Field ~ 2003, 2008
- Bailey Jay Wilson ~ 1999
- Brasha Chantell Chandler ~ 1997
- Marissa Dawn Shipp ~ 1977
- Colton Michael ~ 2000
- Kamryn ~ 2002
- Matthew Edward Jr ~ 2009
- Cassandra Elizabeth Goldyn ~ 1999
- Baby Goldyn 1997,1998, 2001
- Baby Angel Gabriel ~ 2011
- Isaac Aaron ~ 2008
- Isaiah Aaron ~ 2008
- Twins Mark and Darryn Harris ~ 2008
- Addison Lovely ~ 2011
- Jayden Michael Stephenson ~ 2006
- Silas Hunter Beck ~ 2011
- Journey ~ 2011
- Jacques David ~ 2009
- Alexandra Helene Biek ~ 2005
- Dakota & Dylan Muzzi ~ 1997
- Noah Muzzi ~ 1998
- Quaid Keith Kleckner ~ 2012
- Jáqnel Alexander Rivera ~ 2012
- Sachelys Michelle Rivera ~ 2002
- Nevaeh Ángel ~ 2009
- Silas Hunter Beck ~ 2011
- Journey ~ 2011
- Amanda Rae ~ 9/8/1982
- Cassie Alexandra Kay Maron ~ 2005
- Violet Novemeber ~ 2011
- 4 Ember angels ~ 2012-2013
- Amiel Baydon Clark ~ 2005
- Alexander Ashley E. ~ 2009
- Tatianna Jeney E. ~ 2003
- Baby Angel Sica ~ 2011
- John Allen Abbott Jr ~ 2009
- Zeni Lynn Abbott ~ 2013
- Kathryn Grace Newell Sherbondy~2011
- Dominick Carter ~ 2010
- Erin Christine Yee ~ 2004
- Baby Angel Yee ~ 2012
- Trevor M. ~ 2011
- Baby Ward twins ~ 2013
- Baby Ward ~ 2013
- Xavier Ahren ~ 2006
- February ~ 2007
- Tristan Alexander ~ 2008
- Chloe Morgan Phillips ~ 1999
- Carolyn Rose O'Steen ~ 2013
- Caleb James Brafford ~ 2012
- Baby Santos ~ 2008
- Tatum Isabella Drews ~ 2012
- Breanna Lynn Boyer ~ 2011
- Nora Elizabeth Grothe ~ 2001
- Mackenzie Grothe ~ 1996
- Peyton and Jamie Grothe ~ 1996
- Angel Hannah Elizabeth ~ 2007
- Chloe' ~ 2005
- Paige & Angel (twins) ~ 2006
- Mark Jnr ~ 2007
- Baby Raisin ~ 2013
- Buck baby ~ 2003
- Buck baby ~ 2004

Angels

Deanna Roy

- Caitlin Elisabeth Baker ~ 2009
- Brooke McKenzie Bunasky ~ 2006
- Tessa Marie Sale ~ 2009
- Baby Harris ~ 2010
- Lucah Brayson Clark ~ 2010
- Baby Drumheller ~ 2012
- mc ~ 2012
- Angel Baby Strader ~ 1999
- Legacy Thunder Lee ~ 2007
- Spencer Lee Nash ~ 2004
- Finely Storm Nash ~ 2000
- Peyton Reese Nash ~ 1993
- Baylee Jordan Nash ~ 1992
- Amber Skye Pixley ~ 2013
- Justin LaFette ~ 2010
- 4 Lil Cowboy/Cowgirl Angels 1996-2008
- Alexis Rose Lashbrook ~ 2006
- Sophia Anne Spear ~ 2012
- Baby Angel Spear ~ 2011
- Brianna Marie Dille ~ 1999
- Baby Rust ~ 2010
- Ashley Grace Lechtrecker ~ 2010
- Shawn Douglas Duncan ~ 2004
- Cameron Marie Duncan ~ 2005
- Baby Liam Patrick ~ 2006
- Liam David ~ 2011
- 5 McBride babies ~ 2000-2004
- Jordan Lynn ~ 2005
- Baby Campbell ~ 2002
- Lyric ~ 2012
- Alexis Jade Holliday ~ 2005
- Colton Thomas Oursler ~ 2012
- 18 Holliday angels 1995-2003
- Rhys Martyn Burn ~ 2003
- 11 Baby Burn Angels ~ 2002-2013
- Noah Joel Hoyt ~ 2008
- Alexander Michael Sawyer-Sullivan ~ 2007
- Adam James Atkinson ~ 2009
- Conner ~ 2011
- Zackary Allen Gehring ~ 2010
- Olivia Madilynn DeBouver ~ 2011
- Asher James DeBouver ~ 2012
- Spencer Douglas Dyess ~ 2005
- Mattie Bell Horton ~ 2004
- Johnnie Iaun ~ 1992
- Crystal-Lee ~ 2010
- Baby Angel Davis ~ 2003
- Kamryn Davis ~ 2005
- Angel Edward ~ 2012
- Payslee Lynn Busler ~ 2012
- Sierra Jean Harris ~ 1999
- Alyssa Rita Mendoza ~ 2008
- Aubrey Rebecca Faith Hammond~2012
- Tyson Angelo Cortes ~ 2004
- Ethan Thomas Leavitt ~ 2012
- Elise Corinne Leavitt ~ 2013
- Jeremiah Zachary Young ~ 2010
- Corbin Westin Wilson ~ 2010
- 4 Wilson babies 2004-2008
- Katherine Jane ~ 2010
- Amelia Grace Kniskern ~ 2013
- Parker William Novac ~ 2009
- Alexis Jade Holliday ~ 2005
- Colton Thomas Oursler ~ 2012
- Holliday babies ~ 1995-22003
- Parker William Novac ~ 2009
- Zarah Catherine Ann ~ 2011
- Seraphina Rose ~ 2008
- Emma Kate ~ 2004
- Abraham Arthur Abergel ~ 1967
- Cameron Matthew Wesley ~ 1974
- Erin Aileen Wesley ~ 1975
- Justin Eric Tingler ~ 2005
- Sawyer Noreen Stish ~ 2009
- Zen William ~ 2004
- Elijah Jerome Stinson ~ 2006
- Quinten Howard ~ 2007
- Baby Kevin Pino ~ 2005
- Baby Bertin ~ 2011
- Franklin Joseph Riley ~ 2008
- Daniel Barton Riley ~ 2011
- Thomas-James Chipp ~ 2006
- Heaven Lee Hayes ~ 2010
- Alijah Shayne Wilhelm ~ 2011
- Aaliyah Kristine Wilhelm ~ 2011
- Amanda Ruth Riley ~ 1977
- Baby Faith Riley ~ 2008
- Ella Marie Petiniot ~ 2009
- Angel Baby Nemecek ~ 1996
- Angel Baby Nemecek ~ 1998
- Carter Issac Tucker ~ 2011
- Alfie Jason Stephen Allen ~ 2008
- Joyce Jamielynn Mikesell ~ 2005
- Parker Arden Schroeder ~ 2013
- Baby Schroeder ~ 2013
- Dalton Jay Schuster ~ 2007
- Shayna Grace Schuster ~ 2008
- Emma Lindsay Warch ~ 2008
- Baby Warch ~ 2009
- Hayden Trent ~ 2004
- Jordan Jared Davis ~ 2009
- Drew Connor Junod ~ 2005
- DrewAnne Lillie ~ 2005
- Andrew & Quinn (Twins) ~ 2007
- Ella Grace Spalding ~ 2011
- Alex Ember Spalding ~ 2006
- Hope Suzanne ~ 2012
- Dylan Joseph Carr ~ 2010
- Hannah Marie Carr ~ 2011
- Dreyton ~ 2009
- Connor Rion Ikemeyer ~ 2010
- Ethan Audain ~ 2006
- Baby Angelo ~ 2009
- Ariel Marie Suddarth ~ 1996
- Baby Baumann ~ 2005
- Elijah John Williams
- LilyAnna Tamatha Klingle ~ 2007
- Kaitlyn Marie Engness ~ 2006
- Baby Brayden Josiah Swett ~ 2012
- Elijah John williams ~ 2009
- Baby Boy Lauer ~ 2012

Angels

Forever Innocent

- Carly Elia ~ 2009
- Baby Holden ~ 2009
- Tyran Kyle Ireland ~ 2004
- Callum&Kye Manley ~ 1998
- Brianna Ruth Falkner ~ 2008
- Steele Edwin Carpenter ~ 2012
- Morgan Carpenter ~ 2012
- Baby Rivera ~ 2009
- Baby Knapp ~ 2013
- Faith Marie E. ~ 2004
- Aidan Jonathan ~ 2009
- 2 Evarts angels ~ 2007-2008
- Kerri Reynolds ~ 1992
- Journey Alcala' ~ 2012
- Rance Wade Leighton ~ 2007
- Braylon & Myles ~ 2009
- Atticus Erin Rubiss ~ 2011
- C.E. Rubiss ~ 2012
- Briar Kiku Rubiss ~ 2012
- Riot Alexis Rubiss ~ 2013
- Liam Garrett Duthie ~ 2013
- Nehemiah Martinez ~ 2009
- Malachi Martinez ~ 2009
- Eden Martinez ~ 2010
- Meilee Gailann Spurlock ~ 2013
- Lily Katherine Allen-Ball ~ 2010
- Luke Shiloh Allen ~ 2009
- Weston Dradan Kester ~ 2006
- Landen French ~ 2009
- Zoe Eileen Alonzo ~ 2009
- Hunter Breinlinger ~ 2013
- Deacon Alexander ~ 2013
- Justice John Joesph Soulliere ~ 2007
- Angel Baby Soulliere ~ 2010
- Angel Baby Kelly ~ 2010
- Angel Baby Wallace ~ 2012
- Erika Elizabeth Derr ~ 2012
- Casey Derr ~ 2013
- Gabriel William Costello ~ 2010
- Mary Patricia Costelli ~ 2012
- Samuel Peter Costello ~ 2013
- Mason Riley Brotherton ~ 2013
- Jacob Alexander Villalva ~ 2010
- Lily Grace Villalva ~ 2013
- Ava Victoria Capoccioni ~ 2011
- Patrick Mclean Cupit II ~ 2010
- Brianna Elise Farnsworth ~ 2011
- Trista Joy Booth ~ 2007
- Jaydon Wayne Smith ~ 2009
- Kerry Wayne Whitlow ~ 1964
- Spencer John ~ 2013
- Angel Baby Duke ~ 1999
- Angel Baby Kring ~ 2006
- Charles Lee Belcher ~ 1964
- Sophia Marilyn Seymour ~ 2013
- 5 Seymour angels ~ 2008-2012
- Michaela Jane Orbacz ~ 2012
- Taylor Marie Kent ~ 2009
- Zaylee Rayne Collins ~ 2010
- Jocelyn Rose Lahr ~ 2011
- Michaela Jane Orbacz ~ 2012
- Baby Beavers ~ 2007
- Michaela Louise Buck ~ 1994
- Ava Lily Talbot ~ 2012
- Thomas and Homer Mason ~ 2004
- Seve Mason ~ 2010
- Andrew Milan Martin ~ 2013
- Penelope Anne Miller ~ 2013
- Paige Nicole Ivey ~ 2009
- Alex Richard Long ~ 1990
- Nicky ~ 1990
- Katie Long ~ 1998
- Skyler Raine Roberts ~ 2012
- Beatrix Elizabeth ~ 2010
- Baby Angel Ramirez-Postigo ~ 2012
- Aria Carmen ~ 2013
- Baby Kory Magyar ~ 2008
- Angel Baby Magyar ~ 2011
- Astrid "A.J." Magyar ~ 2012
- 7 Angel Babies ~ 2001-2005
- Nadia Love Komakhuk ~ 2009
- Haven Lael A. ~ 2012
- Angel Casey Chapman ~ 2007
- Angel Kellie Chapman ~ 2007
- Angel Jordan Chapman ~ 2008
- Erica Ann ~ 2009
- Lily Rose Carney ~ 2007
- Mason Robert Dey ~ 2013
- Angel Cristian Gutierrez ~ 2011
- Wyatt Nathaniel Finchum ~ 2009
- Carter Hagenow ~ 2008
- Amanda Grace Sanchez ~ 2003
- Wyatt Nathaniel Finchum ~ 2009
- Aimee-Sara Egan ~ 1984
- Jarrett Lee Frye ~ 2001
- Justice Ray Frye ~ 2005
- 5 Kaltenbach babies
- Andrew William Schmidt ~ 1999
- Dawson Samuel Badger ~ 2002
- Benjamin Andrew Russell ~ 2012
- Lydi Ann ~ 2009
- Baby Angel Prohinsie ~ 2006
- William Richard Prohinsie ~ 2007
- Isaac Christian ~ 2013
- Brianna Dawn ~ 2008
- Tanner Eugene Richards ~ 2012
- Andrew Darryl Ross ~ 1997
- Kendrick Evan ~ 2001
- Elijah D ~ 2006
- Jellybean Bradford ~ 2009
- Bradford Angel ~ 2009
- Blueberry Bradford ~ 2012
- Herrmann baby ~ 2005
- Baby Jane Kelly ~ 1996
- Sweet Jeremiah Shepherd ~ 2012
- Hannah Faith Moore ~ 2012
- Baby triplets Aurora, Jackson and Alexander Green ~ 2011
- Hudson Levi Snell ~ 2010
- Hannah Faith Alley ~ 2009
- Joey Q. ~ 2010
- Baby angel Dietz ~ 2006

Angels

Deanna Roy

- Baby angel boy Dietz ~ 2006
- AnnMarie JoLynn Dietz ~ 2009
- Jacob Lambert ~ 2006
- Erica Lynn Williams ~ 1982
- Jade Hearty ~ 1989
- Sam Hearty ~ 1993
- Jordon Cally Kinniburgh ~ 1991
- Camdyn David Bangart ~ 2013
- Isabella Grace Harmon ~ 2012
- Mason Barnard ~ 2006
- Jessica Skye Sylvester ~ 2010
- Bub Sylvester ~ 2012
- Harley Kayleen Carson ~ 2009
- Avery Diane Hanson ~ 2012
- Carleigh McKenna Haas ~ 2009
- Jordan Leigh Haas ~ 2002
- Collin James ~ 2010
- Baby Charmian Bone ~ 2013
- Baby Lyra Flynn ~ 2013
- Baby Chloe Jordaan ~ 2004
- Baby Lewis Ham ~ 2009
- Kaleb Lee S. ~ 2008
- Baby Angel Stegaman ~ 2012
- Deshaun Ray ~ 2006
- 2 Crystal babies ~ 2010-2013
- Scarlette Marie Lynch ~ 2011
- Lil Lynch ~ 2012
- Wade Albert Smith Jr. ~ 1983
- 4 Butterfly Babies ~ 2008-2011
- Gabriel Joshua Smith ~ 2012
- Alexander Robert Smith ~ 2013
- Liam Jason Creegan ~ 2012
- Aamber L. Peugh ~ 2011
- Jenna Grace Liles ~ 2011
- Isabelle Louise Hutchens ~ 2012
- Peyton Arnold ~ 1987
- Riley Arnold ~ 1987
- Michael Thomas Waldron ~ 2012
- 3 Waldron angels, 2010-2013
- Mason Alexander Wallace ~ 2013
- Oliver Franklin Conkle ~ 2011
- Anna Caroline Flores ~ 2004
- Matthew Joseph Flores ~ 2006
- Ileana Marie Owen ~ 2012
- Shianne Michelle Greene ~ 1999
- Khyre Leelynn Kintay Boyd ~ 2013
- Parker Benjamin Papcke ~ 2010
- Jacob Paul Lee Winter ~ 2002
- Hadley Aryn Bergey ~ 2010
- Xavier Ian Swords ~ 2009
- Owen Robert Balda ~ 2010
- Seth Josiah Schamburg ~ 2012
- Abiageal Grace Dwyer ~ 2009
- Olivia Jane ~ 2007
- Austin Lee Otts ~ 1992
- Carlos Carrasco ~ 2013
- Skylar Nicholas Wachsmuth ~ 2001
- Camden Marshall Haun ~ 2013
- Jacob Ryder ~ 2013
- Nathan Fuller ~ 1993
- Logan Simmons ~ 2010
- Brandon Wilson ~ 2009
- Heaven Wilson ~ 2010
- 2 Baby Wilson's ~ 2004-2010
- Jonathan Taylor LeRoy Cash Redhouse ~ 2003
- Baby Redhouse ~ 2001
- Bryson Eugene Smolinski ~ 2008
- Payton Virginia Smolinski ~ 2008
- Scarboro Angel ~ 1987
- Brown Angel ~ 2008
- Brown Angel ~ 2009
- Florence Valentine Dallison ~ 2009
- Katelyn Miriam Matthews ~ 2000
- Angel baby Burke ~ 2005
- Angel baby Burke ~ 2006
- Angel baby Kruse ~ 2008
- Baby angel Glasstetter ~ 2009
- Seth Edward Johnson ~ 2001
- Baby Ava Kristine ~ 2013
- Angel Baby Mathews ~ 2013
- JesseJames Castro Ignacio ~ 2012
- Abel ~ 2013
- Trinity Hope Burough ~ 1996
- Isreal Jorden Burough ~ 2012
- Max Joshua Truman Kajma ~ 2008
- Ashtyn Leroy Holcombe ~ 2013
- Dresdin Rosaire Phillips ~ 2012
- Kyler & Krischan Thibodeaux ~ 2002
- Owen Nelson Osbaldiston ~ 2012
- Samuel Ray Vargas ~ 2011
- Raymond Russell Mack ~ 2010
- Spencer Hargove ~ 1998
- Emma Nerisse Lucas ~ 1988
- James "Jamey" Robert Shish Jr. ~ 2013
- Madyson Alaina Morales ~ 2010
- Baby Rivera ~ 1990
- Baby Casper ~ 2012
- Angelina Marie ~ 1986
- Baby Angel ~ 1987
- Linkon Albert Meyer ~ 2012
- Isabelle Grace F. ~ 2005
- Jeremiah Alan Stewart ~ 1980
- Baby Leo ~ 2013
- Ellisyn Rae Nunn ~ 2012
- Samantha Lynn Phillips ~ 1995
- Arabella Marie Thomas ~ 2012
- Elizabeth Michelle Hamburg ~ 2006
- Dylan Henry Denbin ~ 2011
- Evan August Riebeling ~ 2008
- Jordan Graeme Kai Dobbin ~ 2007
- Angel Baby Letzkus ~ 2006
- Alyana Karley ~ 2013
- Jack ~ 1967
- Raelynn Marie ~ 2011
- Our Eight Wingham-Sherrell Angel Babies ~ 1999-2012
- Gabrial ~ 2011
- Darby Grace Worrell ~ 2013
- Noel Basey ~ 2010
- Jayden Basey ~ 2011
- Declan Ty Gregory Basey ~ 2012

Angels

Forever Innocent

- Noah Aaron Emmanuel Alcorn ~ 2012
- John Joseph ~ 1999
- Grace Angelica ~ 1999
- Mary Anne ~ 2004
- Grace Brown ~ 2011
- Kalani Faith Brown ~ 2013
- Donnell Jr ~ 2010
- Leonidas ~ 2013
- Kashes William Karch ~ 2013
- Jewel Leeann Boswell ~ 2008
- Jeremiah Joseph Boswell ~ 2009
- Eudora Rose Boswell ~ 2010
- Lily Ann Boswell ~ 2011
- Harper Lynn Graham ~ 2013
- Nathan Joseph Mccumbee ~ 2007
- Baby angel ~ 1997
- Emily Rose Anthony ~ 2000
- Jasmine Mariah Anthony ~ 2003
- Nicholas P. Auclair ~ 2001
- Roseanna Robison ~ 2006
- Ethan David Robison
- Leah Elizabeth P. ~ 2013
- Anthony Israel Uy ~ 2008
- Christian Allen Morrison ~ 2011
- Baby Morrison ~ 2010
- Paityn Lilee Ladner ~ 2010
- Megan Marie Blazek ~ 2007
- Tucker William Mills ~ 2013
- Andrew Douglas Cannon ~ 2011
- Lily Abigail Cannon ~ 2010
- Angel Cannon ~ 2004
- 3 unnamed Cannon angels ~ 1995-2011
- Baby "Biscuit" Himes ~ 2011
- Alessandra Love Campa ~ 2011
- Angel Reed ~ 2012
- Baby Girl ~ 2008
- Andrew William Schmidt ~ 1999
- William Bert ~ 2012
- Annabelle Rae Croghan ~ 2010
- Gracie Iris Moran ~ 2012
- Donovan Ace Mount ~ 2009
- Jack Scott Braidwood ~ 2003
- Gabriel Michael Ramierz ~ 2013
- Angel ~ 2012
- Matthew Knierim ~ 2005
- Nate Dewberry ~ 2012
- Sam O'Neill ~ 1996
- Baby Natasha Elizabeth Norwood Copeland ~ 1993
- Joshua Caleb Brooks ~ 2000
- Isaac Patrick Myers ~ 2006
- Tharryn Joseph Noah Avery ~ 2012
- Jaxen Patience Frankl ~ 2013
- Raelynne Kaya R. ~ 2013
- Madisen Peyton Acors ~ 2010
- Aden Jackson Wiggins ~ 2006
- Baby CJ Sangster ~ 2010
- Damian Wayne Safran ~ 2013
- Saro Parmanan ~ 2007

- Jessie Drapeau ~ 2006
- Aaron Drapeau ~ 2007
- Baby angel ~ 2010
- Baby angel ~ 2012
- Baby angel ~ 2013
- Jake Whitehead ~ 2011
- Jackie Carter ~ 2012
- Faith & Dustin Laughlin ~ 2009
- Meghan Elaine Gartland ~ 1995
- Kieran and Bryce Gartland ~ 1990
- Grace Gartland ~ 1997
- 2 Gartland angel babies 1996
- Baby Boo Traudt ~ 2011
- Allan Cason Fox-Cordingley ~ 2012
- Brandon Dewitt Avila ~ 2013
- Emily Rose Frost ~ 2005
- Aubrey Brennan Bender ~ 2013
- Nicholai James Byrne ~ 2012
- Donovan Ace Mount ~ 2009
- Mary-Lynn Gehrs ~ 2006
- Emily ~ 2008
- Samuel ~ 2011
- Thaddeus Joesph Sellmer ~ 2011
- Gabrielle Noel ~ 2012
- Danielle Rayann Petras ~ 2008
- Baby angel Nina ~ 2012
- Little rainbow ~ 2013
- Cecilia Alexandra ~ 2012
- Aiden Jonathan ~ 2013
- Joel David Johnson ~ 2013
- Michael ~ 1993
- Hanna Nicole Rushing ~ 2007
- Shelby Brooke Rushing ~ 2011
- Royce LaMara Caster ~ 2013
- Joshua H. Greer ~ 2012
- A. Faith Greer ~ 2013
- A. Hope Greer ~ 2013
- Hope Salome Heth ~ 2013
- Jacobi Smith-Watson ~ 2011
- Mason Alexander Wallace ~ 2013
- Emily or Geraint Painter ~ 2013
- Calypso Paikea Rhyder Lane ~ 2007
- Alaena Isabella Jiminez ~ 2004
- Ari Lynn Peters ~ 2013
- Norah Brown ~ 2012
- Ruskin Joseph ~ 2009
- Baby Angel Perez ~ 2013
- Jazzlene Adabella Delgadillo ~ 2010
- Marco Antonio Delgadillo ~ 2011
- Madison Bailey Martinez ~ 2009
- Karis Adachi Amaezechi ~ 2011
- Joshua Tyler Podsobinski ~ 1993
- Esperanza Gemini & Carina Gemini Olvera (twins) ~ 2010
- Baby Olvera ~ 2011
- Baby Olvera ~ 2013
- Jonathon Cook 2013
- Jardiel Maldonado 2011
- Eli Thomas ~ 2012

Angels

CPSIA information can be obtained at www.ICGtesting.com
Printed in the USA
LVOW12s1125060414

380512LV00004B/257/P